Any of David Dorris's books that involve Stunning Steven Edwards or the West Side Kids dives deep into classic movies like the Bowery Boys, Martin and Lewis, Abbot & Costello, and even Kenan & Kel - but updates them with modern humor and adventure. One minute the heroes are playing word games and making me smile, and the next minute they are dashing through bullets, time machines, and maniacal madmen! A great adventure for young readers and readers young at heart!

Books by David Dorris

The West Side Kids Meet The Small Fry

Stunning Stephen Edwards and The West Side Kids in The Invisible Man

The Adventures of Stunning Stephen Edwards as The Stunning Kid in The Time Traveling Marshals

Stunning Stephen Edwards as Detective Stunning Stephen Edwards in Wrestling With Death

I was honored to receive an advance reading of this book. And thrilled to know that Davenport, Iowa is well protected by this group of daring do-gooders- Some bumbling and some brave- but all are the finest "detectives" that the Quad Cities will ever know! Not too shabby for this small part of Iowa!

Christopher Murphy
Burlington By the Book
301 Jefferson Downtown Burlington Iowa- 52601

I would like to thank Christopher Murphy for encouraging me to write this book, coming up with the tittle of the book and the great design of the cover of this book.

I would also like to thank Chris for the pictures he sent me for the book and the book review.

I would like to thank Mike Boblit and his Grandson, Benjamin Hendricks for spending hours looking for mistakes and corrections of this book.

I would also like to thank Michael for allowing me to use him as one of the characters in chapter one, the book review and the pictures of him and his grandson, he sent me to use in this book.

I would like to thank Robin Rollins, Tammy Franklin and Suzy VenHorst for taking the time to read my book and giving me their book reviews.

I would like to thank Bob Applegate, owner of The Book Rack, in Davenport for letting me use a chapter of my story in his store.

I would also like to thank Bob for the pictures he sent me of his store to use in my book.

The West Side Kids in A Pocket Full of Wishes

Fifth Book of the Series

DAVID DORRIS

authorHOUSE®

AuthorHouse™
1663 Liberty Drive
Bloomington, IN 47403
www.authorhouse.com
Phone: 833-262-8899

Published by AuthorHouse 01/21/2022

ISBN: 978-1-6655-4982-0 (sc)
ISBN: 978-1-6655-4981-3 (e)

Library of Congress Control Number: 2022901008

Print information available on the last page.

CONTENTS

Professor Boblit

Scooter - Scooter, The Brick

Scooter - Scooter, The Brick

Professor Boblit

Scooter - Scooter, The Brick

Chapter One

Scooter talks to Professor Boblit

It is now May 5, 2019, six months later since Dr. Zodiac was arrested for the blow gun killings by Detective Stunning Edwards. Due to the publicity, the trial was moved to Burlington Iowa. After being in court for three weeks, Dr. Zodiac was set free for lack of evidence.

Christopher Seven Murphy, who owns Burlington By The Book, is Dr. Zodiac's twin brother and attended the entire trial in hopes that his brother Michael Shawn Murphy, alias Dr. Zodiac is proven innocent. After Dr. Zodiac was set free, Christopher invited his brother Michael to stay at his home for a couple of weeks.

Meanwhile back in Davenport, Iowa, The West Side Kids have purchased Dr. Zodiac's home, one block east of the intersection of Sixth and Gaines on top of the hill. To reach the row of houses on top of the hill, you have to come down the alley in back of these houses.

The ten members of The West Side Kids, Hannibal, the leader, Scooter, Who, What, I Don't Know, Because, Smiley, You Don't Say, I'm Not Sure and Whatever all moved their Detective Agency to the home and now live there.

It is now Saturday morning, May 6 and Scooter is in his bedroom listening to station, WMBO radio, his favorite radio station as Professor Boblit is interviewing an author about a book he just had published.

As Scooter listened, he thought to himself, "I am very interested in lamps that genies come out of. I wonder if Professor Boblit can tell me if there are any books on lamps with magic genies?

I like things that are very magical. My invention that I made with my chemicals when I was in Rex Tarillo's chemistry class, Rex Tarillo drank the chemicals and he turned into a forty inch small fry. Then within minutes another of my inventions with my chemicals turned out to be a bomb. I threw the bomb out of the class room window and it landed on Rex's brand new car and it blew up.

When I stayed at my Uncle Columbo's house for a few days, I created a new invention with some chemicals. I drank them and they made me very strong. I could crush beautiful red bricks with one hand. That's why I like working with my chemicals.

Now if I had a magic lamp with a genie, I could wish for several ideas to make more great inventions. I could even wish for a collection of a boat load of very nice red bricks. There are a lot of possibilities I can think of if I had my very own genie.

Sigh, I guess all I can wish for is a genie that comes out of a lamp. I guess there will be no lamp, no genie, no boat load of bricks in my future.

Monday I'm going to call Professor Boblit where he works at station WMBO radio about books with a genie and a lamp. Professor Boblit is a very smart person. He knows about authors and books. If anybody can help me, Professor Boblit can."

It is now 10 am Monday morning and Scooter calls Professor Boblit at station WMBO radio about books with lamps and magic genies.

"Hello Professor Boblit. I don't believe we've been formally introduced. This is Scooter Hickenbottom. I want you to know that I listen to you on the radio as often as I can. Because I know you're very smart, I thought you could help me. You are a man of capabilities," explained Scooter. "I wish I was like you because I'm always doing stupid things. I have a chemistry set. I like to mix up my chemicals to make great inventions. I also like to collect very red bricks. My nick name is Scooter, The Brick."

"You have some very unusual interests and amazing hobbies. How can I help you?" answered Professor Boblit as he was thinking, "What kind of nut am I talking to now?"

"I am very interested in magic genies and lamps. Can you tell me where I can find these kind of books?" pleaded Scooter.

"I can name a couple of books with magic genies and lamps," replied Professor Boblit. "There is "The Forbidden Wish" and " Three Wishes". You can also go online to find several other books with lamps and genies.

I would also suggest you go to The Book Rack, 4764 Elmore Avenue in Davenport and talk to Bob Applegate about these kind of books you are looking for. You can also check with Christopher Seven Murphy who owns Burlington By The Book, at 301 Jefferson in Burlington, Iowa. He also would be glad to help you."

"Isn't Christopher Seven Murphy the twin brother of Dr. Zodiac alias Michael Shawn Murphy?" asked Scooter. "Me, Hannibal and The West Side Kids own The West Side Kids Detective Agency here in Davenport. We bought Dr. Zodiac's house west of Sixth and Gaines here in Davenport. We worked with Detective Stunning Stephen Edwards to help capture him for the blow gun killings.

We have no respect for a man who plays alone and we tried to stop him. It was just like he was playing a game with the jury, called stump the jury. He was just found not guilty by the jury. I didn't think he would be set free. He thinks he is so clever. He says he was the victim of a cruel and tasteless hoax. Just what kind of animal is he? When I met him, I had the feeling he was looking right through me."

"Just what are you getting at?" asked Professor Boblit.

"Somebody needs to put some sense into Dr. Zodiac," answered Scooter. "I know for a fact that he murdered innocent people. We don't need that kind of person who is a murderer around here in Davenport.

I have a deep respect of the law. You would think that the law would be anxious to balance this out with a jail sentence or an execution. Of all the fool things that can happen to this man."

"Just who do you think you are, judge, jury and executioner?" questioned Professor Boblit. "It seems you are prejudice to things a decent man holds valuable. I hope that you admit you were exaggerating. What it does, is add fire to this situation. You talk too much and if you want to think that way, I can't stop you."

"The jury at his trial didn't really take the time to listen to the truth. No one knows. Not even one," explained Scooter. "Just what do you think they were doing here? They just wasn't thinking straight, because they didn't listen to words. The jury was given every chance to convict him of murder. The problem with the jury was by doing nothing, they never knew when they were finished. They just didn't realize that he did murder people. What's the matter with them, anyway? How could they do a thing like that?"

"Just what gave you that idea?" insisted Professor Boblit. "Just what are you talking about?"

"Don't they understand what the law in Davenport was trying to do here?" asked

Scooter. "The jury should have had a go about with this, by fighting fire with fire. A tooth for a tooth. The jury should have been run out of town from ignorance and prejudice. I bet this is the first time a man has brought back the posse. The only thing this jury can handle is a dog fight."

"Why are you saying this?" inquired Professor Boblit. "Has anybody been harmed?"

"Dr. Zodiac was harming innocent people. Now he has had his big moment and was set free. It doesn't seem right for a no good like that," exclaimed Scooter. "It didn't work out very well. I never figured it would go that far. The jury sent him a more urgent invitation by just waving a red flag in the face of Dr. Zodiac who now thinks he is bigger than the law. I suppose I could congratulate him, but I won't.

There was only one way to settle it. The jury should have given him a short trial with an execution. Since the jury let him go, that's what the town of Burlington deserves."

"This is hardly the same thing as a fair trial. Dr. Zodiac is not beyond the law, because that would be kind of a drawback, wouldn't it?" insisted Professor Boblit.

"I'm afraid our friend Dr. Zodiac was overanxious to get rid of his temptations and to get rid of his temptations, was to yield to it," Scooter went on to say. "The things he did and got away with. Dr.

Zodiac didn't need anybody, because he was self sufficient. He killed three people who made themselves perfect targets for murder and now Dr. Zodiac goes unpunished. This is a dangerous situation."

"What do you suppose he's up to now?" asked Professor Boblit.

"I'll tell you what he's up to now," answered Scooter. "He's staying with his twin brother, Christopher Seven Murphy. That may not be the best place to hide. Right now, he doesn't have any choice. He can go anywhere and belongs nowhere."

"Murder is police business, because this is necessary. Just what side of the badge are you going to stand behind?" asked Professor Boblit. "The law is the law. After talking to you, I find you never know when to quit. Now that's too much."

"Dr. Zodiac is three people. He is also known as Dr. Nejino and Michael, The Magnificent. An ugly man who doesn't want to be stopped," Scooter went on to say. "We can't be too careful of the change of our enemies. Maybe he wants to die."

"Do you expect me to believe that?" asked Professor Boblit.

"Don't you think that was a serious charge? Maybe you do and maybe you don't. So far nobody else has been murdered. I think we need to try and keep it that way," reasoned Scooter. "Dr. Zodiac is a menace to society. He is quite a man with his fists around women. He's a vulture that can't wait to prey on the dead and does prey on the living. How could he do a thing like that? You really think I'm making this up, don't you?"

"Why that's terrible what you're saying. Scooter, is that all you know? I think you have been out in the sun too long. Maybe you don't know it, but it sounds to me that you're just guessing," insisted Professor Boblit. "I would like a few answers if you don't mind. How well did you know him?"

"Well enough to know he's crazy enough to kill people. Who can explain the thinking of a killer?" replied Scooter. "Don't that give you any ideas as to what I'm saying? There are certain things in life that are triggered by very dangerous, careless, thoughtless people. He probably kills for amusement. That's all he wanted, because it gave him a false sense of security. There sure are a lot of strange people in this world."

"Scooter, you seem to be very strange yourself," reasoned Professor Boblit.

"You think I'm lying, don't you?" insisted Scooter.

"No, what your saying is plausible. Even though something seems to be missing," reasoned Professor Boblit. "What you're saying could have happened that way. I'm not questioning what the jury in Burlington was trying to do, because it's too late for that now. This Dr. Zodiac as you call him had his day in court.

It isn't quite that simple. No, on the contrary you've got it all twisted around. Dr. Zodiac can't be bruised up for what the jury thinks he did and can't prove. That won't hold up in any court. Now let's get the rules straight. I think the show was worth the price, because the jury has to use due diligence to be sure he was guilty of those murders. They all knew what they were doing here and why."

"That's a black lie. Can you give me one reason to believe you?" demanded Scooter.

"It doesn't look like the jury had any choice and neither do you," replied Professor Boblit. "I know I would like to be sure. This Dr. Zodiac is a man that sounds like he means business and doesn't know when he is through.

Where do you draw the line? Those who think are the incredible are those who do the impossible. You can only fight one fight at a time. There are only two truths. Not getting what you want and getting what you want. It must have been a bad time for them, because the jury ended up being on a blind trail. Knowing it and proving it are two different things."

"Let's agree on one thing. You think you are so smart. You always have to make sense. Don't you?" insisted Scooter. "Are you trying to impress me or convince yourself?"

"Good judgment is very important. For some of us it is forced on us by age and experience," replied Professor Boblit.

"Professor Boblit, do you think I'm making all this up?" growled Scooter.

"I don't rightly know. You have a round about way for asking for trouble. Someday you're going too far and start more trouble than you can handle. Somebody is going to teach you a lesson by chewing you up and swallowing you to pieces," promised Professor Boblit. "Do you think I'm bluffing? It's sure not me that is going to hurt you. You're asking for a life. Are you willing to give yours?"

"Wait a minute. I'm not your enemy. You think I'm a stupid crazy kid who is a childish fool," insisted Scooter. "You really want to get rid of me by hanging up, don't you?"

"Yes, I wanted to get rid of you after we first began to talk," answered Professor Boblit. "No, you're not a crazy kid as you put it. Now I want to help you get your thinking straight. I don't know how old you are.

Just remember it's no tragic thing to remain a child. That's the best age. Their world is mysterious, wonderful, half real, half make believe. The world we live in is not so perfect. That's why at your age you are interested in lamps with magic genies, because you like the mysterious world of make believe."

"You're right. I do like the world of make believe. That's why I like working with my chemicals. I was in Rex Tarillo's chemistry class at The University of Davenport a couple of years ago," explained Scooter. "I had a great invention. I made up a batch of chemicals that Rex accidentally drank. He shrank from over six feet to forty inches and became a small fry.

I accidentally switched the chemicals he was going to drink to help him control his temper. After I got his chemicals by mistake, I accidentally made a bomb and I had to throw it out the class room window into the parking lot. It landed on Rex's new car and it blew up."

"Are you serious or just making this up about everything you have told me?" asked Professor Boblit. "You couldn't possible have done all these things. I think this is a travesty and you're you trying to play me for a fool?"

"I'm sick of you asking me if I'm making all these things up. I've got nothing to confess. Everything I told you is the truth. If you don't believe me, you can ask Rex Tarillo and my Uncle T. J. Columbo," reassured Scooter. "They are both Davenport Police Detectives.

As far is Dr. Zodiac is concerned, I'm trying to prevent trouble. Not cause it. This is something I've got to do, I would be a little less proud if I didn't do this, if you don't mind."

"I do mind and I know what you mean. You better listen to me as to what I have to say. I urge you to change your mind," pleaded Professor Boblit.

"Do you really think I would consider that after what I have been telling you?" asked Scooter. "I'm sorry. I can't be made to bargain."

"I just have a different opinion. A man should know when to quit. Leave it be. It's finished. You should know when to cut your losses. Come off of it. I'm going to tell you for the last time to keep your mouth shut about this Dr. Zodiac," replied Professor Boblit as he began to scold Scooter. "I'm not going to give you time to think it over. I'm not going to tell you again. I want your answer right now. That's not too much too ask."

"I ain't skewered of nobody. Do you hear? I have no intentions of being frightened away," answered Scooter. "It's not so absurd or tragic as a man willing to give his life to fight for what he believes is right. I'm willing to take my chances. My primary purpose is to stay alive."

"Like it or not, we need each other. Friendship, warmth and understanding are all worth looking at. With most people, you need to be as polite as pie," explained Professor Boblit.

"The most gentle kitten can have the fury of a tiger. I told you to start with, I always do stupid things and because of that I am always getting into trouble," replied Scooter. "I ain't looking for more trouble. Davenport Detective T. J. Columbo, Hannibal Columbo's' uncle is my friend. So is Rex Tarillo, who is also a Davenport Detective. They are both always on the look out for me. I just want to stay out of trouble."

"I don't think they are always going to appreciate fighting your battles for you all the time," protested Professor Boblit.

"You have that all wrong what you're thinking," explained Scooter. "Detective Rex Tarillo, Detective T. J. Columbo and Hannibal are like family to me. Ever since I was knee high to a grass hopper, T. J. Columbo taught me a very important lesson."

"Just what are you saying?" asked Professor Boblit. "If you have something on your mind, tell me what it is."

"You must have seen a lot of westerns," Scooter continued to say. "Have you ever heard of The Cowboy Code?"

"Is that like The Dallas Cowboys?" questioned Professor Boblit.

"Bite your tongue. Wash your mouth out with soap. You never heard anything about The Cowboy Code?" answered Scooter. "The Cowboy Code goes like this. Never shoot first. Never hit a smaller man. Never take an unfair advantage of another man. Never go back on your word. Be kind to kids, elders and animals. Don't have any religious, racial or intolerance. A cowboy is always a patriot. The most important thing he taught me was about being honest with another person and about one man's word against another.

Jerry Dickerson and his gang were released from prison and moved back to this same hotel and into their same apartments they lived in before they went to prison.

A few years ago, Jerry Dickerson and his gang were after Stunning Stephen Edwards for not taking a fall at his boxing match. Rex had invented chemicals when mixed together, would make a person invisible after they drank it.

Even though I didn't want to do it, I was expected to go into the ring and box Ace, The Assassin. Stephen drank these chemicals and became invisible. Then he went in the ring to box Ace while everybody thought it was me doing the boxing."

"Come on now. Just what do you expect me to believe?" asked Professor Boblit. "Against my better judgment, I think I'm starting to understand how you think. You really do have the innocence of a child. That explains why you're interested in magic genies and lamps. Where do you come up with stories like that?"

"That wasn't a good neighborly question? That's what you say. I don't care how you say I think. I don't care what you believe as to how I think. It's all true," insisted Scooter. "Maybe I shouldn't be telling you what I know."

"Now to get back to what we were talking about. I know we have our differences and I think they can be resolved," reasoned Professor Boblit. "Now I'm going to tell you a few things. It's not your courage that is being tested. It's your respect for the law. Come on and wake up. You need to try and get your mind off of these things.

Dr. Zodiac, if that is his real name is a free man, because the court couldn't prove he killed anyone. I think this is a good place to stop. Maybe after you get a book or two about magic genies and lamps, you will forget all about this Dr. Zodiac. Then you won't have a problem anymore."

"I have been having second thoughts about this since I have been talking to you," reasoned Scooter. "Those are my sentiments exactly. That seems reasonable enough. I would really like to forget about Dr. Zodiac. I think you are a wise man. Because you are a remarkable man, I will do as you say. Everything you do is well done and you are very efficient. When you have something to say, you come right out and say it.

I want to apologize about what I said to you. I really hope you didn't think I was impolite. I want you to be my friend. Who could ask for more? I want you to know that I will always listen to you on the radio.

Getting back to why I called you, I'm going to call Bob Applegate next at The Book Rack. If I had a magic genie, I would ask the genie to give you a wish. Thanks for the advice and your helping hand. I am so grateful. Good bye my friend."

"Good bye Scooter. It was a pleasure to talk to you. Good luck my friend with finding a book about a genie and a lamp," insisted Professor Boblit.

Chapter Two

SCOOTER AND THE MAILMAN

After talking to Professor Boblit, Scooter searched the internet for the telephone number and address of The Book Rack as the mailman was walking toward Scooter's house.

As the mailman was delivering mail to the neighbor down the block, the mailman asked the neighbor if he knew the people who bought Dr. Nejino's house.

The neighbor replied, "There are several men who live there. They run their Detection Agency out of the house, known as The West Side Kids Detective Agency. Scooter Hickenbottom is the only one that I have talked to that lives there."

"Maybe I'll run into him one of these days," replied the mailman.

"You will. I guarantee it. Scooter will tackle anything," answered the neighbor as Scooter found the number to The Book Rack.

"I found it," said Scooter to himself. "The Book Rack's phone number is 563-355-2310. The address is 4164 Elmore Avenue in Davenport, Iowa. I can't decide. Should I call The Book Rack or go to the store? I want to get one of those books with a magic genie and a lamp as fast as I can. I think I will go to the store. If Hannibal is not busy, maybe he will go with me. I'm going to ask him right now."

A few minutes later, Scooter found Hannibal in his office, sitting at his desk.

"Hannibal, you know how I have been interested in lamps with magic genies," beamed Scooter." I just called Professor Boblit at the radio station WMBO radio where he works to ask him about books of lamps with magic genies."

"Scooter, what did you say? I am sitting here trying to catch up on my work." replied Hannibal.

"Son of a gun. Did you catch her?" laughed Scooter.

"Did you think that was funny?" asked Hannibal.

"No, I was just thinking of a joke," answered Scooter.

"I didn't hear everything you said. Who did you call at a radio station?" asked Hannibal. "What's with you? What are you grinning about?"

"I'm not grinning," insisted Scooter.

"Just what is tickling you? Did somebody stick an ice cube down your jockey shorts?" asked Hannibal. "If you keep grinning like that, somebody is going to put you on a bus leaving for The Funny Farm."

"I called Professor Boblit at WMBO radio where he works," answered Scooter. "He is a very smart person and knows everything about books. I asked him if he could help me find a book about magic genies and lamps. He told me about two books, "The Forbidden Wish" and "Three Wishes". He also told me to go to The Book Rack and talk to Bob Applegate. I want to get one of those books as soon as possible. Would you go with me?"

"Ya, I'll go with you if you give me fifteen minutes to finish my paperwork," promised Hannibal. "It's a nice day for a ride on our motorcycles. Will you get our motorcycles out of the garage while you're waiting?"

"You bet I will," insisted an excited Scooter as the mailman was coming up to the mailbox by the back door. "I really like to ride my motorcycle."

In seconds, Scooter ran out the back door knocking the mailman to the ground as he ran to the garage, the mailman began screaming with all the mail flying through the air. Hearing the mailman scream, Hannibal ran out the back door and to his surprise saw the mailman laying on the ground with mail everywhere on the grass.

"Are you OK? Can I give you some assistance?" asked Hannibal.

"Just what on earth happened to you? What's going on over here? Here, let me help you up."

"I don't really know. Where did everybody go? You must think I'm nuts," answered the confused mailman. "I was walking up the sidewalk, sorting through the mail and the next thing I know, I'm laying on the ground with mail scattered everywhere. It was like a garbage truck ran over me."

"I intend to find out what that garbage truck was and why you were knocked to the ground. I think that garbage truck goes by the name of Scooter," reasoned Hannibal.

"This Scooter, did he play professional football? Is he a friend of yours?" asked the mailman. "He has to be a professional football player by the way he knocked me to the ground."

"No my friend, Scooter never played professional football," answered Hannibal. "He was just over excited to get our motorcycles out of the garage. Scooter and myself are leaving to go to The Book Rack on Elmore Avenue to try and find a book about magic genies and lamps. That's all Scooter thinks about is magic genies and lamps. I'm sorry he knocked you to the ground. I don't even think Scooter even saw you as he ran out the door. Are you hurt?"

"No, just dazed. That was a close call and my mail is scattered from king to come," cried the mailman.

"You just sit there and take it easy. I'm going after Scooter right now. When Scooter comes out of the garage, he will be picking up all of your mail with an apology," insisted Hannibal.

As Hannibal walked towards the garage, Scooter was opening up the garage door from inside with the garage door opener.

"Scooter! Scooter! You come out of the garage right now and leave those motorcycles alone!" yelled Hannibal. "Scooter, do you hear me?"

"Did you call me?" asked Scooter.

"Yes I called you. I was just getting lonely and I thought we could dance," replied Hannibal. "Of course I called you."

"I'm coming. I'm coming. Aren't we going to The Book Rack?" asked Scooter as he began to shut the garage door.

"Not right now. Something terrible has happened and because of that you have something else to do," replied Hannibal.

As Scooter came out of the garage, he saw the mailman sitting on the ground with mail scattered all over the yard.

"Hey man. What's up? What happened? Did the mailman have an accident?" inquired Scooter. "Now how did that happen?"

"You really don't know, do you?" reasoned Hannibal. "It's like this. You are his accident. When you came flying out the back door, you knocked the mailman to the ground and his mail went flying everywhere. Were you having a good time? First you apologize to the mailman. Then you pick up every piece of mail and put it in his mail bag where it was this instant."

"Now I have to sort all my mail all over again," exclaimed the mailman. "I just hope you find all my mail. If I lose something important, I could lose my job!"

"It looks like everything is here," replied Hannibal. "Now Scooter, why don't you watch what you're doing? A fellow can get hurt doing something like this. Apologize and get this mail picked up right away."

"I'm sorry Mr. Mailman," insisted Scooter. "I guess I was so excited to go to The Book Rack I was a little hasty and I didn't see you when I came out the back door. I'm sorry we bumped into each other and I owe you an apology. Did I hurt you? I always believed that there was nothing like physical fitness to keep a man physically fit."

"It's OK Mac. I'm alright. You see. You got me and just knocked the wind out of me and now it's all over. I will tell you one thing, I know that lightning never strikes twice in the same place. From now on when I come to your house, I'm going to be very cautious," promised the mailman."

"I guess from now on, I have to quit being in a hurry when I go out the back door," reasoned Scooter. "Believe me. It won't happen again."

"Was that a prediction or a promise?" asked Hannibal.

"I'm the kind of person who keeps his word. When I give my word, I keep it," insisted Scooter. "Seeing you sitting on the grass with mail scattered all over will be a permanent reminder for me to be careful. You sit quietly and talk to Hannibal while I clean up the mess I made."

"Thank you for the thought. Don't take too long. I'm suppose to be on time to deliver my mail and now the time is short. I'm behind schedule," explained the mailman.

As Scooter bent over to pick up the mail, he stood there gazing at an envelope he had in his hand.

"Looking at Scooter, the mailman asked, "Do you want to read it? Do you always read someone's mail?"

"Oh, I wasn't interested in the mail," explained Scooter. "I was thinking about going to The Book Rack to buy books about lamps and genies."

The mailman then stood up and was bent over.

"Why are you bent over like that? Did you hurt your back when I knocked you to the ground?" asked Scooter.

"No, I'm waiting for the game to start," replied The Mailman.

"Let me see if I can fix it," insisted Scooter. "First of all, I want to know if you have a bad back?"

"No, I have a bad marriage. After I got married, I always burned the midnight oil with my wife. Now that we've gotten older, we have to be careful. We don't have much oil left to burn," answered the Mailman.

I'll be alright. You go to The Book Rack while I shuffle along to deliver the mail," pleaded The Mailman. "Go, just go. I'll be alright."

"Come on Scooter. Hurry it up, so we can go the The Book Rack," ordered Hannibal. "We would have been on our way by now if you had been slower going through the back door."

"Wait a minute. Give me a chance. I'm hurrying. I'm hurrying. I know. I'm always doing something stupid. You still don't have to get into a snit about it," laughed Scooter.

The Book Rack

Chapter Three

SCOOTER GOES TO THE BOOK RACK

It was ten minutes later and the boys were finally on their way, riding their motorcycles to The Book Rack. Thirty minutes later, they had entered the parking lot to The Book Rack and drove past The Dairy Queen.

"Before we go home, I would like to get some ice cream from The Dairy Queen," said Scooter.

"That does sound like a right smart idea. I think I would like to get some ice cream on the way home," replied Hannibal as they pulled up in front of The Book Rack.

Once inside the store, Bob Applegate approached Hannibal and Scooter and said to himself, "Look what the wind blew in." After he stood in front of Hannibal and Scooter, Bob greeted the boys by saying, "Hello boys. Nice day isn't it?"

"You wouldn't be Bob Applegate," asked Scooter.

"Yes, I'm Bob Applegate. I own The Book Rack," replied Bob. "How did you know who I was? I never seen you in my store before. Why are you here?"

"I know. We have never been here before. Our bus broke down and we were on our way to India. Do you have anything to read like a book?" beamed Scooter. "Right now I'm reading a book about anti gravity. I just can't put that book down.

I came to your store because I am looking for books about lamps with magic genies. Professor Boblit told me that if I came to your store, you would help me find these kind of books."

"You know Professor Boblit?" asked Bob. "He sounds like a man with great wisdom that I would like to know."

"I don't know Professor Boblit personally. I listen to him on the radio all the time. Professor Boblit is very smart. I like it when he talks to authors about the books they wrote," exclaimed Scooter. "I called him this morning at his radio station, WMBO to ask him where I could find books about lamps with magic genies. He told me of two books, "The Forbidden Wish" and "Three Wishes" would be the kind of books I am looking for."

"You're in luck. I just happen to have both of those books," recalled Bob. "I've had those books for a while. Nobody that comes in my store seems to want books about lamps with magic genies. Why are you interested in these kind of books?"

"Scooter is obsessed about lamps and genies,"reasoned Hannibal.

"Dissatisfaction is a symptom of ambition. It's the coal that fans the fire," replied, Bob.

"I have a chemistry set where I mix up my chemicals to make great inventions. I also collect very red bricks," explained Scooter. "Last October, I wrestled three tough, mean, wrestlers and won the matches without laying a hand on them. My wrestling name was Scooter, The Brick.

When I talked to Professor Boblit, he said I like mysterious and magical things because of my age. I told him about mixing up my chemicals in a chemistry class at The University of Davenport. My instructor, Rex Tarillo drank them and became a forty inch small fry. Then I made a bomb and threw it out the class room window into the parking lot and blew up Rex's new car."

With a funny look on Bob's face, he replied, "I think somebody could easily write a book about the things you have done. After reading this book, the reader may think it's all fiction. Nobody is going to believe you really did these things."

"Well it's all true. Scooter is my best friend and I know he isn't lying to you," replied Hannibal. "I saw these things happen and so did Detective Rex Tarillo and my Uncle Detective T. J. Columbo."

Thinking he was dealing with a couple nuts, Bob blurted, "I'll be glad to show you where these books are. In fact, I'll go get them for you right now. I'm sure you're in a hurry to buy them and go home and read them."

"Now that's what I call service," reasoned Scooter. "Professor Boblit said you would be glad to help me. I just didn't know it was going to be this fast."

"I'll be right back. Don't go away. Don't even move. Just wait here," instructed Bob as he quickly disappeared.

While Hannibal and Scooter waited for Bob, a nice looking woman entered the store and started to walk past them.

"I wish I had an aunt that looked like you," said Scooter to the woman.

"You have to take that up with your uncle", replied the woman. "For your information, my husband was going to divorce me and then his eye sight got better."

"I can't," insisted Scooter. "He died when he was over in England. His wife caught him with another woman. Since he died, his wife was looking for someone to take his place. Are you planning to stay married?"

"Yes, I am planning to stay married, if it is any of your business," insisted the woman. "The reason I was going to divorce my husband is that I would knit things for him. Then he would get even with me by making furniture."

"Listen to this. I read an article that said that single people are healthier than married people," exclaimed Scooter. "It said that a government study concluded that single people are healthier than married people or people who have been married. Look at you. You look like you need a check up from a doctor."

After looking at Scooter, the woman went on to say, "There is something big about you."

"And what would that be?" asked Scooter.

"Your nose," answered the woman. "Hey, don't be so free with your hands."

"I was just trying to guess your weight," replied Scooter. "How do you think I got this nose?"

"On a blind date," replied the woman. "Stay out of the sun. You could spoil. You do have a weak chin. With your face, you couldn't judge a livestock show. Have you ever thought of growing a beard?"

"If you ever decide to divorce your husband. I would be glad to marry you and another woman at the same time," boomed Scooter. "Why I would do that is, that it can't miss. Women always want what they can't get."

"That's bigamy," reasoned the woman.

"No, that's big of me," beamed Scooter. "You know why I never got married? It's because of this face."

"I can see that. You know what you look like? A man on welfare that was told he had four ex wives to support," replied the woman. "It's because of that face, you will never get and stay married"

"Don't worry about me. I already have a foxy mama," answered Scooter. "My friend Hannibal has a foxy mama and all of God's Children has a foxy mama," laughed Scooter.

"You know the saying; you're beautiful you are angry? Well that doesn't apply to you. I would rather lie down next to a dead goat than to keep company with you.

I had another girl who waited for me to ask her to marry me, yet she married another guy."

"How long did she wait for you?" asked the woman.

"Seven and a half years," answered Scooter. "You know something? After that, I tore up her picture; she looked a lot better that way.

You lose one chick, you get another. I buy every girl I take out a glass of wine. This way I can say I have a port in every girl, instead of a girl in every port."

A man standing behind the woman with a pointed beard snarled at Scooter saying, "I don't know what you think you are doing here. Who made you a judge of beauty?"

"You don't understand. When I turn up the charm, it's like a roller coaster ride into paradise." reassured Scooter.

"You may think that you are courteous and a gentleman by trying the romantic approach with her by trying to sweep her off her feet," said the man.

"No I'm not. I don't even have a broom," answered Scooter.

"She likes her men tall, dark and handsome," replied the man.

"If that's the case, you are zero for three," laughed Scooter. "Why don't you take her roller skating? You'll have a lot of fun, because you'll fall down on each other."

"I'm not going to tell you again. Leave your hands off of her and quit bothering her or I'm going to take you apart," demanded the man.

"You sure are a cranky old man. What's biting you? Who are you and why are you butting in," asked Hannibal. "What is she to you?"

Looking at Scooter, the man replied, "I'm her husband. Are you trying to have fun with my wife? What makes you think we're going to have time for fun and games? That isn't the decent thing to do. You open your mouth again and I will put my foot in it. Just remember, three is a crowd."

"You don't have to worry. I don't like crowds anyway," boomed Scooter. "Why don't you take a cab into the river with all the windows down?"

"That is quite enough. Her coming and going is no affair of yours," exclaimed the husband. "You made your point, so leave it be. If you don't, I'm going to introduce to you a couple of my friends you will absolutely hate. They are a real fountain of sympathy and won't stop halfway. If they see you, they won't wait to say hello. They will get you for this. First they will step on your glasses and then they will burn your nose off.

They caught up with another man who insulted my wife. Now he's selling toy alligators to the kids in Florida. You don't have to apologize to me, but you better apologize to her."

"Just because you're fighting for her honor, don't point that beard at me; it might go off," boomed Scooter.

"Don't talk about my beard like that," snarled the husband. "I didn't like my beard at first. Then it grew on me."

"Fighting for her honor is more than she ever did," beamed Scooter.

"A man does what has to be done or he tries," explained the husband. "That's the only way a man can live. Scooter, I don't like your looks."

"I'm not crazy about you, either." objected Scooter.

"There is nothing wrong with you that a good case of lockjaw wouldn't cure," answered the husband. "If you would really like to save some lives, take a shower. If you don't take a shower, you will start to spoil."

"How would you like it if I sucked up your shoes and made your body shrink?" asked Scooter. "Do me a favor and take a cab."

"Well, what do you know? I remember who he is now," said the woman to her husband. "There is one thing I remember about him. He was in the restaurant where I work as a waitress a couple of weeks ago. He ordered a round steak with mashed potatoes and gravy. He showed me an article he was reading in the newspaper about somebody that had their horse stolen as he was trying to cut up his round steak.

He is the only person I know of that puts mustard on his gravy. Then he went on to complain to me about breaking his fork in the mustard and gravy.

Come on. We're wasting time. Let's continue to look for the books we came it to buy, so we can get him out of our sight."

"What were those books named?" asked the husband?

"The West Side Kids Meet The Small Fry" and "Stunning Stephen Edwards and The

West Side Kids in The Invisible Man" by David Dorris," answered the woman.

A very short time later, Bob was standing at the register with the books about lamps and magic genies.

Showing the books to Scooter, Bob offered Scooter the two books for $5.00.

"I'll take them," insisted Scooter. "I finally have books about lamps with magic genies of my very own."

"Is there anything else I can do for you?" asked Bob.

"No, we have to go," answered Scooter.

"Don't forget about The Dairy Queen. Scooter. Let's walk down to The Dairy Queen right now to get some ice cream," beamed Hannibal. "I want to get a chocolate shake. You will have plenty of time to read your books when we get home."

"Right Chief. A chocolate shake also sounds good to me," replied Scooter.

A little while later Scooter was home sitting in his bedroom reading "The Forbidden

Wish" and then fell asleep. As he was sleeping, Hannibal knocked on his door and then said to Scooter, "If you're not busy, can you come here for a minute?"

"Did I wake you?" asked Hannibal as he entered Scooter's bedroom. "Maybe I should have phoned first. Why don't you put a "do not disturb" sign on your door or leave a wake up call at the desk?"

"I'm sorry. I'm really, really; sorry I fell asleep while I was reading my new book, "The Forbidden Wish," pleaded Scooter.

"It's such a nice day. Would you like to go for a walk?" asked Hannibal. "It will get the whole blood flowing. I think it's a healthy thing to get more exercise and we need to walk our milkshakes off."

"I was exercising," answered Scooter. "Who do you think has been turning these pages before I fell asleep?"

"That's not the kind of exercise I'm talking about," insisted Hannibal. "Are you going or not?"

"I will take that walk tomorrow," promised Scooter. "Right now I am too excited about reading my two books, if I can only wake up."

Burlington By The Book

Christopher Seven Murphy and Michael, Alias Dr. Zodiac

Chapter Four

Christopher Seven Murphy Goes To Davenport As Michael, Alias Dr. Zodiac

It is now Tuesday May 6, 2019. Meanwhile, back in Burlington, Dr. Zodiac, alias Michael Shawn Murphy is at his brother's store, Burlington By The Book. There are no customers in the store as Christopher Seven Murphy and his twin brother Michael began to talk about Michael's future.

"Well Michael, What are your plans now that the jury has found you innocent of killing three people?" asked Christopher.

"I'm glad I am staying with you, because up to now, I have been all alone in the world," reasoned Michael. "You were always the strong one. I was the weak one and I had to be helped by you. As Dr. Zodiac, I thought I was a big shot. Now, I can't believe it. I have been all alone in the world and it has made me sad."

"I'm glad you're staying with me. It's nice to have you here and now you're not alone," insisted Chris. "You're my twin brother and you have never been alone. You should still meet some new people.

You have two choices. You can start by being nice and meet people or you can live alone for the rest of your life."

"Because we're twins, all I want to know is that I'm number two in your life?" asked Michael.

"You have always been number two and you always will be number two since I am your big brother and older than you," answered Chris.

"Just because you are a few minutes older than me does not make you my older, big brother," snapped Michael.

"What can I say? It says right on our birth certificates that I am indeed older than you and that also makes me your big brother," laughed Chris. "Now what did you say your plans were?"

"OK older, bigger, brother," snarled Michael. "Do you have time to listen to your twin brother who is going to change the course of his life and your life and our families lives?"

"What are you talking about?" asked Chris. "You must have thought about this a lot? Is this another stupid idea that you have?"

"You don't sound very happy about what you think I'm going to tell you," insisted Michael.

"I guess that's true," reasoned Chris. "It just seems like I have been very busy, because I have so many customers who buy books from me. It just seems like it never ends. I'm just exhausted all of the time."

"I don't mean to upset you. I am planning on going back to Davenport to get some thing I have hidden in my house that I sold to The West Side Kids," answered Michael.

"No!" answered Chris. "That's a stupid plan."

"That's not a stupid plan. I'm going to Davenport, because it's something I have to do," reasoned Michael.

"No!" answered Chris.

"Since I don't have a car, I am going to have to take a bus to Davenport," reasoned Michael.

"No!" answered Chris. "I said that was a stupid plan."

"You don't need to keep saying no. That's not a stupid plan," reassured Michael.

"I just said it. I can't believe you're doing this," replied Chris.

"Ever since we were kids, you was always telling me what to do. You was always right. I was always wrong. I'm getting sick and tired of this," reasoned Michael.

"When we were kids, just what did happen? Why did you come to me when you had a crisis?" asked Chris.

"I thought you could help me. When I was known as Dr. Zodiac,

I had no use for you as my twin brother. I went my way and you went your way. At that time, that wasn't far enough apart.

Now remember, I'm Michael Murphy and I'll do as I please. You're Chris Murphy and you own a book store and you do as you please."

"Just what are you cooking up? Why do you have to go back to Davenport? What do you have hidden in your house?" asked Chris.

"Maybe you were right on some things. Now I'm going to do this my way. Is that
clear?" replied Michael. "It's not the way you think. You don't understand. Chris, I never did break the news to you. I have a winning lottery ticket worth fifty million dollars," beamed Michael.

"How do you know that? You didn't get this winning ticket illegally?"boomed Chris. "Maybe things aren't going to turn out the way you want them to. I don't want you to be getting in trouble with the law again. I want to make sure I have this right, so this is not going to be an ugly scene. I deserve an explanation and want the whole story from the start. Mom had a struggle with your arrest for killing three people. She had a hard time moving on.

As an older brother, I don't know what I could have done different to keep you out of trouble. You have always raised the fear in other people. I can't change the hate you have for others and I can't blame myself for your mistakes."

"Oh, no, no, no. Don't ever worry about me getting into trouble again," reasoned Michael. "What I'm trying to say is the way I figure, I'm not like that, because that's not who I am. I haven't changed a bit. If you can accept that, that's fine. If you can't that's fine.

Just think positive. I entered the lottery contest and won. It sounds like everything is working out perfect. I'm really on a roll. Do you know that? Don't you think it was wonderful that I won? The key is that this time, I'm going to play my cards right.

Do you realize this is the only time in our lives we have the chance to get rich? This could be the greatest day of our lives. After we cash in on that winning ticket, we will be set for life. Even the words sound like a ceremony.

It is only as it should be. I'll be OK. I can take care of myself. That's the last thing I want to do is get in trouble with the law again.

I just don't want certain people in Davenport to find out that I have this winning ticket. If they do, they will try and take it away from me. If they find out, we will be in trouble. Big trouble. Big, big trouble.

There is an old recipe for tiger stew. First you have to catch the tiger. Don't you have faith in me? Ain't it enough that I'm your brother? I was planning on sharing the money with mom, Kelly, Tim and you."

"That's really nice and very thoughtful of you. What would I do without you? It sounds like you are a very generous brother and you don't want help. You want praise." insisted Chris. "Where do you stand on all of this?"

"Where I choose. When that day comes, I will get even with them after I claim the money," promised Michael. "Because of the kind of people I associated with, it was the cause of my troubles. I know what I'm going to do next. I'm going to try to right a wrong."

"Tell me what's going on with this. I demand. I insist. Why are you trying to be so secretive about this?" questioned Chris as the phone rang and a customer walked into the store. "Hold that thought for a second. I w ill get right back to you. Michael, we'll talk about this later. Burlington By The Book. Can I put you on hold for a minute? Can I help you?" asked Chris to his customer?

"Excuse me. I'm sorry. I don't want to interrupt your phone call. My name is Henrietta Vanderstopper and I just want to look around," replied the customer. "I find television very educating. Whenever somebody turns on the television, I go into my bed room and read a book. By the way, do you have "The Time Traveling Marshals or "Wrestling With Death" by David Dorris?

I understand that "Wrestling With Death" is a great murder mystery with lots of laughs, twists and turns and most of all a surprise ending. The picture of that character on the upper left hand corner of the cover, portraying Dr. Zodiac is a very scary person. I sure wouldn't want to meet him on a dark corner at night here in Burlington.

"The Time Traveling Marshals" also sounds like a great book. I'm sure that also has a surprise ending. In David's books, he says it all. That makes his books so much better. Since I can't decide, maybe I'll just have to buy both books."

"Yes, I have both of those books. I'll find them and leave them here on the counter for you. Take your time and look all you want. Do you want anything else? If you need any help, tell me if there is anything I can do for you," insisted Chris.

"I also have a section of books called, "Do-It-Yourself" and one right next to that section called, "Do-It-Yourself-With-Good-Friends-Pizza-And- A-Few-Beers" if you're interested."

Going back to the phone, Chris said to the caller, "Thanks for waiting. Can I help you? We're located at 301 Jefferson in downtown Burlington. We close at five. Thank you."

"What was that about? Who was that woman? There are attractive people who love life, because life loves them. She really looks like a bow wow," laughed Michael. "Ugly people are depressed and neurotic. They hate life because life has no time for them, because life is busy loving attractive people. She must have been the pick of the litter. Do you have a leash for her? She looks like she wants to go for a walk."

"That bow wow as you call it, is a very good customer of mine," scolded Chris.

"Don't let her hear you talk about her that way. Please cut it out, because she won't come back."

"OK, I won't say another word about her," replied Michael. "I really don't want to know this woman. If she makes a mess here in the store, I'm not cleaning it up.

You know that dog, that big dog I adopted from the kennels last week? I decided to name him Lucky. When I'm not there, I always keep him in the bedroom. You know that Burlington has so many trees? When Lucky saw all of these trees, he had a nervous breakdown. You know how boys are about their dogs? That's why I always had a dog when I grew up."

I always had a cat,"replied Chris.

"Wasn't he a fluffy little cat?" laughed Michael. "Did he shed like crazy?"

"No he didn't. He was a very big cat, who was a Tom Cat and I named him Mighty Joe," answered Chris. "All the dogs were afraid of him. Now I don't have a cat."

"You know how dogs are? Cats can't be much different," laughed

Michael. "That's why I always liked having dogs. Outside of a dog, a book is man's best friend. Inside of a dog it's too dark to read.

You tell that bow wow over there looking for books, if she doesn't have anything better to do, she can come to my room and get Lucky."

"I told you to quit talking about her. Now be quiet, scolded Chris. "Now tell me, when are you leaving for Davenport?"

"First I have to call The West Side Kids Detective Agency to see if they will let me back in the house I sold to them," replied Michael. "If they do, I will leave for Davenport by bus tomorrow. Would you give me a ride to the bus station?"

"I have a better idea. I don't want to cramp your style. If you and our sister, Kelly will watch the store for me, since we are identical twin brothers, I will take your place as Michael, alias Dr. Zodiac and go to Davenport to find the winning lottery ticket."

"We may be twins, but remember, there is only one Dr. Zodiac and that's not you," reasoned Michael.

"Because we're twins, I'm sure I can pass as Dr. Zodiac. Don't worry about me. I can take care of myself," reasoned Chris. "Since today is Tuesday and Wednesday is my day off, I can leave after we close and be back by Thursday. I don't want you to get in any more trouble with the law."

"That's nice of you, but I don't know anything about running a book store," reasoned Michael.

"Kelly will be here to help you. You will be fine," reasoned Chris.

"If you go in my place, you could be in danger," insisted Michael.

"What are you talking about?" asked Chris.

"First of all, The West Side Kids aren't going to be too kindly about you coming back to the house I sold them," explained Michael. "Then there is Jerry Dickerson and his gang plus Dr. Fine and Charlie, The Chill you may have to deal with."

"Just as I'm going to give you some education on running the store, you can tell me what I need to know about dealing with your friends," reasoned Chris. "I deal with people all day long in my store. I have a plan. I think I won't have any trouble getting The West Side Kids to let me in the house."

"I guess it's alright to go in my place," answered Michael. "You seem to know what you are doing."

It was finally six o'clock and Chris, alias Dr. Zodiac was on the bus heading for Davenport. As he sat looking out the window of the bus, he thought to himself, "With these certain people that could be after my brother's lottery ticket, I think I better see if The West Side Kids would let me hire them to take me back to Burlington safely? They don't need to know about the winning lottery ticket or the people that may be after me to get it.

I still haven't been able to get a hold of Hannibal. From what my brother told me about Scooter, I can't wait to meet him. I just have to remember to watch out for the crazy things he does.

Even though my brother was at odds with them over Dr. Zodiac, I really hope they take the job and let me in the house to find the lottery ticket. If they don't let me in the house, I'll have to find another way to get in. Even though I want to meet Scooter, I just don't want to have to deal with of all the stupid things he does.

This lottery ticket will make my brother, Michael and me millionaires, if I can find it. Then maybe Michael can live a normal life in Burlington. I think I will try calling Hannibal again on my cell phone. Good, the phone is ringing."

"Hello, this is Hannibal Columbo, owner of The West Side Detection Agency. May I ask who is calling, hmm?"

"This is Michael Murphy calling. Would it be possible to get in your house to look for something I left behind after I moved out?"

"Who did you say you were?" asked Hannibal. "If you tell me what you left behind, maybe I can find it for you. By the way, how could you leave something behind at our house when you don't even live here?"

"I said my name was Michael Murphy. Dr. Zodiac to you. I have some business to take care of at my house that you bought from me. There is a personal thing I left behind and I feel mighty poorly about leaving this behind. To tell you the truth, I really need to get it back. You can't find it, but I can. Can I stop over today for a visit? Right now, I'm on a bus going to Davenport from Burlington."

"What happened? Why would you leave that behind?" asked Hannibal.

"There was just too much confusion when you bought my house at the time, because I was in jail," answered Chris. "My brother Christopher Seven Murphy was involved in selling you my house and moving all of my things out of the house. You know how it is? You put something off and it's left behind.

I have some personal business to take care of. This personal thing was hidden in the house and my brother, Chris didn't know anything about it. This is really bothering me that you may not let me back in the house."

"Don't be a fool. You don't have a chance. I don't think I want to let you back in the house," replied Hannibal. "You know how it is? I'm here alone. I'm not sure that what you're asking for is what I want to go along with. I don't trust you or even want to be nice to you, because of the trouble you gave us and they set you free at your trial."

"Would you let me in if it makes you happy to see me tap dance at a press conference?" asked Chris.

"I'm going to wait until the gang is back at the house. Then I guess I can let you back in the house to get your belonging," answered Hannibal. "Everyone will be back at 7 p. m. Can you come by then?"

"I should be in Davenport, by eight p. m. If I can come to your house at nine pm, that will give me a chance to get something to eat and then walk up to your house," answered Chris. "Will that be too late to come? After I find this personal thing, maybe I can interest you in a business proposition?"

"What did you have in mind?" laughed Hannibal. "Why do you even have the nerve to ask if I want to do business with you after all the terrible things you did?"

"Because a man does what has to be done or tries. That's the only way a man can live," explained Chris. "Because you and your agency are honest and can get the job done, I'm willing to pay you a good price for your troubles."

"Hmm, Even though we don't need the money we do need the work. I just sent Scooter to the bank with a large deposit," reasoned Hannibal. "After you get here and find your belonging, you, the gang and I will sit down and discuss our future together."

"That sounds reasonable. I'll see you at nine," promised Chris.

Chapter Five

WHERE IS SCOOTER?

It is now seven o'clock and the gang is back home except for Scooter.

"Where is Scooter?" asked Hannibal. "I sent him to the bank at nine o'clock this morning to deposit the money we made from the last job. I think we have a problem. I never saw such a man. That boy is never around when you need him."

"You know Scooter. Maybe he got lost," answered I'm Not Sure.

"How can Scooter get lost? He knows every street in Davenport. He better not let anything happen to that bank deposit," insisted Hannibal as Scooter came through the back door. "Hello Scooter, where have you been? Where were you?"

"Around," answered Scooter.

"I have some fresh coffee. Can I bring you some? I think we should sit down and have a cup of coffee and talk about where you've been all this time. Did you get to the bank to deposit our money or did you lose it along the way?" asked Hannibal. "Well."

"Well," added I'm Not Sure.

"Well, I, I, I, lost it all," answered Scooter.

"Don't tell me you lost it. Why do you always do things like that?" screamed Hannibal. "That's just typical of you. I want to know what you're planning on doing about it?"

"Just hit me. I deserve it," demanded Scooter.

"If I did, I would be held for murder. Nah, this isn't going to make it. It would serve you right if you choked on that coffee," scolded Hannibal. "I don't understand you, you big dummy. Just how did you lose all of that money?"

"I lost it at the casino," replied Scooter.

"And what machine did you lose it on? Was it called Brainstorm?" asked Hannibal.

"That sounds like it, but that's not it. I never play on Brainstorm. I don't know why, but I never win on that machine," answered Scooter. "I was playing on a machine called Thunderstorm. I thought I was beginning to get lucky, because I started to win. I wasn't able to win because of the elements out of a clear blue sky, I lost it all. I really am sorry about losing the money at the casino I was suppose to deposit."

"I hate to tell you this, you big dummy. You big moose. I'm afraid we have trust issues here and your apologies are pointless. You need to change your ways or stay out of my life," scolded Hannibal. "You're not very bright and you don't know what is ever going on, because you don't even know a little about anything. I wish you would stop doing stupid things.

You gambled our money away and didn't even think of the consequences. It's quite common with you. It makes me so mad, because you keep doing the same stupid things.

You are so disgusting. You never use any part of your brain. I think you have parts of your brain missing. I never know what you are going to do next."

"Why are you always making cracks about me?" asked Scooter.

"I make cracks about you, because everything you do is stupid," replied Hannibal. "If you don't like it, quit doing stupid things."

"I think you're right. It was all my fault that I lost all that money. You don't have to lose your temper over this," insisted Scooter.

"We never agree on anything. So don't tell me not to lose my temper," demanded Hannibal.

"Am I in any real danger over this?" asked Scooter. "You look like you have blood in your eyes. Anymore, I feel real nervous when I'm around you."

"Why would that make you nervous?" reasoned Hannibal.

"I think it's like when I had early toilet training," replied Scooter. "You're always standing over me waiting for me to do something."

"It can be very dangerous if you keep asking dumb questions and continue to do stupid things," boomed Hannibal. "Then you shouldn't be here. Remember when we thought it would be so nice to run a detective agency? Well, we was wrong."

"You know and I know I have to quit doing stupid things," answered Scooter.

"You're not like most people. You have to get your act together. I should have known better to send you to the bank with all that money. Sometimes I think you don't know the difference between a horse and a banana," yelled Hannibal. "How do you come up with these stupid things you do? Next you're going to tell me to hold on, because that whole thing I told you was a joke.

Scooter, you're one of a kind. You would think that I'm surprised at you and disappointed at you at the same time. Why can't you pay attention to the important things in life? You're never on time. I thought you would have been more careful with our money and didn't do anything foolish with it.

It's about time I stopped lying to myself about how responsible you are. Trust is earned. Respect is given and loyalty is demonstrated. I gave you more chances than anybody. The first rule is, you need to be responsible for the jobs I give you. You didn't follow the rules and this is it. Come on. Rules are rules.

The second rule is that you have to quit doing stupid things. Instead you went to the casino and spent the bank deposit like a rich millionaire. I must have been out of my mind to let you take the deposit to the bank.

Now, I can't stand the sight of you. That's the only way I can think anymore. There is no free room and board here. I don't think this is your kind of place to live. If you don't want to follow the rules, there's the door. I don't want to discuss it anymore. I don't have any other choice. Get out of here by morning, before I throw you out or commit murder."

"Listen to me. Listen to me. I'm your friend. I will pay you back by selling my car and giving you all of my blood," muttered Scooter. "You're one hundred per cent right. Hit me. Take your best shot."

"Oh, you're going to get what's coming to you alright. This is just you and me. I would rather have you come out in the backyard and fight me so I can teach you a lesson," ordered Hannibal. "I don't like to be kept waiting. You are a small minded coward. If you don't come now, that will be your last cup of coffee here."

"You talked me into it. Don't threaten me or I'm going to give you trouble. I'm going to warn you to not even try it. I'm a beast when I get mad," insisted Scooter.

"Very cute Scooter. Maybe I should give you a college education by straightening out your nose and breaking both of your heads. Anytime you're ready," demanded Hannibal.

"Are you kidding? I'm not asking for a fight. I'm going to quit while I'm ahead, because I can't stand the sight of blood, especially my own," replied Scooter. "I guess I owe you an apology."

"I would say so. I guess whatever happens, you still have a friend. I really don't want to hit my best friend," cried Hannibal. "Oh gee, I never have any fun anymore."

"You mean I'm going to get to leave in one piece. OK, I'm leaving. I don't know if you're coming or going. Either way this is going to be an empty room," exclaimed Scooter. "Now I'm going to my room to pack before you change your mind. I promise you that I will go away and you will never have to be kind to me again. The next time I see you, remind me not to talk to you."

"And where do you think you're going?" asked Hannibal.

"Out west somewhere. I'm going to shave my head and move to Florida or maybe further west," insisted Scooter. "I'm no good at nothing to nobody. No more. No more. Nobody owns me. I do not care to belong to A Detective Agency that accepts people like me as members and I'm never coming back."

"That's a shame. You're in worst shape than I thought. You're coming back. I will be expecting you," exclaimed Hannibal.

"I'm not coming back," exclaimed Scooter. "I told you that, I don't want to belong to any group that will accept me as a member."

"You don't fool me. You're thinking with your mouth as usual.

Now we have to raise some more dough somehow to pay our bills. Michael Murphy, alias Dr. Zodiac is coming to our house at nine tonight, to recover some personal property he left behind," muttered Hannibal. "He wants to hire us for a job. I don't trust him and would rather not take it. When he gets here, first I want to let him in and then let him out. Now we have to take the job, because of you."

"My best friend, Hannibal really thinks I'm nuts. Man, I really caught it this time and I can understand that," Scooter said to himself. "I'll get the money back somehow. What am I going to do? I may know a way out of this.

Maybe if I put an ad in the newspaper to sell my roller skates and ice skates I can get some of the money back. Now lets see. To get these skates sold fast, I think the ad should read, "If you are interested in roller skates or ice skates, call and ask for cheap skates at The West Side Detective Agency." I know. I also can sell my old 1980 Dodge Aspen."

"Where are you going?" asked Because. "You really caught it this time."

"I'm going to settle some business. I'm going to take my car to Friendly Freddy's Used Cars on West Kimberly Road. Maybe he will buy my 1980 Dodge Aspen from me so I can pay Hannibal back the money I lost at the casino," answered Scooter as he went out the door.

"Hannibal," yelled Because. "Scooter just told me that he was going to take his 1980 Dodge Aspen to Friendly Freddy's Used Car Lot to sell it to Friendly Freddy. What a stupid idea. You've got to stop him before he gets into more trouble."

Chapter Six

SCOOTER AND FRIENDLY FREDDY

Twenty minutes later, Scooter was pulling in the used car lot of Friendly Freddy's. As Scooter climbed out of his car, Friendly Freddy came out of his office and greeted Scooter by saying, "Hello neighbor. How can I help you today? You look like a one legged shopper to me. Would you like a cup of coffee neighbor?"

"Hello Freddy. Do you feel friendly today?" asked Scooter as he was looking at his old Dodge. "How about $500 for this Dodge?"

"I'm here to help you. That's a good choice. This is a very popular car. This car is a special edition. Isn't this a beauty, a cream puff? That car is a real honey," exclaimed Friendly Freddy. "That's in great condition and runs like a top.

Ah, this is perfect timing. This car is special to me. I was saving it to give to my daughter for her birthday. My wife drives one just like this and she loves it.

This is a limited time offer. But for you, I could let it go for $500.00. We would have to charge you a dealer prep to clean your vehicle. Why don't you look elsewhere to see if anybody can match my price?

I, myself wouldn't own a car like that for anything. I have my own means of transportation. I hitch a ride."

"That could be very dangerous Freddy. You could be taken out in the country and stripped," answered Scooter.

"So far that hasn't happened. She hasn't come along yet," laughed Freddy. "What's the matter? You look worried.

Allow me to let you take it for a test drive and you can keep it over night. You can drive the car now and we'll check your credit later.

I'll tell you what I'm going to do. If you buy it and after a week you don't like it, I will give you your money back. Do you have some money for a down payment?"

"That sounds very nice. Hold it. Just wait a minute, this is my car, all mine," insisted Scooter. "Would you buy it from me for $500?"

"That piece of junk. That car looks more like a lemon to me. They don't make cars like they used to. I might give you $350 for it," reasoned Friendly Freddy. "Start your engine to see if it is making any tell tale noises. It will indicate any faults that you have. What is that awful smell coming from your engine? This car can sure use some air freshener. That car should have been buried a long time ago.

Look at that rusty old bumper. It's ready to fall off", Freddy continued to say, as he yanked off the bumper of the car. "Those tires are really old," Freddy continues to say as he kicked the left front tire, with the air coming out. "That windshield is very dangerous. It is made with very inferior glass. If you were to be driving on a gravel road and a car comes from another direction and with all the dust, a rock flies through the air and hits your windshield and it will break the windshield like this," said Freddy as he picked up a large rock and through it through the windshield.

"You know what I think," suggested Scooter. "It just needs a tune up. I have a friend of mine who is addicted to brake fluid. He says he can stop anytime.

How would you like to play gas station? I'll put a bell on your nose and drive over you."

"A tune up won't fix that pile of junk. I'll tell you what the repairs this car needs. Because I'm known as Friendly Freddy, I'll give you $350 minus the cost of the repairs. Let's see, that will be $60 for a new tire, $125 for a new windshield, $154.90 for a new bumper and I will deodorize the engine for free."

"Don't forget the tax," reminded Scooter.

"Oh yes. The tax will be $10. That makes it a dime that I owe you," replied Freddy.

"Just make sure you pay me every nickel of it," replied Scooter as Hannibal road his motor bike into the used car parking lot.

"Just what do you think you're doing?" asked Hannibal.

"I just sold my Dodge Aspen to Friendly Freddy for $350 to get back the money I lost at the casino," explained Scooter. "My profit was ten cents after expenses."

"You did what? You sold your car for a dime? I thought you had better sense than that. I didn't expect you to do something foolish like this. No man would ever do that to me. Did you sign the paperwork?" questioned Hannibal. "If you did sign the paperwork and want to get your car back, you better get yourself a mask and a gun. On second thought, you already have the mask."

"Freddy said he would guarantee me a refund if I bought one of his cars. Only it wasn't in writing," explained Scooter. "I'm sure he would guarantee to sell me my car back."

"I've got a surprise for you," promised Hannibal.

"Is it bigger than a bread box?" asked Scooter.

"A guarantee that is not in writing is not worth the paper it is written on," replied Hannibal. "How about those apples?"

"I didn't know that," answered Scooter.

"I knew that," reasoned Hannibal.

"You stay out of this," ordered Friendly Freddy. "I ain't saying anything about our deal."

"It's no use fighting over this. If you didn't sign the paperwork, that's one way out. Get in your car and lets go home," instructed Hannibal. "It took us five years and we just got your car paid off. It may take us another five years before we can buy you another car. Well?"

"Well? Well? Just a minute. You guys aren't going anywhere with that car. We didn't sign the paperwork yet. That doesn't change anything. When I make a deal, I never miss. I already paid him for his car," explained Friendly Freddy.

"I didn't know that," exclaimed Scooter.

"I'm Scooter's life long friend and I'm in this as far as a friend can get," vowed Hannibal. "That's important to me. I like being Scooter's number one friend."

"I told you to stay out of this," snarled Friendly Freddy. "I'm known as Friendly Freddy. I'm Scooter's friend, because he is the best."

"I didn't know that," replied Scooter.

"Which one, Scooter? Ask yourself, which one is your friend? It can be anyway you want it," replied Hannibal. "Let me know anytime you're ready. Well?"

"Well," boomed Friendly Freddy.

"Well. I had to pay Friendly Freddy for the repairs of my car. Mr. Friendly Freddy. I guess I can't sell you my car," laughed Scooter. "Here is your dime back. Who needs money when you've got friends. On second thought, I wish I had friends with money. Now I don't have a nickel in the world. What I wouldn't give for a hundred bucks."

"I didn't know that," answered Friendly Freddy.

"I knew that," beamed Hannibal.

"Well sir, I'm feeling really bad that you don't trust me anymore. We made a deal and now you're backing out of it. Get that piece of junk off of my used car lot and take that old rusty bumper with you," demanded Friendly Freddy.

"And you call yourself Friendly Freddy! You're no friend of mine!" screamed Scooter.

"I knew that," laughed Hannibal.

"That's the last time I'm going to call you friendly," promised Scooter. "Next time I'll just call you Freddy. That's the last time I'm going to do business with you, Freddy."

As Hannibal and Scooter was driving off the used car lot, Friendly Freddy thought to himself, "That's never happened to me before. I can't understand it. I don't know, but I must have done something right."

Chapter Seven

SCOOTER, THE LAMP
AND THE GENIE

It is now nine o'clock and the boys are back home talking to Chris, alias Dr. Zodiac.

"I left my personal belonging in the room hidden behind the office which goes down to the basement," explained Chris. "I can find it and be back in five minutes."

"We didn't see anything in that room," replied Hannibal.

"That's because it's well hid," answered Chris. "Would you wait here while I go get it? When I get back then maybe I can explain to you what I want to hire you for."

"Since the ten of us are here, we can talk business after you get back," reasoned Hannibal. "Go get your belonging."

"What could he possibly have hidden in that room?" asked Scooter. "Ooh it's probably something from the supernatural or maybe a nice red brick. Na, it can't be a brick. I really wish it was a lamp with a magic genie."

"You and your lamp with a magic genie. If it was, I know what I would wish for," replied Hannibal as he was looking at Scooter.

"Don't say it. Don't say it," insisted Scooter as Chris returned and threw something in the wastebasket.

"What is it? I'm trying to think what that could be," boomed

Scooter as he reached down in the wastebasket and pulled out the object that Chris had put in the wastebasket.

"We must be tidy. Oh wow. Do you know what it is?" asked Scooter. "Oh boy! Oh

boy! A lamp. A real lamp. Can I have it?"

"Sure, go ahead and take it," offered Chris. "For some reason I bought this lamp at a yard sale a couple of years ago. I don't have any use for it. Its yours for $5.00."

"Thanks Michael. You know something? This is my lucky week. My lucky day. Now I have a lamp. My very own lamp," said an excited Scooter. "I owe it all to you Michael. I'll never forget you for this. Hannibal, can I take it to the kitchen and polish it? There is so much dust on it that you can write your name in it."

"Education is a wonderful thing," replied Michael.

"What are you going to do with that broken down teapot?" scolded Hannibal. "You ought to have your head examined throwing your good money around like that. Next, you're going to have to buy some tea to go with it and you don't even drink tea."

"It will look a lot better when I get it all shined up," answered Scooter.

"The tea pot or your head? Just rub the lamp. Try it and see how it works. And then get it out of here before I rub your head," exclaimed Hannibal. "Go ahead, polish your lamp. Maybe a genie will come out of the lamp and you can wish for the money you lost at the casino."

"That's a great idea. It would help all of us if a genie came out of the lamp. You don't like it, do you?" asked Scooter. "I was going to make it look nice enough to give it to you for your surprise birthday party tonight."

"Now you spoiled the surprise party for Hannibal tonight," insisted Who.

"Who cares. So I spoiled the surprise party for Hannibal. You didn't tell me it was a secret. Besides, Hannibal made it clear that he doesn't want it, because he called it a broken down teapot." objected Scooter.

"What surprise party?" asked What.

"I didn't know it was a surprise party," added I Don't Know.

"I wasn't sure we were even going to have a surprise party," replied

I'm Not Sure. As Scooter left the room to go to the kitchen to get a polish and a rag.

"If I could tell you all about the surprise party, it wouldn't be a secret," yelled Who.

"In the meantime, the rest of us have to sit here and talk about a job Michael wants to hire us for, because Scooter gambled the money away that he was suppose to take to the bank and deposit," explained Hannibal.

As Scooter disappeared into the kitchen with his new lamp to get some polish and a rag, the rest of The West Side Kids sat in the office listening to the job Michael wants to hire them for.

"Now that I have my personal belonging, I want to hire two of you to drive me to Burlington where my twin brother, Christopher Seven Murphy lives," explained Chris. "I just want the three of us in the car without anybody knowing about the trip or having to answer any questions about the trip. I'm going to give you a very good offer. If you can get me there safely, I will pay you $3,000 plus expenses. Do you want the job? How about it?"

"Nothing about it. Because we don't want to do business with you and we don't trust you," replied Hannibal. "Just why do you need us to escort you to Burlington? Just what are you afraid of?"

"I told you more than I wanted to tell you. I don't want you to ask me any more questions about the trip," objected Chris. "The less you know, the better."

"Since this is going to be a mystery, make it $4,000 and it's a deal," reasoned Hannibal.

"That's a lot of money for a job like that," answered Chris. "How about $3,500?"

"I don't know," replied I Don't Know. "I agree with Hannibal. There is too much of a mystery in it and we don't know what we're getting into. I think we should have more than $4,000."

"I'm not sure we should even take the job if there are things we don't know," added I'm Not Sure.

"Who is going to be in the car?" asked Who.

"I'll tell you what I'll pay," offered Chris. "I give you $4,500 as long as Scooter doesn't go. I'll be glad if he doesn't go on this trip. He is somebody I can do without."

"I'm way ahead of you. That's where you're wrong. Scooter has a job to do too. I'll tell you who's going and who isn't," explained Hannibal. "Scooter and myself will do the job for $4,500. I know Scooter goes on and on about stupid things that you don't want to hear about.

Scooter gambled our bank deposit away at the casino. Now Scooter will have to be part of this job to get the money back. That's my final offer. Take it or leave it."

"I guess I'll have to take it," reasoned Chris. "I don't like Scooter going along anymore than you want to do business with me."

While The West Side Kids were talking to Chris about taking him to Burlington safely, Scooter went to his bedroom to start polishing his new lamp.

"Oh boy. Oh boy. I finally got a lamp of my very own," Scooter said to himself as he sat on his bed and then laid down. "Well Mr. Lamp. I'm going to shine you up good. When I'm done polishing you, I will be able to see my face in you. First I have to clean all that awful dust off of you. Then I'm going to get you all shined up.

Why you were kept in that dark dirty room, I'll never know. Don't worry, I'll take care of you from now on. This polish won't work. Now I have to go back to the kitchen to see if we have some better polish.

First, I'm going to rest now that I have some peace and quiet. I am so tired, so tired. I won't be here long after I get some peace and a quiet rest."

After Scooter laid down, he kept thinking about the lamp and getting it polished.

"A minute later Scooter said to himself, "I just never seem to get enough rest and I am so tired. That's enough rest for now. Now that I had a long peaceful rest, I feel fine and I am ready to get up and go, go, go.

Now that I'm rested up, I am going to go polish my lamp that Hannibal calls a broken down teapot. It would serve Hannibal right if a real genie came out of my new shiny lamp."

After Scooter entered the kitchen, he walked over to the pantry to find some more polish. Finding some different polish, Scooter sat down at the kitchen table and began to rub the lamp with a rag to clean the dust off, he said to himself, "I wish something would happen to this broken down." and a puff of smoke came out of the lamp and a male Arabian Genie appeared before Scooter.

"Greetings," said The Genie. "I'm a slave of the lamp."

"Who are you with? Where did you come from?" asked a surprised Scooter.

"I'm The Genie of The Lamp. I'm a magical spirit and you just freed me from my imprisonment of the lamp. To reward you, I will grant you a wish for anything you want and I will get it for you," replied The Genie. "What do you wish for, gold diamonds, dancing girls?"

"There is no such things as genies. Na, you can't do that unless you're a rich millionaire," reasoned Scooter. "This is The United States and it's against the law to have slaves."

"Oh boy. What a day this is going to be. This is going to be tougher than I thought," answered The Genie as Lefty and Ace, The Assassin were looking through the kitchen window.

"Oh gosh. Oh dear. Hey Lefty, do you see what I see? We have to find the boss and tell him about this. Let's spread the good news," said Ace to Lefty. "The boss would like to get this information."

"I'll be right behind you," reassured Lefty.

"Just wish for something, so I can show you what I can do," insisted The Genie. "Now do you get it?"

"I may get it, but I don't know what to do with it," laughed Scooter.

"All you have to wish for is something you really want and I will grant you that wish," insisted The Genie. "This is the nicest part of my job."

"OK. I'll give it a try Mister Slave of The Lamp. Let me see. Like what? Like what do I really want? I know. I'm going to wish for, a lamp with a magic genie," wished Scooter.

"For two thousand years, I have had masters that really had some good wishes that I could grant and you wish for a lamp with a magic genie. You have no imagination at all. That's not even a dignified wish. I have spoken," scolded The Genie as he disappeared.

"Oh Genie, did I wish for the wrong thing? Please come back and give me another chance?" asked Scooter. "If you want to be a slave of the lamp, it's OK with me. Come back Genie. Please come back ole buddy, ole pal."

The Genie then reappeared and said to Scooter, "Now that you believe I am the slave of the lamp, can I grant you some wishes. Throw out the nonessential wishes. Think of something else that you want. I'm not going to compete with another genie."

"Oh Genie, I'm glad you're back. I didn't know you were so sensitive. Where have you been? I was worried sick that I said something wrong. I was afraid that you weren't coming back," exclaimed Scooter. "You promised to give me what I wanted. When I did, you got mad and left.

Everybody always says I'm doing stupid things. That must have been a stupid wish, so I'm going to try again. I'm going to wish for six nice red bricks. Is that too many?" asked Scooter."

"Of all the things you can ask for, you ask for six nice red bricks," laughed The Genie.

In a flash, six nice red bricks appeared on the kitchen table while Lefty and Ace rubbed their eyes in disbelief.

"These are a lot better than the bricks I've got," reasoned Scooter as he picked each one up to examine them. "Your incredible."

"So are you. I never had a master quite like you. In my opinion, you're one of a kind," replied The Genie as Hannibal walked into the kitchen. In a flash, The Genie turned himself into a monkey. "Your wishes are getting better than your last dumb wish. Now think. What do you want next?"

After seeing this, Hannibal went back to the office. Scooter then said to The Genie, "That was my best friend, Hannibal who just walked into the kitchen. After I bought

this lamp for $5.00, he called my lamp a broken down teapot. He always thinks he's my master. I want some muscles where I'm big and strong so Hannibal can't push me around anymore," wished Scooter as The Genie disappeared.

"Oh Genie, where did you go? Where did you go Mister Genie? Oh Mister Genie, please come back. Why won't you come back? Didn't you like that wish because you thought it was stupid? Did I ask for too much?" asked Scooter as he looked in the mirror to see his new muscles. As he looked in the mirror, Scooter said to himself, "Now, I've got enough muscles for everybody. Broken down teapot. I'll show Hannibal whose the master and whose the slave." Then Scooter picked up one of his new red bricks and crushed it with one hand.

"I have to watch those muscles. They have a mind of their own. Now I only have five nice looking bricks," cried Scooter. "Oh Mister Genie, would you put another fine looking brick on my kitchen table? It seems that my new muscles and my new bricks don't get along."

Scooter then said to himself, "I know something that Hannibal doesn't know that I know."

Scooter then went to the office where the gang had just finished talking to Chris.

"It's a deal. Now that you're our new client, we're back in business again. Michael, you be back here at nine o'clock tomorrow and we will leave for Burlington, just the three of us," replied Hannibal.

"Hey fellows. Look at my muscles," insisted Scooter as Jerry and Ace entered the back door to take the lamp off of the kitchen table. "You rub the lamp and The Genie gives you anything you want."

"Scooter, was that you calling us from the kitchen," asked Hannibal.

"No, it was a coyote and it's mating season," answered Scooter. "Of course I was calling you from the kitchen. If you promise not to say nothing to nobody, I will tell you what just happened to me."

"Quit bothering me about a genie that comes out of lamps. Right now, I have my own problems because you gambled our bank deposit away. What I wouldn't give for $1,000," replied Hannibal. "There is no such thing as magic genies and you know it. Next you're going to tell me that a beautiful Genie comes out of the lamp and grants you every wish you want and now you are an Astronaut.

That's a fairy tale that you're reading out of those books you just bought at The Book Rack. All you think about are genies. I just went into the kitchen and saw you talking to a monkey. You're in worst shape than I thought."

"Who do you think you're talking to. You don't understand. For a guy without muscles, you talk like a big man. Now that I have these new muscles, don't ever get out of line with me," scolded Scooter as

Jerry picked up the lamp from the kitchen table and Scooter's new muscles disappeared.

"My muscles. Their gone. Somebody else has gotten the lamp. Let's get to the kitchen now," ordered Scooter.

The boys then ran to the kitchen, seeing Ace with the lamp and pushed him against the wall. Ace dropped the lamp: along with Lefty escaped out of the back door.

Hannibal then picked up the lamp, locked the back door and threw the lamp in the waste basket.

Jerry Dickerson, Ace and Lefty

Dixie Doneright

Chapter Eight
THE POT WITH THE MAGIC GENIE IS REAL

Back in Jerry Dickerson's apartment, Ace and Lefty is telling Jerry, Danny, Shorty and Dixie about the pot they saw as they looked through the kitchen window at The West Side Kids Detective Agency.

"We followed Michael, The Magnificent, alias Dr. Zodiac like you told us to do," explained Lefty. "He took us straight to The West Side Kids Detective Agency on Sixth Street. Ace and myself looked through the kitchen window and we saw that menace to society, Scooter holding a pot.

Hold on to your socks. You won't believe what I am going to tell you next, because there is nothing like it. I know this sounds crazy and really has a ring to it. It looked like Scooter rubbed the pot and a puff of smoke came out of it. This odd looking character who was a male Arabian, who had a beard, was wearing a turbine on his head and the fancy clothes that Arabians are known to wear came out of the pot. You could have knocked me over with a feather after I saw what was coming out of the pot.

I heard him tell Scooter that he was a slave of the lamp and that Scooter freed him from his imprisonment of the lamp. Whoever is holding the lamp can wish for anything they want. And just like that you get it. Scooter wished for six nice red bricks and just like they, appeared on the table. I saw it with my own eyes."

"Come off of it Lefty. This is not the kind of eye sight I want. That don't make sense and never happened. Sometimes I think you look like an idiot and talk like an idiot. I never let that fool me, because I happen to know you're an idiot," insisted Jerry. "Ace, you were with Lefty. What's he been nipping?"

"That ain't the word for it. Could it have been a lamp instead of a pot that you saw?" asked Danny. "It won't take long to find out. I have a book that I checked out from The Davenport Library about a lamp with a magic genie. It's right here on the coffee table. I'm fully convinced there is such as a thing as a real genie. It must be on the level, because it's here in the book. Haven't any of you ever heard of Aladdin and The Lamp?"

"I know what you're talking about," added Shorty. "I once saw a cartoon about Aladdin with a magic lamp."

"The understanding of theory and the acceptance of reality are two different things. It says here in the book that Aladdin told the genie that he was hungry and the genie gave him a huge steak dinner with a couple loaves of bread and a couple of pies." explained Danny. "That proves there are real genies or they wouldn't even make cartoons about lamps and genies. For your information, people stood up for what they believed and they were executed for it. People called them nuts."

"Speaking of nuts, what a stupid idea it is to have to deal with Scooter to get this lamp. I can anticipate a nervous break down coming on," insisted Jerry. "We have to find some other way around it.

If that is true, Ace and Lefty go get that lamp and don't come back without it. I don't want you crowing about how you're going to get the lamp. I don't want any alibis by being five minutes late and a dollar short.

Be sure that nobody follows you. I don't want Dr. Fine and Charlie, The Chill to find out that Michael, The Magnificent is in town or about the lamp. They will be following Michael to see what he's after, just like us."

"We're on it boss. We'll do our best. We won't even bring our shadow along," promised Ace.

"I agree with Jerry. With that lamp, I could wish for some real diamonds instead of that cheap jewelry that Jerry gives me," reasoned Dixie.

"Give us some time to think about how we are going to get the lamp from Scooter without dealing with his stupidity," promised Ace. "Now that we're sure we weren't seeing things, we will definitely bring back that pot."

"That's a lamp, not a pot," insisted Danny. "Make sure you bring back the lamp without Scooter."

Chapter Nine

HANNIBAL RUBS THE LAMP

After Hannibal followed Scooter to the office, he decided to sneak back into the kitchen to get a better look at the lamp. After looking at the lamp in the wastebasket, Hannibal picked up the lamp to look at it.

This time, Dr. Fine and Charlie, The Chill stood outside the kitchen window watching Hannibal as he stood there for a minute trying to decide to rub the lamp or throw it back into the wastebasket. After making a decision, Hannibal began to rub the lamp. In a flash, a puff of smoke came out of the lamp and a genie appeared before Hannibal.

Rubbing his eyes Hannibal said to The Genie, "I don't believe what I'm seeing. Will you wait until I get my senses back? I thought Scooter was pulling my leg. I thought this was just a big joke."

"I don't believe what I'm seeing. I'm beginning to believe it myself," insisted Charlie, The Chill. "It is true. There really are lamps with magic genies."

"Somehow we have to get that lamp," replied Dr. Fine. "Let's go home and get our guns and come back later. Then we can just watch through the window and wait for our chance to get the lamp."

"I'm the slave of the lamp," said The Genie as Scooter entered the kitchen. "You have just freed me of my imprisonment of the lamp. It's surprising how simple it is. I will grant any wish that you want because you are holding the lamp. What will you wish for, gold, silver, diamonds, dancing girls?"

"Hannibal, I want you to meet my pal, The Genie. Genie, this is my life long friend, Hannibal. Any friend of mine is a friend of mine," Scooter informed the two standing in front of him. "Come to think of it, you never offered me any diamonds to wish for. What happened? Were you out of diamonds when it was my turn to make a wish?"

"This may seem silly, but now I'm going to have my big day. I'm jumping into the thrill of having a lamp with a magic genie and I'm really excited. From now on, he's taking orders from me," demanded Hannibal.

"Who are you talking to?" asked Scooter.

"I was just talking to The Genie," answered Hannibal.

"It's hard to tell. He looks bored," laughed Scooter.

"I almost forgot myself. I'm talking to you, Scooter," answered Hannibal.

"Good, because I hate to be left out of the conversation," replied Scooter.

"I take orders from whoever holds the lamp," insisted The Genie.

"I'll be the judge of that," demanded Hannibal.

Scooter then pulled the lamp out of Hannibal's hands and ordered The Genie to tie Hannibal to the kitchen chair. A chair was then pushed behind Hannibal and he was forced to sit on the chair, tied up.

"I don't like the way the day is starting out. I thought we were buddies, friends," Hannibal began to say as tears came out of his eyes. "Don't I always share things with you?"

"Nope!" replied Scooter.

"Don't you always share things with me?" asked Hannibal.

"Yep," answered Scooter.

"Didn't you say you were going to give me the lamp at my birthday surprise party?" reasoned Hannibal.

"I may have said those words," replied Scooter.

"I have something to say and I don't care no never mind how mean you are to me. The lamp is mine. Give it to me. I deserve this," ordered Hannibal.

"Nope, quit saying that. This is true that I said I was going to give it to you. I'm going

to keep this lamp, my lamp. That's the birthday surprise I have for you," laughed Scooter. "This is my very own genie."

"I thought we were buddies, that we shared everything," cried Hannibal. "I thought that was all that mattered. Right now, I am very sad, because it just poured on the greatest day of my life. Owning the lamp would take my mind off of my troubles."

"For the sake of our friendship, don't ask me to go along with this," reasoned Scooter.

"I'm asking. I'm asking," cried Hannibal. "I don't understand what you're doing, wanting to keep the lamp to yourself."

"I knew this would happen, because I know exactly how you feel. You must be devastated by now and really jealous. You just can't take it, can you?" insisted Scooter.

"I'll tell you what that means, because I know you don't understand. You think I'm weak and you always expect me to do anything you want me to do. It's my lamp. I won't do this and I will enjoy not doing this for you.

I was interested in magic genies and lamps to begin with. I paid for it with my own personal money," Scooter went on to say. "You never really wanted the lamp to start with, because you made fun of it by calling it a broken down teapot."

"You really think you're the center of the universe! I have my opinions! They may not be right! You know I'm still mad at you for gambling our deposit away! Maybe you should pack your things, shave your head and go to India!" screamed Hannibal. "You should never forget your friends on the way up, because they will be there on the way down."

"Don't be mad at me. I'll share the lamp with you. You're going to have to make it up to me," promised Scooter. "Genie, release Hannibal from the chair. Hannibal, just relax and do whatever you like. Are you happy now Hannibal?"

"That's a fine idea. I can't promise anything, but I will try," answered Hannibal with a smile on his face. Hannibal then stood up and bent over, putting out his right hand and said, "Shake partner. So far, so good."

"What's the matter? Did you hurt your back when the genie pushed the chair behind you?" asked Scooter.

"No, I'm paying my respects to The Queen of England," answered Hannibal. "Genie, from now on, you will take orders from both of us regardless as to who holds the lamp. You will take orders from no one but us, jointly and together. Let's keep it that way. Is that clear?"

"That's quite irregular. That is the dumbest thing I ever heard of. Of course I can't. This wish is a disaster. Over the years, I have only taken orders from one master at a time. He always made it simple, but significant," answered The Genie.

"So what? This is a wonderful moment. I'm glad I didn't miss it. Well now Genie, you've got two masters. Just think positive and consider this your lucky day," laughed Hannibal. "That's a sweet deal. Don't you just love it?"

"Wait a minute. I want some more red bricks," cried Scooter.

"Scooter, you're breaking my concentration about wishes. I'm in charge here. I'm feeling good and you're not going to spoil it. If you don't be quiet, I'm going to grab you by the legs and make a wish.

Oh yes. Check this out. First of all Genie, get us fifty million dollars in cash and forget the bricks," demanded Hannibal. "I think that does it. Come on. Let's get with it."

"Hey what happened to our partnership?" asked Scooter. "You sure put on a swell act."

"I changed my mind," answered Hannibal. "I think a lot of that lamp with the magic genie."

"Would you explain that to me again?" asked Scooter.

"What's it take to teach you a lesson. It was touch and go there for a while, then it was a cinch. You fell for it hook, line and sinker," answered Hannibal. "You messed up, although it was a nice gesture. I told you not to try and stop me. The last time you did this, you got into a lot of trouble. Our partnership disappeared the minute after we shook hands. From now on, I'm going to do the thinking around here."

"Where do you want the fifty million dollars?" questioned The Genie.

"Over on the table where we can count it," replied Hannibal.

"What's with all of that junk anyway? Those are gold bars. I asked for cash, folding money.

I can't carry around gold bars in my billfold. How am I going to buy things with gold bars? No business will take them. Get rid of those gold bars and give me the cash I asked for."

In an instant, the gold bars and The Genie disappeared.

"Well, that didn't take long. Now where did he go?" asked Hannibal.

"Mr. Genie, I know you're here. Come out, come out wherever you are and show yourself. I don't think he's here. I don't know where he went. Maybe he went to lunch," reasoned Scooter.

"Just leave the lamp on the kitchen table. Let's go to your bedroom to get the books you bought about genies," insisted Hannibal. "Maybe if we read about and understand genies, we can get The Genie to come back and get our wishes granted."

After Hannibal and Scooter left the kitchen, Ace and Lefty came in the back door to the kitchen. In an instant, Lefty grabbed the lamp off the kitchen table and then ran out of the back door and disappeared.

Chapter Ten

WHERE IS THE LAMP?

A while later, Hannibal and Scooter returned to the kitchen with the books about magic lamps and genies only to discover that the lamp was gone. After returning to the kitchen window, Charlie, The Chill and Dr. Fine saw Hannibal and Scooter in the kitchen.

"I don't see the lamp anywhere," said Dr. Fine to Charlie. "I don't think we better wait any longer to get the lamp. Let's see if the coast is clear and get the lamp now while we still have a chance."

In the kitchen went Dr. Fine and Charlie, The Chill, holding guns in their hands.

"Where is the lamp?" asked Dr. Fine. "I'll take the lamp now."

"I'm not sure, what you are talking about?" asked Hannibal. "Where did you get the notion that we had a lamp. If we did have a lamp, it would be none of your no, never making business."

"He's talking about the lamp with the magic genie," replied Scooter.

"Scooter, we don't have a lamp with a magic genie," reasoned Hannibal. "You and your delusions. Do you see a lamp anywhere?"

"Don't you remember? We left the lamp on the kitchen table and now it's gone," explained Scooter.

Showing Dr. Fine and Charlie, The Chill the books about the lamps and genies, Hannibal replied. "We all know there is no such thing as lamps with magic genies. Scooter is just pretending to have a lamp, because that is all he talks about."

"We know you have a lamp with a magic genie," answered Charlie. "Dr. Fine and myself, Charlie, The Chill was looking through the window and saw the genie come out of the lamp. Now give us the lamp and we will leave peacefully."

"OK, so you got us. Now your acting like a first class hood," muttered Hannibal. "The lamp was here on the table when we left the kitchen ten minutes ago to get these books about genies and lamps. Now the lamp with the magic genie is gone."

"That's a lie. You can't tell the truth to a mirror. You don't have any proof that you don't have a lamp. I ought to skin you alive for lying to us," answered Dr. Fine. "Come clean. You still have the lamp and you know where it is. Because you know the value of the lamp, you wouldn't be so stupid as to leave the lamp here on the kitchen table while you went trotting off to get those books."

"Yes we would," objected Scooter. "Before we left, I had just mopped the floor." "Why didn't you come back to get the lamp sooner when you knew the lamp was so
valuable?" asked Dr. Fine.

"The floor was still wet," insisted Scooter. "Besides, we can't be every place at once." "OK, you got us Dr. Fine. You're making a big deal about a lamp we don't have," insisted Hannibal. "After leaving the lamp on the kitchen table, we left to get the books about lamps and genies. I don't know anything different.

We don't know where the lamp is, unless Jerry Dickerson and his boys beat you here and took it after we left the room. You just have to take my word for it. Now may I show you out?"

Still with the gun in his hand and pointing it at Hannibal, Charlie answered, "I don't want The West Side Kids stopping us from what we have to do. I know you, Hannibal. There is a hole in your story. You're just trying to do a head trip on us. You're both coming with us, someplace where we can make you talk."

A half hour later, Hannibal, Scooter, Dr. Fine and Charlie, The Chill were sitting in a room at a motel on North Brady Street, by Interstate 80.

"As of now, I am going to give you some free information. Charlie and me have recently fallen on hard times," explained Dr. Fine.

"What's it have to do with us?" inquired Hannibal. "I don't know what your game is. What is it this time. You want to run that by me again? Just what do you want to talk to us about this time? Who do you think you are and what are you trying to do?"

"I'm the question and answer man and we want to talk to you. I think you know exactly what Charlie and me want to talk to you about," answered Dr. Fine.

"What is this, truth or consequences?" asked Hannibal. "What makes you think we can help you?"

"No it's not truth or consequences. As I said before, you know what Charlie and me want to talk to you about," exclaimed Dr. Fine. "Charlie and myself looked through your kitchen window and saw in fact a real for goodness genie come out of your lamp," Dr. Fine continued to say.

"Charlie and me need the lamp and the wishes as soon as possible. We have been reaping a lot of long lean years, hoping and going without. Instead of saving and slaving, the lamp and the genie are what we were looking for. We need to start driving and conniving. This is our ticket, our big break and we want it all. You really think you have both of us fooled, don't you?"

"So that is what you want. So you are trying to get the lamp? That did cross my mind," laughed Hannibal. "If we give you the lamp, we are digging our own graves. Why don't you go lock lips with a gorilla?"

"A word to the wise. You better be on your best behavior and tell us where the lamp is. If you don't, I will definitely kill both of you. Are you willing to take everything we can give you? There is no point of both of you getting hurt," exclaimed Dr. Fine. "You both are pig headed fools. If we can't get you to change your mind, there is a way to get around your stubbornness. I don't want to have to give you a hard time about figuring out how to get the lamp and the wishes. You better not make any long term plans, because you don't have much time.

I'm sorry I will have to do this to both of you. Don't get too comfortable. There could be some changes made if you tell us where the lamp is. If you don't tell us where the lamp is, I'm going to take you to never, never land."

"I keep telling you that we just don't know where the lamp is," reasoned Hannibal. "Why don't you go do the tango and screw yourself to the floor?"

"This gun says that you can," replied Dr. Fine.

"You really think you're tough guys and you sound like real mad men. You may think that I'm scared because I have never seen you with a gun before. Go ahead. Shoot me dead. Stomp on my grave," screamed Scooter.

"This is different," replied Dr. Fine.

"Sometimes when a man's mind is made up, it can't be changed. The lamp is my investment! I'm going to protect my investment by not telling you anything about my lamp! If you kill us, our death is on your head," answered Scooter.

"OK Scooter, you sit in this chair. Now tell me what I want to know," instructed Dr. Fine as he pointed his gun at Scooter. "Answer me and quit flashing your teeth. You're starting to give me a pain. Just don't try to remember, just remember. Try harder. Think really hard.

I was hoping I could get a little more cooperation from both of you. If both of you think you're going to get a nice and easy punch, you are very much mistaken. Now it's between you and us. I promise you if you don't tell us where the lamp is, you will be down for the count."

"You're beginning to sound like Jack, The Giant Killer," insisted Hannibal. "Your just plain poison. A rattlesnake wouldn't keep company with you. Why don't you go rent an empty store and live with a gypsy? You will have to cut us loose sooner or later."

"You are a real pair. Why are you putting us off? You better tell us what we need to know before it's too late," demanded Dr. Fine. "Hannibal, start slapping Scooter in the face until he tells us where the lamp is. I'm only going to ask you once. As old friends, tell us where is the lamp? We're going to get nasty if you don't tell us."

"Now that you mention it, you do have a nasty streak, if you get my drift. I don't know how I can sell you on the truth," insisted Hannibal. "Hold on. Now, listen. I can't hit my best friend. We don't know who has the lamp or where it is."

"I know you think you are very good at your job," screamed Scooter. "It's people like you that make people like me hate people like you, that want to hit you in the socks, yell at your mother, and spell your name wrong.

You have no feelings. No feelings at all. I feel like beating your head in, but I hate violence. I'm a sensitive guy. The cowboy code says you can't hit a smaller man, but I'm ready to make an exception. I've taken all I'm going to take from you. You're getting too far out of line. If you want to fight? I'll hold your coat for you."

"Maybe you think you can hit a smaller man, but not one that is as smart as me. How would you like to have your head stuffed through your collar?" replied Dr. Fine.

"No, I wouldn't," objected Scooter.

"It's nice to have loyal friends and you think you're going to get off easy. You're going to talk to me. Do it or else the lamp won't do you any good,"replied Dr. Fine holding the gun to Hannibal's head. "Now tell us, before it's too late."

"That's how I no never mind feel about you people. Put that gun down and now." scolded Scooter. "I don't like to be questioned at gunpoint. Besides, I think we have a fifty-fifty chance of getting out of here."

"How do you figure to get out of here? You're just stalling for time. Unless you tell us where the lamp is, it's more like a fifty-fifty chance you have of living," answered Dr. Fine. "Tell us where the lamp is and be quick about it. After you give Charlie and myself the lamp, by this time tomorrow Charlie and me will be clear out of the country."

"Or in the cooler. Does that mean we have until tomorrow morning to tell you, or do we?" asked Scooter. "You make me so mad that I just want to spit at the sun and bark at the moon. Why don't you let me and Hannibal do our thing and you and Charlie do your thing? That will allow all of us to do our thing together and that's the whole thing."

"What an idiot Scooter is. I don't think Scooter will ever stop being stupid because he either isn't here or not all the way there. Boy was that stupid what Scooter said to me," reasoned Dr. Fine. "Scooter, I don't know how come you have lived so long being stupid?"

"Scooter just has a bad streak in him from watching too many cartoons," laughed Hannibal.

"I think you are both too mule headed to to tell us what we want to know and you think this is some kind of an idea of a joke.," exclaimed Dr. Fine. "I don't think our threats are doing us any good now."

"Now you're catching on," insisted Hannibal.

"Hannibal, start slapping Scooter before I do, just to knock some sense into him if

that is possible," demanded Dr. Fine. "Give it up. You only have one chance."

Hannibal then began slapping Scooter ordering Scooter to tell him where the lamp was.

"I don't know! I don't know!" screamed Scooter. "I don't know where the lamp is!"

"Hit him harder until he tells you where the lamp is," demanded Dr. Fine.

As Hannibal began to hit Scooter harder, Scooter screamed, "I don't know! I don't

know! I don't know where the lamp is!"

"OK Hannibal. It's your turn to sit in the chair," ordered Dr. Fine. "Scooter, start

slapping Hannibal as hard as you can until he tells you where the lamp is."

As Scooter began to slap Hannibal, Hannibal yelled, "I don't know! The lamp is gone! I don't know where it is!"

Scooter then pulled Hannibal out of the chair. He then grabbed Dr. Fine by the arm, shoving him into the chair.

"Wise guy, huh? Where is the lamp?" yelled Scooter as he began slapping Dr. Fine.

"Where is the lamp? You took the lamp! Where is the lamp? Have you had enough?"

"I don't know! I don't know!" screamed Dr. Fine. "I don't know! where the lamp is."

"That's just enough," ordered Charlie, The Chill. "Stop it right now. Nobody is

leaving here until you tell us what we need to know. Nobody is going to help you."

"Who needs help? All I want to do is to get out of here!" yelled Scooter.

"You can say that again," insisted Hannibal. "Scooter, you know what our best defense is?"

"Running?" insisted Scooter.

"Something like that. Scooter, remember the routine we use called Look at us go?" explained Hannibal. "It begins by me saying, On your mark. Get set. Look at us go."

At that moment Charlie looked at Hannibal with a confused look as Hannibal pulled the gun out of Charlie's hand and hit him in the chin, knocking him on the floor. Then Hannibal and Scooter ran out of the door as Charlie, The Chill watched them go.

Chapter Eleven
Jerry, We Got It

As Ace and Lefty entered Jerry's apartment, Ace exclaimed, "Jerry, I told you that we would think of something to get the lamp. Now we've got it. Everything went smoothly and now we're in the money."

"What is it? That looks strange. That's the pot?" questioned Jerry. "That piece of junk doesn't look like anything a genie would come out of."

"This piece of junk as you call it may not look like anything, but it sure acts like something," replied Ace.

"I don't want it. Throw it in the trash," ordered Jerry.

"Don't pick it up that way. You're going to break it. Here, let me rub it?" insisted Danny as he grabbed the lamp out of Ace's hand.

As Danny rubbed the lamp, a puff of smoke came out of the lamp and in an instant, The Genie appeared.

"Where did you come from?" asked a surprised Jerry.

"You sent for me. I am the slave of the lamp. You have just freed me of my imprisonment of the lamp," replied The Genie. "I am here to grant any wish that you have."

"I'll want money," replied Ace as everybody requested their wish from the genie.

"This is quite embarrassing," replied The Genie. "You're going to hate me for this. I can't grant those wishes, because I have to obey those wishes of those I am suppose to serve."

Holding the lamp next to the picture of a lamp in the book Danny replied, "That doesn't sound right. It's not the way it's told. It doesn't check out? There is no doubt about it. This book is a blue print for genies. You have to grant those wishes. You're a slave of the lamp and whoever is holding the lamp gets those wishes. It's a sign of respect. It says so right here in the book."

"You are so right. I don't know what I can do for you. For over two thousand years I have done that for my masters," explained The Genie.

"How old did you say you were?" asked Danny.

"Over two thousand years old," replied The Genie.

"You can't be that old," reasoned Danny.

"I really am," answered The Genie. "As I was saying I can't grant you wishes anymore because of the last master I had holding the lamp. Perhaps that's the reason for all of this. Are you going to believe the book over me?"

"Say what?" interrupted a surprised Danny. "We have the lamp now and you have to grant those wishes."

"That's impossible. I'm afraid I can't go along with this," explained The Genie. "That doesn't make any difference what you ask me to do. I just can't go along with this.

You ask, why can't I do that? It's not what I want to do. It's what I have to do. There is a purpose in all of this and because of that it won't be so easy to get your wishes. You don't seem to realize what kind of ordeal this is going to take."

"Why don't you educate us?" asked Jerry.

"I don't know if I should tell you this, because it would sort of be like a betrayal of confidence. I was expecting to find a higher form of intelligence when I was summoned out of the lamp and found Scooter and Hannibal by mistake. They are second rate opportunists," explained The Genie. "I swear that it wasn't my fault. When Scooter rubbed the lamp last time, I thought I was home free because Hannibal was standing next to Scooter. Hannibal, who was my last master took the lamp from Scooter and made a wish that from now on I was to take orders from him and Scooter only, jointly and together regardless of who is holding the lamp."

Walking up to The Genie, Dixie put her arm around him and

asked, "How would you like me to play Dracula and let me suck on your neck? Why can't you make this one exception and give us one free wish? I'm sure we can get together on this."

"Bright eyes, you're pretty formal for a girl. Are you trying to entice me? You make it very tempting young lady. You are a very industrious lady and may think it was worth all of this," replied The Genie. "I learned to say no to women before. You learn to do that when you have a body like mine. Now you think you can try another way to get the wishes you want?"

"Why can't you make this one exception and give us one free wish?" cried Dixie.

"Don't you have a shred of dignity? It has to be business before pleasure," replied The Genie. "The wishes are something you can't have because of the wishes from my last master."

"So what if I don't have a shred of dignity. If I did, I wouldn't have done it," answered Dixie.

"Excuse me. This may be a poor chose of words. Here it goes," explained Jerry. "Dixie is just teasing you. She's a crazy lady with a crooked smile. If you let her, she would tease the pants off of you.

When I met Dixie, she worked at a bank. Before that, Dixie was a bar room brawler. Dixie turned down my loan. The loan didn't work, but she was crazy about me. After that she called me and told me that she loves me more than she can tell me. I didn't understand why she had a crush on me.

Dixie got her looks from her father. He was a plastic surgeon. She used to play the harp and was very good at it. I was so highly strung, my body was starting to tingle. When she touched me and jumped on my lap like a little old puppy she would bite my neck. She made my body dance because she has great hands.

With Dixie, it was like a Sunday Night Football Game. Only we got to do the replays. Because of that, I'm a lucky guy. Dixie turned out to be an angel of mercy.

For some odd reason, she believes that if a man is tired among us, he is tired of life. Why is it that thrills a woman more than a man's blood?

In the telephone call she approved me and said Smart Pants, I think I'm in love with you. After that, she nicknamed me Smart Pants.

A man and a women are like a meal on a card of life. One will not turn without the other. We have been through a lot together."

"That's not life. It's a stupid paperback novel,"laughed Ace.

"Thank you Mr. Sensitivity," boomed Jerry.

"I'm sorry if I'm not a hopeless romantic," answered Ace. "Why couldn't you just look at each other and fall in love?"

"You have to face reality. It was just a little awkward when we met," insisted Jerry. "There was really no awkwardness. We were just having trouble thinking about what we wanted to say to each other."

"These wishes are not for sale. There is no rhythm to the universe. Everybody wants the things they don't have and they don't appreciate what they do have," The Genie continued to say. "I know that sounds ridiculous, but as a slave of the lamp, I have to grant my last master's wishes and they were from now on I was to take orders from Scooter and Hannibal only, jointly and together regardless of who is holding the lamp. What do you want me to do about it? Tap dance on your head."

"OK, let me handle it. This is a job somebody has to do. and that's my specialty. I really want the job. It looks like the ground rules have changed and they won't get us to second base. I'll tell you what I have to do," reasoned Ace.

I think we have been asking the wrong questions and whatever it is, The Genie is going to tell us what it is that is biting him. If I work The Genie over by using him as a punching bag, he will tell us and then grant us our wishes.

The Genie is going to do what any man would do right now to survive the pain, discomfort or maybe death. Because you're hard to convince, you're ruining our mission. Lefty, stand behind The Genie and hold his arms."

"That's rude. I tell you that ain't going to work," replied The Genie.

Lefty then grabbed The Genie's arms as Ace swung at The Genie's face. The Genie disappeared and showed up sitting at the bar and Lefty was hit in the face.

"That won't do you any good," laughed The Genie. "I told you that wasn't going to work. When are you going to believe me?"

Pulling out a gun and pointing it at The Genie, Shorty replied, "I'm beginning to catch on. You interest and fascinate me. I know it may sound crazy, but I am beginning to believe you. That's what worries me. I never turn back once I start.

Now I am going to find out if this is a good bet or a bluff. Genie, you make a decision right now or do I have to order you to start granting wishes?"

"You think I am so unnerved by you. I have discipline and control. Nobody owns me," replied The Genie. "You haven't caught me yet"

Again, The Genie disappeared across the other side of the room, standing there with a bottle of gin and a glass.

"Boy, you're tough. I bet nobody can push you around," reasoned Shorty.

"I just love gin," laughed The Genie as he took the cap off of the bottle and poured gin in the glass. "I have been in the lamp so long that I forgot what it tasted like."

"Genie, you're taking this remarkably well. I didn't know that Genies drank. Shorty, can't you stop him?" asked Jerry.

"I'm not sure I want to. That's not the point. I've got it. I certainly do," answered Shorty. "I just noticed something that makes me think it's not going to be so easy. We have ourselves another whole kind of problem."

"I don't want to hear no more. I'm afraid what we tried is not going to work out at all. I want to straighten out a few things about my concern for this lamp. This whole thing is for the birds. As of now this lamp is a piece of trash, because The Genie isn't going to grant us anything. Throw it in the wastebasket," demanded Jerry.

"Wait a minute. We tried everything we could to discourage The Genie from not granting our wishes," reasoned Danny. "I have a better idea. It's so simple, it's beautiful. Sometimes I amaze myself. Maybe we have been operating a different way that we should have and have been going about this all wrong. We still have the lamp. At least we know how to get our wishes. To get our wishes, we just need to convince Hannibal and Scooter to come to your apartment."

"You win another cigar," added The Genie.

"I sure don't want to deal with Scooter again," explained Jerry. "He makes me so mad. Scooter is a real bummer, a weirdo, a crackpot, a loony who is a one dimensional person with problems. You never know what he is going to do next. Ace, what's your opinion?"

"I think Scooter is a loony," insisted Ace. "It's one thing to have a lamp with a genie. It's another thing to be stupid. Some people are confused with education and intelligence. They broke the mold first. Then they used it to do a stupid thing by making Scooter. Sometimes I think Scooter makes every one around him act stupid. I guess we don't have any choice."

"OK, then you need to all go back together you nit wits. Danny, Ace, Lefty, Mugs and Shorty go get those two and bring them back here. You do it and you do it fast," demanded Jerry. "You know where to find them."

"Is anybody thinking the same thing I am thinking?" asked Ace.

"I don't know. What are you thinking?" asked Jerry.

"I don't want Dr. Fine and Charlie, The Chill to find out about the lamp and the magic genie. If they find out, I suppose they will try to get the lamp, sometime, someplace, behind our back," insisted Ace. "We better find Hannibal and Scooter before the storm hits in case Dr. Fine and Charlie, The Chill finds out about the lamp.

Here's a bulletin for you. Watch yourself. Dr. Fine and Charlie, The Chill may come to your apartment and try to get the teapot from you while we are gone."

"Why those dirty crooks. Sometimes I think you are always exaggerating. Now I get it now," reasoned Jerry. "I wouldn't wish Scooter on my worst enemy. Since I don't have a worst enemy, Dr. Fine and Charlie, The Chill will have to do.

We can't let those crooks get away with this. There is just no honor among thieves. Then in that case, I will hide the teapot and put it in a secure place."

"That's a lamp, not a teapot," corrected The Genie as he gulped down the glass of gin. "I'm a slave of the lamp, not a slave of the teapot. Call me when you're ready for business. I have spoke."

"Give me that bottle of gin or you're not going to be in any shape to grant wishes to anybody," demanded Jerry.

In a flash, the genie disappeared with the bottle of gin.

71

Chapter Twelve

Our Rainbow Fell From The Sky

Meanwhile back at The West Side Kids Detective Agency, Hannibal and Scooter were sitting in the office with the rest of the gang telling them the whole story about the lamp with the genie.

"Why I'm associated with you, I'll never know. I've known you all my life and I still can't tame you. You make me crazy and you're nothing but a dream killer." Hannibal said, scolding Scooter. "I thought this was going to be the best time of my life, because I thought we were sitting on a rainbow. I was hoping we could continue to be lucky. We had a genie that could give us anything we wanted right in the palms of our hands and cashing in was just a matter of time.

Because of you, our rainbow fell from the sky and disappeared. You're turning out to be a very expensive friend. You let Lefty grab the lamp right out of your hands."

"You were a big help letting Ace sock you in the face knocking you to the floor," answered Scooter. "The problem with you doing nothing is that you never knew when you were finished. You didn't even try to defend yourself. That would have been a strong and courageous thing to do, to defend yourself with your martial arts. I didn't even need those new muscles to defend myself against you."

"Well. Ace took me by surprise before I could do anything," insisted Hannibal. "I don't know what I can say to make you believe me."

"Well nothing. Lefty took the lamp from my hands before I knew what was happening," reasoned Scooter. "You know, I feel a little tension around here and I really feel that you are being unfair. It looks like I have to be careful how I answer this?

Maybe I should rephrase what I said. It may sound weird to you. I'm really sorry about the mess I got us into. I know it's a difference of opinion, but I'm sorry how I acted and just can't tell you how sorry I am that I let Lefty take the lamp from me."

"You can show me how sorry you are by hanging yourself!" screamed Hannibal.

"What's that suppose to mean? Are you upset about something?" asked Scooter.

"No, I always relax like this. Of course I am upset about something!" yelled Hannibal.

"It seems that you have a very irritating manner about you today!" yelled Scooter. "Is this some sort of cruel joke or are you going to be like that all day Mr. Happy Face? Are you trying to spread your happiness all around to the gang today?"

"There is a moral here," replied Hannibal. "Shut up. You're starting to steam me. So keep your mouth shut."

"Hannibal seems to be a little upset. What drives me crazy is that Hannibal is always right," mumbled Scooter.

"Do you think I have been too rough on you?" asked Hannibal.

"Let me sleep on it?" replied Scooter.

"Thanks to you, I've already started," laughed Hannibal.

"Your always too rough on me and it hasn't been a picnic," answered Scooter. "You are always barking at me, calling me crazy and lazy and trying to show me up."

"That's because you are a bad boy. I do not like a bad boy," exclaimed Hannibal. "I want the entire world to know you're a bad boy."

"That's what I'm talking about. You never show any compassion for me. You are a real worrier," reasoned Scooter. "That's why the skin on your nose is all pinched up and pulls your eyes together. It makes you look like an angry owl."

"What do you mean? Who me? Mr. Warmth. You're putting me on," answered Hannibal. "Oh, I see, you want me to change how I treat you, by starting to pay more attention to you, by being nice to you, by saying if you have any problems, come to me.

Well I have a surprise for you. If that doesn't work, I 'm going to lock your knees together and you will find out how hard it is to ride your motorcycle."

"That's impossible. It won't work. Scooter, you're going to be alright," promised Who. "Hannibal can be a hard man at times and he holds you up to ridicule you to anybody. Sometimes Hannibal can be the cause of your problems. There you have it.

So what? You said all the right things to Hannibal and you were beautiful. You are a bigger man than he is. Scooter, you're a real nice kid and we all like you. We all know you want to stay in the gang. You like the gang and the gang likes you."

"It may not make any sense, but why do I suddenly feel better?" replied Scooter.

"Maybe if you two get something to eat, you both will feel better. We all know what happened and it didn't work," reasoned Who. "What, what do you think?"

"I agree. It's not important if you win or loose. We need to roll with the punches and face reality. If you want something and can't have it, let it go," laughed What.

"Never let your brain idle. Just have as much fun as you can. Laugh often, long and loud. Laugh until you gasp for breath. Be alive while you are still alive. You just need to keep cheerful friends around you. The grouches pull you down.

Life is not measured by the number of breaths we take, but by the moments that take our breath away. The only person that is with us our entire life is ourselves.

Hannibal you do have a short temper. You shouldn't get so upset like that. There is no reason to blow your stack like that. You have to learn to rise above that. You have to learn a new way. When life gives you a hundred reasons to lose your temper, show life that you have a million reasons to smile and laugh."

"The trouble with people, they keep everything all locked up inside," added Scooter. "People should be able to say what they want to say. Hannibal, I thought I knew you and we should just be able to shoot the breeze."

"OK, you're boring me. I'm a cowboy and I come from Texas. Now you know me," insisted Hannibal. "There is nothing wrong with being stupid, but don't abuse it."

"I saw your face go from white to red to purple," What continued to say. "Sometimes we have to blow our stack instead of letting everything being bottled up inside of us. A certain amount of blowing off steam is healthy. If you really feel like your going to burst, let it go. Just don't over do it. It may seem like a vicious circle, but it will come back to you if it was meant to be. Don't even worry if you blow off some steam. You will bounce back."

"I think What is right," added I Don't Know.

"I agree with I Don't Know," laughed I'm Not Sure. "It's written all over Hannibal's face. I don't like being around depressed people. We might as well brew up some coffee and relax. Hannibal, how come this is the first time today, I've seen you smile?"

"You know something? After thinking about what, What said, I'm starting to feel better already." insisted Hannibal. "There is nothing wrong with me. I'm in perfect shape. I'm as free as a bird."

"If your blood pressure gets out of control, it's bye, bye birdie," laughed What.

"I suppose it's out of the question. What really sounds good to me are some nachos," added I'm Not Sure.

"I don't really care for nachos myself," replied Scooter. "Nachos are just tacos that don't have a life together. Sometimes after I eat tamales, they keep me up all night. Then they are here today and gone tamales. Do you like it?"

"I thought it was a very bad joke. Jokes about German sausages are the wurst. What I can go for is some nice pizza," added What. "I can really go crazy over that stuff."

"What I can really eat is some good fried chicken," reasoned I Don't Know. "It seems that my favorite place to get fried chicken has made the portions of chicken smaller and smaller. If the portions get any smaller, they will be handing you the eggs. Their french fries are getting so bad that they taste like shoe leather cooked in oil."

"I have an idea. Why don't each of us go into the kitchen and make something to eat of our own, so we can have a pot luck?" suggested What. "There will be plenty to eat and drink for everyone."

"What? I don't like pot lucks. People serve food to others that they wouldn't eat themselves," replied I Don't Know.

"I Don't Know, what you're saying is that the pot luck hot-line suggests that we give up and order some pizza?" asked What.

"When you stop to think about it, pizzas are round. They are cut into triangles and put in a square box," reasoned Hannibal. "If you can understand that, then you may understand how Scooter thinks."

"What, you really can put away the groceries," laughed I Don't Know. "I don't know how all those groceries ever get into your stomach."

"They don't. They just lay in my chest," laughed What. "I think it sounds fun to me. I always say you should never miss out on a good pot luck. Does anybody know what a clock does when it's hungry? It goes back four seconds."

"Gang, do you remember when we took the class trip to the Coca Cola Factory?" asked Because. "Because when we got back, I was surprised there was no pop quiz."

"I'm sorry that I'm a wet blanket. I guess you're right. I'm not crazy about reality, but it's the only place to get a decent meal. Why don't we all tie on the feed bag? Scooter, why don't you go in the kitchen and get us all some coffee and cookies?" asked Hannibal.

"You don't deserve any coffee and cookies after what you did. Get some for yourself anyway and then maybe we can all forget about the genie.

Maybe the whole thing was figmentation of the imagination of my brain. I'm sure there is a logical explanation. I wouldn't know if it really happened or I dreamed it. There was no genie in the kitchen, because there are no such things as genies. Make my coffee black," added Hannibal.

"Naturally. Who ever heard of white coffee," replied Scooter. "Go ahead. Sing like a bird. Eat like a pig."

"Scooter, I don't know where you come up with these things?" insisted Hannibal.

"Well, you know I'm an only child," answered Scooter.

"I wonder why," laughed Hannibal.

"Would you like some cottage cheese to go with that?" asked Scooter.

"No, I don't want any cottage cheese," answered Hannibal. "How would you like it if I put a bell around your neck so we can play Dairy Farm? I've eaten enough cottage cheese in my life time and I don't want anymore. If I eat anymore, I will go snow blind. Scooter, you're starting to get on my nerves."

"Even the people with the best intentions can get on your nerves," reasoned Scooter.

"There is one thing worse than eating too much and that is talking too much. Now go into the kitchen and get our coffee and cookies," ordered Hannibal.

Scooter then went in the kitchen to find the coffee. Smiley was standing on a ladder with the back door open, painting a patch in the wall that he just installed. Realizing the coffee was on the top shelf of the kitchen shelf, Scooter grabbed the ladder from under Smiley and a cup of paint and Scooter yelled, "Hang on Smiley!"

Grabbing the cup of paint, Scooter set it on the counter. A little while later, Scooter returned with coffee and cookies for everyone.

"Well kiss my spare ribs. Here comes Scooter with the coffee now." exclaimed Hannibal. "Scooter, where is Smiley?"

"Smiley is hanging around in the kitchen," answered Scooter.

"Scooter, is that a fire in the kitchen?" asked Hannibal.

"It's not a fire. It's just a little smoke," answered Scooter. "I have some hamburger patties in a pan. I just forgot to turn them over."

Scooter then set the coffee and cookies down in front of Hannibal. Hannibal took a sip of his coffee and spit it out.

"How do you like your coffee?" asked Scooter.

"Isn't this great? It's hilarious. I ask for coffee and you give me a cup of paint!" shouted Hannibal. "What are you trying to do, give me food poisoning? You don't deserve any coffee. You deserve this cup of paint. It's a good thing it wasn't ham that you gave me! Then I would have been ham bushed! You need to laugh at yourself Scooter! I can't do it alone! Can I make a suggestion?"

"Are you mad at me?" replied Scooter. "What is your suggestion?"

"Mad. Are you asking me if I'm mad at you. Of course not. After you turn those hamburgers over, I would just like to send you to France on an inner tube. Before you go to France make out your will," replied Hannibal.

"Somehow when you say this, it doesn't sound funny," reasoned Scooter.

"Funny? I'll tell you what's so funny!" yelled Hannibal. "You giving me a cup of paint to drink instead of the coffee I asked for! Now go back to the kitchen and get me some coffee! Some real hot coffee, instead of more paint! Now get me some coffee this time! Hurry it up before I gum myself! In fact I'm going with you to find out how you gave me a cup of paint!"

"You left your voice in my ear," insisted Scooter.

Chapter Thirteen

WHY DON'T YOU JOIN US?

As Hannibal and Scooter entered the kitchen, there was Ace, Lefty, Shorty, Mugs and Danny waiting for them with guns in their hands. Smiley was still hanging on to the door.

"I never thought you were ever going to come back," growled Smiley. "Bring that ladder over here and get me down."

"What happened to you?" asked Hannibal.

"What do you think happened?" bellowed Smiley. "Scooter, the president of stupidity, took the ladder away from me when I was painting this patch above the door."

"Hold on. I get you the ladder," insisted Hannibal.

"What do you think I've been doing for the last ten minutes?" asked Smiley.

After getting Smiley down, Hannibal asked Ace, Shorty, Mugs, and Danny, "Gentlemen, what can we do for you today?"

"We are here to call on you. You're just the men we have been looking for. Guess who wants to see both of you?" asked Ace. "We came back to get both you and Scooter by Dixie Doneright's request. This is not a social call."

"You don't say," answered Hannibal. "I thought this was a membership drive."

"It's been a long time since we seen you last," reasoned Ace.

"Not long enough," replied Hannibal.

"Why don't you join us? Dixie wants to talk to you. It won't take long," reassured Ace. "Come on! We're wasting time."

"Just a moment. I'll be with you in a minute," insisted Hannibal.

"I was hoping you both would come on your own. Dixie has a girlfriend by the name of Sandra and they both want you to come and have dinner with them. Shall we proceed?" instructed Ace.

"It's a good thing you're asking both of us. Scooter, quit your worrying. Scooter doesn't go anywhere without me," reasoned Hannibal.

"Oh yes I do," replied Scooter as he was looking at the guns. "Oh no I'm not. I always string along with Hannibal. I don't go anywhere without Hannibal. Worrying nothing. I'm scared stiff. Well, shut my mouth."

"I will," replied Ace as he pulled out a gun and pointed his gun at Scooter.

"You did. Now you know. Inside my brain, I'm screaming for help," answered Scooter. "I think you thrive on this sort of excitement. If you shoot me, do you think the cops will think you're celebrating the 4th of July early? When it comes to murder, the cops won't like it. The cops aren't just going to give up and go away."

"I just want to know what you are doing and why are you doing this?" asked Hannibal. "I'm sorry, but I still don't understand."

"Jerry Dickerson wants to speak to you in private, because he wants the wishes from the lamp," replied Ace. "Speed is of the essence."

"I thought you said that Dixie Doneright and her girlfriend, Sandra wanted us to have dinner with us," answered Hannibal. "I don't care what that crazy man wants."

"I have a couple more notions of my own. Instead of shooting you, maybe we should break your arms and legs if you don't want to come with us," insisted Ace. "I am in charge of this show and the waiting is over. Both of you better come with us now, because Jerry Dickerson won't like it. It's your necks, not ours, so come on. Snap into it now. OK, let's go, rush, hurry."

"Don't forget, You still owe us a dinner! yelled Hannibal.

Hearing the new voices in the kitchen, The West Side Kids went into the kitchen to find Hannibal and Scooter gone.

"I thought Hannibal and Scooter went into the kitchen to get more coffee. That's strange that Hannibal and Scooter are gone. They always tell us where they are going," reasoned I Don't Know. "I'm going outside to look for them."

"While you're outside looking for them, I'm going to call Hannibal and Scooter on their cell phones. If they don't answer, What and I Don't Know, will you come with me to look for them?" asked Who. "I don't know where they went. If we're not back in two hours, will the rest of you come and get us?"

"Who is going to come and get us?" insisted I'm Not Sure as there was a knock at the office door.

"I better go answer the door," offered I'm Not Sure. "I'm not sure who it could be. Hey everybody. Look at what we've got here? We have a visitor. It's T. J. Columbo. Come on in."

"We heard you went to Burlington to go to the trial of Dr. Zodiac. When did you get back into town?" asked What.

"Last night," answered T. J.. "It's sure good to see everybody. Is the gang all here?" "No" replied Who. "Am I relieved to see that you are here. Hannibal and Scooter just

left and we don't know where they went. I Don't Know was just going outside to look for them."

"Has there been any word as to where they are?" asked Columbo.

"Not yet. I Don't Know just went to look for them," explained Who.

Five minutes later, I Don't Know came back in the house and said, "Scooter and Hannibal are not outside. Their motorcycles and cars are still in the garage."

"What and I Don't Know come with me. The rest of you spread out and look for them here in the house," ordered a concerned Who.

"Is there anything I can do to help?" asked Columbo.

"Stay here and wait for Hannibal and Scooter to come back. If we're not back in two hours, come with the rest of the gang to look for us," answered Who.

Twenty minutes later, Hannibal and Scooter arrived at Jerry Dickerson's apartment with Ace, Lefty, Danny, Mugs and Shorty.

Acting as if he was a butler, Danny reached for Hannibal's hat and asked, "Your hat sir?"

"Yes it's my hat. I let my hat go to my head and I'm glad I did, because but if it wasn't my hat, I wouldn't be wearing it," answered Hannibal.

"OK mister hat. Whatever you say. We brought you here to have dinner with Dixie and Sandra," explained Danny.

"Alright, alright. A little food won't hurt us," reasoned Hannibal.

"You wait here while I go and get the girls," ordered Danny.

"Scooter, when the girls get here, you be on your Sunday behavior," ordered Hannibal. A few minutes later, instead of the girls, Ace returned with the lamp.

"We have this lamp of yours, that is now our lamp. Instruct The Genie to give us the

wishes we asked for," explained Ace. "The Genie won't grant us any wishes without both you and Scooter, jointly and together, regardless of who is holding the lamp to grant wishes."

"What's this all about?" asked Hannibal.

Holding a knife to Scooter's chest, Ace went on to say, "You know what this is all about. Suppose you tell me. Start talking. If you don't instruct the genie to give us our wishes, I'm going to cut Scooter's heart out."

"I resent that. That's not very friendly. If you do, you will have to buy me a new suit," exclaimed Scooter. "If you break it, you will have to buy it."

"No you don't. You're not going to kill Scooter. You need both of us two, jointly and together to order the genie to grant wishes. How would you like it if I put a pulley in your nose to haul bricks?" asked Hannibal. "You sure are asking a lot of personal questions. I think Scooter and me better go now."

"Now go over there and sit down and no gabbing. All we want you to do is to tell the genie that we're taking over and from now on the two of us, Jerry and myself will be his new masters and he will take orders from no one but the two of us jointly and together regardless of who holds the lamp," replied Ace. "The possibilities are endless. It doesn't look like you have any choice to do this? Either you promise to do this or I will promise to cut Scooter's heart out."

"OK, I'm a trustworthy guy. Scout's honor. I don't want you to kill my best friend," reasoned Hannibal. "People have been told to kill for less. What do you think Scooter is, chopped coyote meat? I didn't know it was going to be that kind of day. Let's get started by giving me the lamp."

Handing the lamp to Hannibal, Ace again ordered Hannibal to do like he was told to do.

Hannibal then rubbed the lamp and a puff of smoke came out of it and in seconds there stood the genie.

"I'm a slave of the lamp," said The Genie. "Have you and Scooter, jointly and together made up your mind what wishes I can grant you? Tell me what you're going to wish for and I will grant you that wish."

"We sure do. This is a no brain er. This is our wish, jointly and together," replied Hannibal. "Scooter and myself need to get out of here. Return you, the lamp, Scooter and myself back to the kitchen in our home where we will be a lot safer."

"Here is another man trying his luck with his wishes. Scooter, do you jointly agree with that?" asked The Genie. "What do you say now?"

"I sure do. Hurry before I need a new suit," exclaimed Scooter.

"I swear that this place is going to be condemned. I can feel the fungus crawling up my leg and because of that Scooter and me have to leave all of you and your family picnic. Have a nice time. Happy trails to all of you," laughed Hannibal.

In a flash, Hannibal, Scooter, The Genie and the lamp were back in the kitchen of their home where The West Side Kids were standing.

"We've got trouble. We've been had," yelled Jerry. "Hannibal sure surprised me. He doesn't play fair anymore."

"Oh boy, they're asking for trouble. They ran out on us. Are we going after them?" asked Ace.

"We don't have to at the moment," answered Jerry. "There is no sense wasting time. They already told us where they are going."

Chapter Fourteen
WHAT'S GOING ON?

"What's going on? What happened to you?" asked What. "Where have you come from and where did you disappeared to? How did you get into the kitchen? Scooter, why are you all smiles?"

"I have a hat full of smiles right now. Would you like one of mine? It seems that somebody up there likes us. Somebody down here doesn't," replied Scooter. "We just left the bad guys. Hannibal and myself were kidnapped by The Jerry Dickerson gang."

"How did it go? Now that it's over with, are you alright?" asked I Don't Know.

"Are there any troubles?" asked Because.

"Plenty. Jerry Dickerson and his crew kidnapped us. Because of the lamp with the magic genie, we were able to escape," replied Hannibal. "Scooter is alright as long as he is talking your ear off."

"Hannibal was terrific. Let me tell you how great he was. Hannibal is a wise man? He always has the right answers and because of that he outsmarted Jerry Dickerson and saved my life again," exclaimed Scooter. "You can't ask for anything more than that.

Before Jerry Dickerson and his crew kidnapped us, Dr. Fine and Charlie, The Chill kidnapped Hannibal and myself. They took us to a motel on Brady Street near Interstate 80 and tried to force us to tell them where the lamp was. Hannibal and me couldn't tell those two bozos anything because we didn't know where the lamp was.

Hannibal and me found out later that Ace and Lefty came into our kitchen and took the lamp off the kitchen table when we went to my bedroom to get my books about lamps and genies. For now, the nightmare has gone away.

I'm not going to lose the lamp anymore. Right now, I have a safe place to hide the lamp. I'm going to lock it up in my car. Hannibal, have you seen the keys to my car? Never mind, I'll keep looking."

"That's ridiculous. Why would Jerry Dickerson kidnap you and Hannibal? How did Jerry Dickerson, Dr. Fine and Charley, The Chill even know you had a lamp with a magic genie?" asked Uncle Columbo. "That is a very interesting question. I intend to find out what is going on. Jerry Dickerson is a good man. I'm only telling you what he seems to me. He was a Davenport Police Detective until a month ago. For some strange reason he quit the department.

As far as Dr. Fine and Charlie, The Chill goes, I find them to be very shady characters. How did these people even know about your lamp and the genie?"

"There is a purpose to it. Well, it's like this," explained Hannibal. "You know how Scooter has always been interested in lamps with magic genies? When he was in the kitchen and rubbed the lamp, the genie came out. Later on, I went in the kitchen to see for myself if it was true about the lamp and the genie. Our friends, Ace and Lefty along with Dr. Fine and Charlie, The Chill were looking through the kitchen window when the genie came out of the lamp."

"I know. Lamps and genies are all that Scooter has been talking about for months," replied Uncle Columbo.

"Michael Murphy, alias Dr. Zodiac came to our house earlier today," Hannibal went on to say. "He asked me if he could find a personal thing that he hid in the house. He disappeared in the dark room behind the office wall and came out with a lamp and threw it in the waste basket. Scooter pulled it out of the waste basket, seeing it was a lamp and asked Michael if he could have it. Even though Michael threw it in the waste basket, he sold it to Scooter for $5.00. Scooter went in the kitchen to polish the lamp and."

"Don't say anymore," interrupted Uncle Columbo. "That's when the genie came out of the lamp."

"How did you know what I was going to say?" asked Hannibal.

"Remember, I'm a detective and solve mysteries," reasoned Uncle Columbo. "The only mystery I'm having trouble solving is Scooter," laughed Uncle Columbo. "It seems that we have an awful lot to talk about. Now tell me what happened after the genie came out of the lamp."

"I couldn't believe my eyes that I was seeing a real genie," exclaimed Scooter. "After the genie came out of the lamp, it was like. It was like the genie gave me a pocket full of wishes.

I told Hannibal about the genie, he didn't believe me. Here, let me show you how it works," boomed Scooter as he picked up the lamp and rubbed it.

In a flash, a puff of smoke came out of the lamp and The Genie appeared.

"I'm a slave of the lamp," said The Genie. "You just freed me from my imprisonment of the lamp. Hannibal, since you and Scooter are here jointly and together I will grant you any wishes that you want."

"I can't believe what I'm seeing," beamed Uncle Columbo. "If it was anybody else than Scooter, I wouldn't believe what I am seeing. People always call Scooter stupid and says he does stupid things. Yet, Scooter is always involved into something remarkable. I think this genie has caused both of you big problems.

Learning about that there are lamps with real genies makes the world less scary and more wondrous with each new thing we learn. This sheds the light on centuries-old myths about lamps with magic genies. If we work it right, the genie can also solve your problems."

"You just gave me an idea, Uncle Columbo," praised Hannibal. "The genie always comes out of the lamp and says that whoever holds the lamp has freed him of the imprisonment of the lamp."

"That's right," interrupted the Genie. "The Blue Gin who has more power than me, put me in that lamp, because of something I did to him. Since then, I have been living in that dusty old lamp for two thousand years.

You know that now I'm set in my ways. I got so lonely living in that lamp from day to day. I was always so grateful to the person who rubbed the lamp so I can get out once in a while. I was more than happy to grant them any wish they wanted."

"Then Genie, lets all talk this over. I think the last time we met, we got off on the wrong foot. I have a neck ales of an idea that we may all like and solve all of our problems including yours," replied Hannibal.

"Tell me about it. I'm all ears," replied The Genie.

"At this moment, you will grant any wish that Scooter and I give you together and jointly. Is that right?" asked Hannibal.

"That's the wish you and Scooter gave me. Now that you are both my masters, wish away," answered The Genie.

"OK, my friend, Mister Genie. If you and everybody here likes my plan, I will make this wish with Scooter and myself jointly and together," explained Hannibal.

"That's my friend Hannibal," reasoned Scooter. "Leave it to the desert fox. All my life I have always done stupid things. He would always get mad at me because I made his blood boil. He would lose his temper so bad that his face would go from white, to red, to purple. Hannibal is my good friend. He always gets me out of my scrapes and solves my problems."

"Hannibal had good parents," added Uncle Columbo. "They taught him well. Scooter also has a good heart and I am proud of both of them."

"All of you are truly my friends that you're going to include me in your wishes, cried The Genie. "All my other masters were very greedy people. They were flawed because they wanted so much more than they had. Then they are ruined, because they get these things and wish for what they never had. They never really cared about me. All they cared about is what I could give them."

"Well, here's my idea," exclaimed Hannibal. "What if Scooter and myself wished jointly and together that you can come out of the lamp and come and go as you please, so that you don't have to wait for Scooter or me to jointly and together rub the lamp?

When you are out of the lamp, try not to be noticed. You can wear the street clothes of your choosing, so you won't look any different than anybody else here in Davenport. Then you can be one of the regular guys. Hide the lamp so when anybody including Dr. Fine,

Charlie, The Chill and Jerry Dickerson and his gang come to our palace of business to look for the lamp, nobody can find it.

Are you with me so far? Least of all, remember that Scooter and me will always be your friends and masters jointly and together. Well, what does everybody think?"

"Hannibal you hit it right on the head. I like it," replied The Genie.

"I like it as well," added Uncle Columbo. "Hannibal really has a good head on his shoulders."

"Mr. Genie, I told you that Hannibal is a good friend and problem solver after his face goes from purple to red, to white," praised Scooter.

"We also like Hannibal's plan," yelled The West Side Kids.

"Then it's settled. I will grant this wish sooner than immediately," laughed The Genie. "It's a great gift about me finally feeling alive. Do you have a bottle of gin so that we can celebrate this wish?"

"How about we wish for enough gin for all of us," replied Hannibal. "While you're here, don't ever let Scooter bring you a cup of coffee."

Chapter Fifteen

Nick Names

"Now that we're all in this together, we have to decide the best way to use our wishes and take care of our friend, The Genie," explained Hannibal. "When I say we're all in this together, that includes you Mister Genie. By the way, what is you're first name?"

"I don't have any other name but Genie," replied The Genie. "After being around all of you, I see that you all have nick names. How did all of you get these wonderful nick names?"

"Well, Mister Genie," explained Hannibal. "We have all been friends since second grade and was on a baseball team together. My dad gave me the nick name Hannibal. Scooter's parents gave Scooter the nick name Scooter. Everybody on the baseball team liked having nick names and the rest is history.

"What's a baseball team?" asked The Genie.

"Well, it's like this. The game of baseball is played by two baseball teams, Hannibal said as he informed The Genie. "There is a baseball stadium here in town where they play baseball. Would you like to go see a baseball game with us?"

"I would like that very much," answered The Genie. "I have been in that lamp for a long time. When people rub the lamp and I come out of it, all I do is grant wishes and go back into the lamp. It looks like there is so much for me to learn."

"Then it's settled," insisted Hannibal. "We're going to take you to a real live baseball game here in Davenport. After you see how the game is played, you can watch it on TV."

"I don't know what a TV is?" answered The Genie. "What an incredible life all of you must have. I really do have a lot to learn."

"With all the trouble we have been having, I have thought of one wish I seriously

need to make," reasoned Hannibal.

"And what would that be master?" asked The Genie.

"Now that you're one of the gang, you don't need to call me master anymore," insisted Hannibal. "From now on, just call me Hannibal."

"That includes all of us," added Who.

"You want me to call all of you Hannibal," asked The Confused Genie.

"No. No. No," instructed What. "Call us all by our very own nick names."

"But what about me?" asked The Genie. "I still don't have a nick name."

"I've got a good nick name for you, Mister Genie," promised Scooter.

"Don't pay any attention to Scooter. Save it for later. Let me do the thinking," replied Hannibal. "It's probably a stupid nick name. Everything Scooter does is stupid. Stupid is as stupid does. In fact Scooter's nick name should have been stupid.

After experiencing failures and setbacks, Scooter should learn to be tough. The wish I was going to make, was about having Scooter quit doing stupid things. As of now, the misunderstandings and grievances I have with Scooter, I just tolerate."

"Hannibal, Scooter is your best friend and you're going to hurt his feelings talking about him that way," insisted Uncle Columbo. "Scooter shows you who he is, but you ignore it, because you want him to be who you want him to be. If you don't see Scooter's own worth, how do you expect Scooter to see it?

It's OK to dislike some of the things Scooter does. It is not OK to disrespect, degrade and humiliate him. If it really matters to you about being Scooters friend, you need to show Scooter the respect and dignity he deserves for you to have a long lasting friendship. When

Scooter faced Dr. Zodiac, he was tough. Now apologize to him," ordered Uncle Columbo.

Looking down at the floor, Hannibal muttered, "I didn't know that. Scooter, I'm sorry what I said about you being stupid. I don't mean to hurt your feelings. Are we still friends?"

"I know I'm always doing something stupid and you are always hurting my feelings," answered Scooter. "I never thought of myself as depressed so much as paralyzed by hope. I guess it was meant to be that I'm always going to do stupid things. But you don't have to keep reminding me of it."

"I didn't know that," answered Hannibal.

"That's right," added I'm Not Sure. "Just because Scooter does stupid things, it doesn't mean you have to always call Scooter stupid."

"None of the rest of us ever call Scooter stupid," boomed Smiley. "I was on a ladder painting a patch I fixed above the back door in the kitchen. Scooter took the ladder from under me and I had to hang on to the open door. I did have a grievance with Scooter. I may have called him some other names, but I never called him stupid."

"I didn't know that," insisted Hannibal.

"I knew that," answered Because.

"Come on boys. All of this is all nonsense," interrupted Uncle Columbo. "You have all been a team since second grade. Stop your fighting. Scooter always tries to be happy. Happiness is something you should spread all around. Do you want to give The Genie the wrong impression about who all of you are?"

"I'm sorry Uncle Columbo. I think we're all sorry what we said," exclaimed I Don't Know."

"Well then lets get back to the business of giving The Genie a nick name of his own," demanded Uncle Columbo. "Now Scooter, before you were interrupted, what kind of nick name did you have for The Genie?"

"No matter. It was probably a dumb nick name anyway," answered Scooter.

"Scooter, tell me what you thought my nick name should be," replied The Genie. "Are you going to tell me or do I have to wish that out of you?"

"All right. I'll tell you as long as somebody doesn't tell me how stupid it is," answered Scooter.

"If they do, I promise you that I will turn them into a toad," laughed The Genie. "Now tell me what you think my nick name should be."

"I think your nick name should be A Pocket Full Of Wishes. Pockets for short," said an embarrassed Scooter.

"That's a great nick name. That fits me just perfect," explained The Genie.

"Well, Pockets. You are officially in our club," promised Hannibal.

Holding up his motor cycle jacket, Hannibal added, "Can you wish up a motor cycle jacket like this one for yourself? Put The West Side kids on the back of your jacket with your new nick name below it. Pockets, let's wish up some gin to celebrate. After that We need to discuss our other problems."

Chapter Sixteen
A New Club Member

"Other than Jerry Dickerson and his buddies, Dr. Fine and Charlie, The Chill, what other problems do you have?" asked Uncle Columbo.

"We have some problems that need immediate solutions. As I began to tell you at the beginning and from the beginning," Hannibal went on to say, "I will start over from the beginning. I told you about Michael Murphy, alias Dr. Zodiac coming to our house to retrieve a personal belonging that was left in his house before his house was our house and now it's our house and not his house anymore if you get my drift."

"Yes Hannibal. I get your drift. Why is Michael a problem as far as the lamp goes?" asked Uncle Columbo.

"After Michael sold Scooter the lamp for $5.00, nobody, but nobody even knew that this very lamp that is setting here on this very table had a genie living inside it," explained Hannibal, as he stood there rubbing his head. "Scooter went in his bedroom to polish his lamp. Not having any good polish in his bedroom, Scooter then went into the kitchen to get some polish.

While Scooter was gone, Michael wanted to hire us to escort him to Burlington safely where his brother, Christopher Seven Murphy lives. It was all a big secret as to why he needed our help. There was to be just Michael, yours truly and Scooter to be in the car. We are to leave at nine o'clock tomorrow morning. As of now, Michael hasn't told us or discussed with us about his big secret. Michael also doesn't know that the lamp he sold Scooter for $5.00 included our friend and new club member Pockets, who indeed is a magic genie in this pot."

"Correction, my dear friend Hannibal," interrupted Pockets, The Genie. "That pot you are referring to, my good man has been my home for 2,000 years and is a lamp, a lamp. Do you hear me? Not a pot."

"Pockets, I'm very sorry I said pot instead of lamp," laughed Hannibal. "I guess pot came out of me while I was rubbing my head just like you come out of the lamp when somebody rubs it."

"I really like my nick name Pockets," replied The Genie. "Scooter, a little while ago, Hannibal kept calling you stupid and said everything you did was stupid. Scooter, my friend, my buddy. I think it took a brilliant mind for you to come up with my nick name, Pockets. Now it's as if you were a genie and granted me a wish to have a great nick name. Now that you boys freed me of the lamp, whenever I need help, I'm going to ask you first."

"Wait a minute," demanded Hannibal. "Are you talking about Scooter? You are misjudging Scooter. I think you have been in that lamp way too long. With Scooter, all the birds are singing and the little humming birds are always coming up to him to say hello. Scooter has always liked Punk Groups."

"A Punk Group? What is a Punk Group?" asked the Genie.

"A Punk Group is a band that is against what all of society believes in," explained Hannibal. "They do things that sounds wild such as the names of their bands. There are Punk Rock Groups called, The Fingers, The Veins and The Skulls."

"I didn't know that," replied Uncle Columbo. "What do they do, play background music for a heart transplant?

Hannibal, I think you have been so over protective for so long, that you never have been able to accept the fact that Scooter is a smart person." insisted Uncle Columbo. "Why do you pick on Scooter all the time? You are the wrong person to pick on Scooter. You are suppose to be Scooter's best friend. When you are always picking on Scooter, you will have him feeling like there is something always wrong with him."

"Because it brings out the best in him. If it doesn't get easier for Scooter, then he will just get stronger," answered Hannibal. "If failure would kill him, he would have been dead a long time ago. It's the bad treatment he survives that makes him gentle. Then it's easier to cope with him."

"Hold it down until you hear the whole story," explained Uncle Columbo. "You need to face reality and stop wasting words on Scooter when he deserves your silence. Sometimes the most powerful thing you can say, is nothing at all.

Scooter always gets excited and looks for any good quality in a person. He always tries to show them respect and dignity. One thing people need to understand about extremely kind, nice and loving people is that their other side is just as extreme. Don't mistake Scooter's self-control for weakness.

An example of how smart Scooter is, when Dr. Zodiac threatened all of us here with the inclusion of Jerry Dickerson and his mob of thieves, Dixie Doneright, Dr. Fine and Charlie, The Chill. Dr. Zodiac showed no remorse for the killing of two people. Because of that, we were all afraid for the safety of our girls and ourselves.

Strength doesn't come from what you can do. It comes from overcoming the things you thought you could do. Every accomplishment starts with the decision to try. Scooter knows that success is a decision. The key to success is to focus on goals, not obstacles.

Never forget who helped us out when the rest of us were making excuses. Scooter is my hero. None of us could ever believe that Scooter stood toe to toe with Dr. Zodiac. Scooter became a man when he faced Dr. Zodiac. I guess Scooter was too smart for Dr. Zodiac. This unselfish man made it possible to outsmart Dr. Zodiac. I cannot express how important it is to believe that.

After Scooter made a small fry out of him, Dr. Zodiac was thrown into a rage. After that, Scooter continued to play his game and Dr. Zodiac was chased by Scooter to the elevator and fell to his death into the elevator shaft.

Then there was the time we talked Scooter into wrestling three tough professional wrestlers. Although he was very afraid of getting hurt and very uncomfortable about wrestling these men, Scooter won all three matches.

Scooter sort of got into a fight with these wrestlers without laying a hand on these tough guys. That was never heard of before. That was a great accomplishment. Scooter was an absolute genius to pull that off."

"It was fascinating for me to wrestle these tough guys," added Scooter. "I finally understand that it is OK to be afraid of little things. There was something about the violence, the brutality, and the talking back at these tough guys."

"We all know that Scooter is not perfect," added Uncle Columbo. "Scooter does his thing and he doesn't care if anybody likes it. Scooter always says and does stupid things. Sometimes he laughs when he is not suppose to.

The scars on his heart didn't come from his enemies. They all came from the people who said they loved him. You and many others have left scars on him and keep looking down on him, calling him stupid. He may believe his alone time is for everybody's safety."

"It's not the stab in the back that kills me. Oh no. I'm used to this," exclaimed Scooter. "It's when you turn around and see who's holding the knife.

I come to realize that some of you think I'm not right in the head. It's not my fault, because that's how the universe works. I'm OK with that. I'm just a person who stopped explaining myself, because I realize that people understand only what they want to understand about me. Everything always ends up working out for me.

Life doesn't give free lessons to anyone. So when I say what life taught me, rest assured I paid the price. You may think I may seem a little crazy and won't change."

"Obviously that is not true. Scooter may be different from what people think he is," Uncle Columbo went on to say. "The problem of having a good heart is, people think you're stupid. The more wisdom you attain, the more conscience you become and the crazier you will appear to others. You're only given a little spark of madness and if you lose that, you're nothing.

Scooter knows the only way we will survive is by being kind. The only way we can get by in this world is through the help of others. Nobody can do this alone.

What people think about Scooter is not important. He

understands what he thinks about himself is everything. Scooter is not afraid of being outnumbered. He knows that eagles fly alone and pigeons flock together.

Scooter knows that people will only love and care for him, when it is beneficial to them. People won't realize how big of a part he is playing in their lives, until he's not playing it anymore.

Remember, you, Scooter and The West Side Kids are a team. It took all of your talents to win those baseball games you were telling me about. Without Scooter, you may not have won all those games.

Scooter really is a wise man. He deserves a break. There aren't many like him. I like his style. He is really in charge when he needs to be. Do I need to go on?"

"I guess your right as rain, Uncle Columbo. I get it. We all need to remain as a team to get our other problems solved," reasoned Hannibal. "I want to explain something to you Scooter. Now I realize that it was all a mistake the way I treated you. Again, I'm sorry what I said Scooter. Are you happy in being part of the gang?"

"Let me think about it for a minute?" answered Scooter.

"If you think too hard. You're liable to hurt yourself," laughed Hannibal.

"Oh yes," replied Scooter. "I'm happy, very happy. I couldn't be happier. I'm as happy as can be."

"You're always there with a grand slam when we need you," reasoned Hannibal. "I would like to give you a $2.00 reward for all the things you have done. Here is $10.00."

"I don't have change for a ten," replied Scooter.

"Consider it as a tip," laughed Hannibal.

"In that case, you can forget the rest of what you owe me," reasoned Scooter.

"Now that you mention it, you do know what a grand slam is?" asked Scooter. "Three men on base with a home run. Did you know you can have a grand slam without three men on base?"

"No way! Impossible!" answered Uncle Columbo. "How can you do it any other way?"

"Simple, very simple," explained Scooter. "You have two women's teams playing." "Very funny Scooter," laughed Uncle Columbo. "Now let's start with you. How do

you think we should solve all these problems?"

"I think since The Genie, my good friend Pockets has vacated the premises of the lamp, we should let the bad guys move in the lamp to live rent free," exclaimed Scooter.

"That's not a bad idea," praised Uncle Columbo.

"What's the rest of you think?" asked Uncle Columbo. "Hannibal, do you have any good ideas?"

"I have a great idea just waiting to be hatched," offered Hannibal. "Do all of you remember the movie, "Ground Hog Day"? What do you say we treat these criminals of crime, Jerry Dickerson and his bunch of thieves and Dr. Fine and Charlie, The Chill the way the movie was spelled out to the audience of movie goers."

"What?" asked The Genie. "Just what is a Ground Hog Movie? Is this a story about ground hogs? What is a movie?"

"A movie is shown on a movie screen at a theater," answered Hannibal. "The Ground Hog Movie is a story about Ground Hog Day being repeated over and over. It also says like in the song Hotel California, that you can check out any time you want, but you can never leave."

"Boy, am I confused?" laughed The Genie.

"There is all kinds of evil in this world due to the love of money. What evil lies in the hearts of men? The Shadow knows," laughed Scooter. "Say, does anybody know how mice communicate?"

"I don't know," replied I Don't Know.

"I'm not sure either," added I'm Not Sure.

"What?" asked What.

"Mice communicate by using mouse code," laughed Scooter.

"Pockets, my boy, my friend. You have lived in that bottle so long, that progress has passed you by. Now that you are a member of The West Side Kids Detective Agency, it is become our duty to learn you everything you want to know about life out of your lamp," promised Hannibal. "For now, just hang on tight and follow our lead as we solve the crimes of our day and along the way, show you the mysteries of life.

Say, you are just the man. If you agree to make it your job to grant us the wishes we need to operate our Detective Agency with a little Hocus Pocus, we can get our problems solved before we can say Hocus Pocus. The very best part of it all is that you are now our new friend, that is worth way more than any wish that you can grant us."

"I don't know what to say," cried Pockets, The Genie. "Nobody has ever treated me like that before. OK, I'll do it. You can rely on me. I will gladly take on this job you gave me. I just hope I don't let all of you down."

"Pockets, would you do me a favor as my friend?" asked Scooter.

"What do you wish me to do?" replied Pockets.

"I want you to do me a favor as my buddy," explained Scooter. "I want you to do this favor because you want to. Not because I wished for this."

"I really think I can get used to doing a favor for each of you. I can also grant each of you a wish to put in your pockets, to save for a rainy day, instead of granting a wish each time you need one," exclaimed Pockets. "Scooter, what do you ask of me?"

"As you know by now," replied an embarrassed Scooter. "I have always been interested in lamps with magic genies. I just bought two books, "The Forbidden Wish" and "Three Wishes". Now that I am friends with a real live Genie, you can tell me things that the books don't tell about. Would you tell me what's it like to be a Genie? I also would like to know how you are able to grant wishes. Would you take me inside your lamp?"

"I would be glad to," answered Pockets. "I will tell you anything you want to know and more."

"Pockets, it looks like you're going to fit in with The West Side Kids," promised Uncle Columbo.

Chapter Seventeen
PROBLEM SOLVING WITH A GENIE

"OK gang, listen up. Tomorrow is the big day. The day we have all been waiting for. Tomorrow, Scooter and yours truly is suppose to escort Michael Murphy, alias Dr. Zodiac, to Burlington," explained Hannibal. "Here's my proposal. Pockets, for your first assignment as a member of The West Side Kids Detective Agency. When Michael Murphy shows up at our door tomorrow at nine a m, I want you to send Michael back to his brother's book store, Burlington By The Book, at 301 Jefferson, in Burlington Iowa.

When you send him back, make the date and time, eleven a m, May seventh. When Michael gets there, I don't want him to ever remember any reason for coming to Davenport or that he ever came. Most of all, I don't want him remembering selling the lamp to Scooter for $5.00.

As of now, the lamp belongs to Scooter and myself and you are now a member of The West Side Kids Detective Agency. Do I have to wish for this or can you just do it on your own?"

"You got it Master, I mean Hannibal," answered Pockets. "I know it's my part of the job to do these things you ask. I will see that the wish is right for you and not right for Michael. But it's right for me, but not for Michael or nobody else. Does that sound right?

Is that right what you asked me? Maybe I didn't understand the question. Anyway what ever you ask, it's the same as a wish. I will see that it gets done if that's alright?"

"You know what I wish?" asked Scooter. "I wish that something would happen to me that I don't deserve."

"Don't be a sucker. I wouldn't wish that if I were you," answered Hannibal.

"What's wrong with that wish? I kind of like it," insisted Scooter.

"Then how about you wish that I sock you in the jaw. Now do you feel better?" laughed Hannibal. "You know what I wish? I wish you would keep your mouth shut. It's just about a wish that everybody in this room would like to make come true.

Pockets, on the other hand, since we can't grant wishes to you, remember if you need anything from any of us," promised Hannibal. "We will try to help you in any way."

"Pockets, since you are now my good buddy, I'll let you read my books about lamps and genies," added Scooter as everybody began to laugh.

"Scooter, I would like that very much. Maybe I can learn something about lamps and genies," insisted Pockets.

"Now to get to the next problem that I recalled to mention," exclaimed Hannibal. "We need to get good ole greedy Jerry and his buddies along with Charlie, The Chill and Dr. Fine out of our ever loving hair. They are hard to discourage. In the past, they have caused us problems from time to time. Jerry really got under my skin once.

I have an idea how we can trap them. Pockets, can you erase the memories in their minds about you and your lamp? If you can do this, that will end granting wishes to new masters. Then you can live a normal life as a member of The West Side Kids."

"That's the best idea you ever had," replied Who.

"That's a good theory. I would like that very much. I hope I never let you down," reasoned Pockets. "There is still something wrong. What if The Blue Gin finds me in this new way of life?"

"What? What? Just who is this Blue Gin Character?" asked Hannibal.

"The Blue Gin is the reason I have been in this tea pot, I mean lamp," explained Pockets. "Now you've got me calling my lamp a tea pot. Anyway, The Blue Gin is very powerful and he put me in this lamp that has been my home for over 2,000 years. If he catches me with all of you as a member of The West Side Kids, he will be very angry and take me and my lamp away with him."

"I know what I can do for you. Pockets, you give me back my muscles and I will tear The Blue Gin apart. I will break both of his arms and legs, replied Scooter. "If that don't work, I'll tell Jerry and all of the bad guys about The Blue Gin. Then they can grab his lamp and if they really want a pocket full of wishes, he's the go guy to get them from."

"No! That's a very bad idea. Like I said. The Blue Gin is very powerful and doesn't have a lamp. He uses lamps to make a home for genies like me. Don't ever say the words, Blue Gin. If you do, he will track me down and find me," exclaimed Pockets. "If he comes to Davenport, we will all be in trouble."

"Is that a prediction or a promise? Well, he's not here now," reassured Hannibal. "Forget about him and let's proceed with my plan."

It is now 9 a m the next morning and Michael alias Chris Murphy is knocking on the office door of The West Side Kids Detective Agency. Hannibal then opened the door with Pockets standing next to him.

"Hello," said Chris. "Are you ready to take me to Burlington?"

"Hello," replied Hannibal. "I want you to meet a new member of The West Side Kids Detective Agency. His name is Pockets. Do me a favor and tell Pockets in these same exact words that you wish to go back to your brother's book store, Burlington By The Book, in Burlington Iowa and I guarantee you will be there before you know it."

"Why should I ask him a thing like that?" asked Chris. "I don't even know who this bum is?"

"Because that's how it happens. My name is Pockets. Glad to meet you John."

"I'm not John. My name is Michael" answered Chris.

"Don't mind me. I call everybody John," replied Pockets as he was looking at Hannibal. "John, I think you better explain to John why he has to say those things to me."

"There are two very good reasons for doing this. The best reason of all is that Scooter won't be going to Burlington with us," explained

Hannibal. "If you do what I ask, I won't charge you the $4,500 we agreed upon."

"I don't get it. If that's all I have to do to keep Scooter from going with us and keep the $4,500, I will do it," answered Chris.

Looking at Pockets square in the eye, Chris asked, "I wish to go back to my brother's book store, Burlington By The Book, in Burlington Iowa."

Michael, Alias Dr. Zodiac and Christopher Murphy

Chapter Eighteen

WHEN DID YOU GET BACK?

In a flash, Chris was standing behind the counter of his book store as the phone rang.

"Burlington By The Book," Chris went on to say to the caller. "Can you hold?" "Michael, what do you want?" objected Chris. "I'm on the phone right now. I will talk to you after I hang up. We close at five Chris went on to say to the caller. Michael, now that I'm off the phone, what do you want?"

"When did you get back from Davenport? I never expected to see you here today," exclaimed Michael as he walked from the back of the store.

"What happened? Did you find the winning lottery ticket that I hid in my house that The West Side Detective Agency bought? What are you doing working on your day off?" boomed Michael. "I thought I was working for you today."

"What are you talking about?" asked a puzzled Chris. "I never went to Davenport and you know it. My day off has always been Wednesday. Today is Tuesday. I've been here all the time. I don't know anything about a winning lottery ticket."

"Are you crazy? I really think so," reasoned Michael. "Today is Wednesday. Our sister, Kelly and I personally took you to the bus station yesterday which happened to be Tuesday and saw you leave for Davenport on the bus. Ask Kelly, she will tell you the same thing that I'm telling you."

"I think you're the crazy one. In fact, I think you're a scream. Don't tell me you forgot what day it is. Today is Tuesday, May 6th," corrected Chris. "I think you were in a very, very dark place telling everybody that you're Dr. Zodiac, and you believe in the supernatural. I think your a cold man getting into trouble with the law and arrested for murdering people with a blow gun.

You really upset our parents. Our mother cried for days on end when she found out about all this. She put on her happy face so no one could ever find out you broke her heart. She was going to put her head in the oven and turn on the gas, until she remembered her stove was electric. If our grandfather was alive, he would be rolling over in his grave.

Where did you get the idea of telling everybody that you are Dr. Zodiac and believed in the supernatural? Then you went by two other names, for one Michael, The Magnificent who is Dr. Fine's manager. Then you have this other name, Dr. Nejino and you have patients who you treat with spooks. Beyond the doors of personality lies a hidden key to identity. People are never who they appear to be. I think you're the one with the personal problem."

"Time always reveals who you are to someone. We are all bad in someone's story. It takes nothing to join the crowd. It takes everything to stand alone. I always believed you would feel better if you dial into your pride in the worth of who you are,"reasoned Michael. "It just never felt right and I've always known what I wanted. At some point, I believe we are all parked in the wrong garage."

"I think your problem could be stupidity?" replied Chris. "Compared to Scooter, you have been doing dumb, stupid things. I think Scooter is way smarter than you will ever be.

OK, I don't want any more fooling around little brother. Your going to have to fix some of what you've been doing. I want you to stop acting like a child and start behaving like a responsible adult."

"And what if I don't?" replied Michael.

"Then you will never work in this town again," laughed Chris. "If you did, would you only be doing this to make me happy?"

"Yes I would. What's come over you? What's wrong with you? Today is Wednesday, May 7. Today is Wednesday, Wednesday," replied a puzzled Michael.

"No Michael, I think you're the crazy one," reasoned Chris. "The last two weeks haven't been great for me. I've been hearing a lot about you. Because I am your twin brother, people mistake me for you. Because of that, I happen to know that people are laughing at you all the time."

"Well, at least they are laughing at something," laughed Michael.

"Well, that's the frosting on the cake. Why don't you just go to all the nursing homes and unscrew the bolts on the wheel chairs?" insisted Chris.

"I thought you were on my side," insisted Michael. "When I talked to you the last time, you wanted to help me by going to Davenport to find my winning lottery ticket. Now you're telling me that you never went to Davenport to find the winning lottery ticket."

Looking out the window of the store, Michael observed Kelly and Tim coming into the store.

Walking up to Chris, Kelly asked, "Chris, when did you get back from Davenport? How are things in Davenport? Did The West Side Kids let you in the house to find the winning lottery ticket?"

"Like I told Michael, I never went to Davenport, by bus, plane or train. I have been here all the time," replied Chris. "I don't know anything about a winning lottery ticket. Are you two trying to play a joke on me?"

"Not at all," insisted Kelly. "Whoa! Put on the brakes. You're always the one playing jokes on me and Tim. Do you think that's funny? You both have the same sense of humor.

I didn't think you would be back from Davenport until tomorrow. While you were gone, I just did something by accident. It was just an accident that I opened up all your mail. Don't worry. I didn't read any of it."

"That's OK Kelly. Accidents will happen," answered Chris.

"Did you know that you're late paying your gas and electric bill? You better pay it before the lights in your store are shut off," replied

Kelly. "They are also out of those books you ordered. What are you doing working here on your day off?"

"Are you serious? I work on Tuesdays. My day off is Wednesdays" protested Chris.

"To settle this whole thing, we have to show you the truth. Let's all take our phones out and look at the dates on our phones," reasoned Michael. "This will be our proof what day it is."

As everybody pulled out their phones, the date on each phone was Wednesday, May 7th.

"This is horrible. I don't believe the dates on these phones. It can't be that it's Wednesday, May 7th. It's not right, because it doesn't look like a Wednesday. It's as if I lost a day in my life," exclaimed Chris. "It can't be, unless this is a dream that I'm having or I'm in The Twilight Zone. Now you're telling me which was last night, that I left on a bus that went to Davenport to find a winning lottery ticket hidden in your old house."

"That's right," replied Michael. "This is no dream and you're not in The Twilight Zone. This part I understand. Maybe it's the strain of me being arrested and put in jail for murders I didn't commit is your problem."

"We need to keep up with the times. Everyday is a complete cycle. It's all slipping away. You build up so much speed and after that it's a day to day thing," reasoned Kelly. "The past is gone. I wouldn't look so hard into your past, because you don't live there anymore. Now it's Wednesday. Chris, when is the last time that you have been to a doctor for a check up?"

"About a month ago. I was told I had type A blood, but it was a type O," answered Chris as he began to cry. "Suddenly I don't feel so good. I don't know what's happening to me. I feel kind of sick."

"What's wrong? What's changed? You are really talking yourself into something. You better sit here in the chair. I think you're getting depressed from feeling so sensitive," insisted Kelly.

Ooh, what happened there? It makes you sound like bad milk. You're no fun now. You're just a sour dumpling. You look like a man on welfare who was just told that his wife had triplets. They are all girls and very ugly."

"Kelly, you're not suppose to take notice of what a man does. If he wants to cry, let him cry," replied Tim as he bent down looking at Chris's nose. "Chris, you look kind of flush. If your nose is hot, that is a sign of a fever. I guess if you get up, you better get up slow, so you don't get a nose bleed. You want me to feel your nose?"

"No, maybe you would like to put your hands under my arm pits and play fog horn," replied Chris. "You know what I think? You've got a lot of hair in your nose."

"Maybe you should take some aspirin with a glass of water," insisted Tim.

"So what? Maybe I should. If that's any of your business?" asked Chris.

"Yes, and business is bad," laughed Tim. "Maybe we should let the doctors worry about Chris's health. That's what we're paying them for.

Chris, you should cherish your health: If it is good, preserve it. If it is unstable, improve it. If it is beyond what you can improve, get help. A friend of ours was told by a doctor to take two aspirin every four hours."

"Did it work?" asked Chris.

"No, his health was worst than the doctor thought it was. He ended up going to the hospital because he was near death's door. His family was in hopes the doctors could pull him through and he died a week later," answered Tim. "That was one time his doctor gave him the wrong advice.

I have the same doctor as he did. When I had a fever the doctor told me to take a laxative once a day. It didn't work either. But I'm regular every day.

I asked the doctor if you can tell if a person is sick by feeling his nose? The doctor replied, No. I can tell if a person is flush by feeling his wallet.

I had another friend who had the same doctor as we did. He was a kind, wonderful, warm friend. That friend didn't look as bad as you do. The doctor gave him the wrong advice also and he was gone in thirty days."

"Why you hockey puck, how would you like to join your friend?"

asked Chris. "I think you're exaggerating. I'm going to keep my eye on you."

"Michael, you stay here with Chris while I go get him a glass of water," ordered Kelly. "I have a plan about him losing his memory. I am going to call his doctor right away. If Chris can get in to see him, then I better take him while you watch the store."

"Kelly, you think of everything. I'm sure glad I don't have the same doctor as Tim and his two friends," insisted Chris. "At least you're not trying to feel my nose."

"What's wrong with Chris?" asked a concerned customer as she approached the counter with a couple of books. "Is there anything I can do to help? He looks terrible. Who is this other man? Why are there two Chris's here?"

"Hello. My name is Tim. This is my brother Chris and this is my other brother Chris," laughed Tim. "Did you know that Raymond Burr had a brother who was a lumber jack? His name was Tim Burr."

"Tim is just fooling with you," answered Kelly. "This is Chris and this is his twin brother Michael. We don't know what is wrong with Chris. I just called his doctor and he said we need to get Chris to the ER and call an ambulance right away. When he gets home, I'm going to nurse him back to health."

"I can face any challenge, but if it's the only way, I'll do it on one condition. I'll take the ambulance to get away from Tim. I feel better already," exclaimed Chris. "Tim, while I'm gone, why don't you go to the zoo and scare all the animals?"

"Michael, I guess it's just you and me to take care of the store while Kelly goes to the hospital with Chris," offered Tim.

"I hate to leave you with all the work," insisted Chris.

"Don't worry about it," answered Tim.

"OK," laughed Chris.

"It's OK," reasoned Tim. "I can handle this until you get back."

Chapter Nineteen
One Down, Two To Go

Meanwhile, back at The West Side Detective Agency, the gang was sitting in the office sipping on coffee as they talked about Pockets sending Chris who they thought was Michael, alias Dr. Zodiac back to Burlington.

"Great job, Pockets. Wow, this is more like it. You did a great job and I'm going to reward you," replied an excited Hannibal. "I'm going to let you be a permanent member of the gang. This calls for a celebration."

"Hannibal, I really got to hand it to you," praised Pockets. "Your suggestion really did the trick."

"That doesn't surprise me," answered Hannibal. "You know, I'm very proud of you. It was just like you to paint a masterpiece."

"I don't know just what to say," answered Pockets "I can't tell you how much I am relieved."

"Pockets, one down. Two to go," boomed Hannibal. "I wish I was a fly on the wall at Burlington By The Book when Michael appeared back in that store."

"I don't think that would be a very good idea," laughed Scooter. "What if Michael came after you with a fly swatter?"

"You're right. That wasn't a good idea," laughed Hannibal. "You should have been the fly on the wall that Michael was chasing with a fly swatter. That would have solved all of our problems."

"I think Pockets should have shaved Michael's head before he sent him to Burlington," laughed Scooter.

"Who are we going after next?" asked Who.

"What do you want Pockets to do with the next guys?" asked What.

"I don't know. What do you think we should have Pockets do with them?" asked I Don't Know.

"I'm not sure what we should do with them," replied I'm Not Sure.

"I guess whatever Hannibal decides to do with them," answered Whatever.

"I think we should make a joke out of it and remove the memory of the lamp and the genie from the hallows of their ever loving mind," added Smiley. "Just like when Pockets sent Michael back to Burlington, Jerry and his gang, Dr. Fine and Charlie, The Chill should lose a day from their mind."

"You don't say," replied You Don't Say. "They would be so confused. That would really drive those guys loony. What do you say, Hannibal?"

"I like that idea," reasoned Hannibal. "Not only would they forget about the lamp and Pockets, losing a day would drive them all insane. What do you think of that idea, Pockets?"

"I really like that idea,"insisted Pockets. "It's nice to be in a conversation where I am being asked my opinion, rather to just grant wishes to a master who rubbed the lamp. Some of these masters that rub my lamp, rub me the wrong way."

"That's very funny what you just said. You are a very funny genie," laughed Smiley. "None of us know you very well. You sound like a fun guy."

"I do? Nobody has ever said that to me before" replied an emotional Pockets. "I have no idea what I sound like. I have been so lonely living in that lamp all these years only to come out and grant wishes. Now I feel like I have a family with a real home."

"You heard what we all thought we should do with these rats," reasoned Hannibal. "Now as a present to you, you grant your own wish in how you think we should deal with these people."

"I think we should keep the scam going. I think Hannibal's idea is very creative," reasoned Pockets. "When I move on to these next group of fellows, should I shave their heads when I make them lose their memory of me and my lamp that has been my home for two thousand years?"

"This is a search and destroy mission. As I said, do as you wish," laughed Hannibal. "Get it? Do as you wish."

"Before you do that to these fellows," added Scooter. "You may want to read my books about genies and lamps to give you some ideas."

"Thanks Scooter," praised Pockets. "As a member of The West Side Kids, I am going to follow through with the idea that Hannibal talked about."

"Now you're catching on," reassured Hannibal. "I forgot to tell you, when you remove the memory of the lamp, a genie and shave everybody's head from The Jerry Dickerson's Gang, do it to everybody but Dixie Doneright. I don't think we will have any more trouble with Jerry Dickerson and his boys since they are going to lose their memory of the lamp and a genie. I bet those scollywags leave us alone after that."

"I hope so, but I have my doubts," replied I Don't Know.

"Pockets, after we all count three together, do as you wish," boomed Hannibal. "Is everybody ready? One, two three."

In an instant, the memory of the lamp, the genie, heads being shaved and a loss of the day was gone from the minds of Jerry Dickerson and his associates, except Dixie Doneright, along with Dr. Fine and Charlie, The Chill.

Back in Jerry Dickerson's apartment, 5025 in downtown Davenport on East 3rd Street, Jerry, Ace, Lefty, Danny, Shorty and Mugs were eating their lunch in Jerry's apartment, talking about the lamp and the genie when everything in their minds went blank about the lamp and the genie.

"Now I forget. What were we talking about?" asked Jerry.

"Not remembering, an embarrassed Ace replied as he was looking at everybody, "When did everybody decide to get their heads shaved?"

"I never got my head shaved," answered Jerry as he reached up to feel the top of his head. "Ace, you have your head shaved like the rest of us."

"I don't either," objected Ace as he reached up to feel the hair on his head.

"We all have our heads shaved," reasoned Danny. "I hope we're not falling for somebody's joke. I would be madder than a bull if I thought that."

"What's the matter with us? The only way that could have happened is that we were all drunk and went to the barber shop together to get this done" reasoned Lefty. "That's it. That's it. I think this is very serious. Don't talk. Don't anybody talk. Maybe we should smell each others breath."

"I'm not that anxious to find out. I think your breath would start a fire. If I was to get down wind of you, you would be murder," laughed Shorty. "Maybe this is just a dream."

"This is no dream," replied Ace. "I don't know what it is with us guys. We must have gone to the tavern and had a party. I think we are all boozers. We taste the liquor, like it and then finish the whole bottle. This is a bad thing. We must have gotten drunk. I think it's stupid, stupid, stupid. I can't even remember what we were talking about."

"Hey, who took my shoes?" asked Mugs. "All of you must think I have a sense of humor. This isn't funny at all. Not one bit."

"I didn't mean for it to be funny. Do these look like your shoes?" asked Lefty. "There is one way to find out. Try them on."

"They kind of look like them, but I don't know for sure," replied Mugs.

"Well, try them on to see if they fit," insisted Lefty as he handed the shoes to Mugs.

Mugs then sat down and put a shoe on his right foot.

"You're batty. Of all the things, what are you trying to do? You deliberately filled my shoes with shaving cream," screamed Mugs. "That's not funny."

"It's not as funny as you look with your head shaved," laughed Lefty.

"I'm going to tell you to you're flat ugly puss what I think of you," yelled Mugs. "I am just finding out that I have an unfortunate choice of associates. I don't have much use for you anymore. You're nothing but a coward."

"Stop it, both of you!" screamed Jerry. "That's enough of that kind of talk. Never mind that now. This is no time to be causing trouble and fighting among ourselves. You two are gumming up the works as to what we have to do."

"I'm sorry, Jerry," insisted Lefty. "I was just having fun with Mugs."

"I'm sorry, Lefty. I didn't mean a thing what I said to you," reassured Mugs.

"I knew somebody who walked in his sleep when he was drunk and he drowned," exclaimed Danny.

"He drowned?" asked Ace.

"He was a minister and he tried to walk on water," laughed Danny.

"We were talking about Michael, alias Dr. Zodiac and how he was set free by the jury in Burlington," insisted Shorty. "Michael and his lawyer were very clever with their defense where the jury couldn't prove he murdered anybody."

"Oh yes. We need to keep on eye out for Michael if he comes to Davenport," reasoned Jerry. "Rumor has it that Michael left something very valuable in his house that he sold to The West Side Kids Detective Agency. Whatever it may be, I want it. We also need to keep an eye on Dr. Fine and Charlie, The Chill. If they are wise to this, they may try to take it away from Michael before we can.

Ace, Lefty, and Mugs, I want you to keep an eye on The West Side Kids Detective Agency in case Michael, alias Dr. Zodiac shows up at his old house. Danny and Shorty, I want you to go to Burlington with me to check out Burlington By The Book to see if we can get a line on Michael."

"When are we going to leave for Burlington?" asked Shorty. "The one thing I want to see when I get to Burlington is Snake Alley."

"Today. First I'm going to call a motel and make reservations in Burlington," answered Jerry. "Here's a good number to call. Hello, this is Jerry Dickerson. I would like to make a reservation for three adults. I would like three rooms for today, Wednesday and Thursday."

"You mean Wednesday, Thursday and Friday?" asked the desk clerk.

"No! I mean today, Wednesday and Thursday," answered Jerry.

"You better look at your calendar again," reasoned the desk clerk. Today is Wednesday May 7th."

"OK, whatever," said a confused Jerry. "I want three rooms for today and the next two days."

"Do you want to pay by credit card?" asked the desk clerk.

"Yes, and will it be alright for the three of us to check in today at one p m?" asked Jerry.

After Jerry gave the desk clerk all his information, he hung up.

"What was that all about?" asked Danny. "What was that confusion all about?"

"The desk clerk told me that today was Wednesday, May 7th, not Tuesday, May 6th,"

replied Jerry. "Did all of us get drunk on Tuesday and really have a gut full. Maybe that's why we don't know its Wednesday? There is something funny about this. We'll soon find out. Dixie must have gone shopping. When she gets back we can ask her."

An hour later, Dixie returned to Jerry's apartment.

"I'm glad I caught you. I thought you would be gone. Have you figured out how you're going to get the lamp with the magic genie from Scooter and Hannibal?" asked Dixie.

"Dixie, what are you talking about?" asked Jerry. "There is no such thing as a lamp with a magic genie."

"Why are you talking to me this way?" asked Dixie. "Say, what is it with you guys? Are you doing this for laughs? I don't know about you, but I want that lamp and that genie with all the wishes I can get the genie to grant me.

Alright. What's going on here? When did all of you get your heads shaved? I wonder what this is all about? Do you know you guys really look ridiculous. I think you all look stupid, stupid, stupid. Did you go to the tavern and party all night?"

"I admit we look ridiculous. This is highly irregular," admitted Jerry.

"Wait a second. You men. You remarkable men are always doing very nice things for me," exclaimed Dixie. "I'm surprised at you. Now you look like the guys in the unemployment line."

"We must have all been drunk and had our heads shaved sometime yesterday," replied Jerry. "We must have done it all at once."

"What do you mean yesterday? Haven't you got anything better to do like going to the dentist and getting a shot of Novocain in your mouth?" asked Dixie."

"There are a lot of jokes out there, but this one is the dumbest," scolded Jerry.

"Last night Ace and Lefty was at The West Side Kids Detective Agency looking through the kitchen window after 9 p m when they saw Scooter rub a lamp with a magic genie coming out of it. When they came back home, all the barber shops were closed," reasoned Dixie. "All of you still had all of your hair.

What happened? What happened? Last night you were dynamite. Today you are just dead batteries. This is dragging all of you down. Maybe we should have stripes painted on your heads and we can use you as beach balls. Something is definitely wrong. Have you ever tried shock treatments?"

"OK, OK, you made your point. Dixie, why are you making all of this up?" Are you doing this for laughs?" demanded Ace.

"Something is fishy that is going on here," replied Danny. "A little while ago we were all sitting here talking and then couldn't remember what we were talking about. Next, we discover that we all have had our heads shaved and can't remember having it done.

Jerry called a motel in Burlington to make a reservation for Tuesday. The desk clerk tells Jerry that it is Wednesday, not Tuesday. Then you come home and talk about a lamp and a magic genie."

"If the desk clerk is right about it being Wednesday and not Tuesday and Dixie is right about a lamp with a magic genie, that would explain everything," insisted Ace. "What is the day of the week and the date, Dixie?"

"You know what the day of the week and the date is," reasoned Dixie. "I just told you that you were looking through the window last night at The West Side Detective Agency and it was Monday night, so today is Tuesday."

"I think the best way to settle this is for all of us is to check the date on our cell phones," reassured Lefty.

Everybody then pulled out their cell phones, looking for the date.

"Hey, what's going on here? I can't believe what I'm seeing," exclaimed Dixie. "Ain't that a kick in the head? I really believed it was Tuesday, May 6th. Now all of our cell phones say it is Wednesday, May 7th. What happened to Tuesday?"

"I'm sure glad Dixie came back to the apartment when she did. Dixie hit it right on about a lamp with a magic genie. Like I said. She knows what she is talking about. That was a twist of fate," replied Ace.

"Wait a minute. Wait a minute. I can't think with all of you jabbering at once. Let me figure out what we have to do next," reasoned Jerry. "You know what they say: the best laid plans of mice and men. In that case, I better make a change in plans. These are my new plans."

"Hey, I had the same idea," exclaimed Ace.

"Now listen up. No more goofing off," instructed Jerry. "I want all of you to be sharp and on your toes.

I want Dixie and Shorty to go with me to Burlington today. Danny, you team up with Mugs and keep an eye out for Scooter, Dr Fine, Charley, The Chill and Michael, alias Dr. Zodiac if he comes to Davenport. Ace and Lefty, you keep an eye on Danny and Mugs. Watch them, in case they don't do their job. I'm going to keep an eye on all of you. As an ex Davenport Police Detective, I think I'm better prepared to solve this mystery.

If you have any questions, I want you to ask them now. Now get to it."

Chapter Twenty

TWO DOWN. ONE TO GO.

Back at The West Side Detective Agency, the gang was waiting for
Pockets to grant a wish of his own that would deal with Dr. Fine and
Charlie, The Chill.

"I don't know what happened to Jerry and his crew," reasoned
Hannibal. "But they are getting what they well deserve."

"That was fun," exclaimed Pockets. "It's really fun granting my
own wishes. I'm so excited that I'm ready to do it again."

"Do it again while you're on a roll," insisted Because.

"I don't know what you did to those guys. Whatever it was, do it
again to Dr. Fine and Charlie, The Chill," added I Don't Know.

"I think you should have Dr. Fine slap Charlie, The Chill over and
over," suggested Scooter. "Then you should have Charlie, The Chill
slap Dr. Fine over and over and neither one of them knows why they
are doing it to each other."

"Scooter, keep quiet before I start slapping you over and over.
Only you will know why I'm doing it," laughed Hannibal. "We all told
Pockets to do things his way. So shut up before I pour a cup of paint
all over your head."

"OK, I'll be as quiet as a mouse as long as you get me some cheese,"
replied Scooter.

"If you don't shut up, I'll get you some cottage cheese and shove it down your ever loving mouth," threatened Hannibal. "And you know I'll do it. Then you can go snow blind."

"Ulp, Genie, save me ole pal, ole buddy," yelled Scooter. "Quick, turn Hannibal into a toad or something small so he can't hurt me."

"OK Pockets. You're up. Do your thing before Scooter opens his mouth again," pleaded Hannibal.

"Oh goody, goody," replied an excited Pockets. "Dr. Fine and Charlie, The Chill, hear my wish ready or not. Your memory will fade of me and my pot. Your heads will be shaved as you slap each other or not. You will remain friends although not brothers. Tuesday, May 6th will be yesterday and no other. It will now be Wednesday May 7th as you will be confused, as you continue the day and your memory will be bruised."

"Not bad," praised Hannibal.

"I don't know what to say other than I liked it," exclaimed I Don't Know.

"What do you know? Pockets did it again," laughed What.

"I think because Pockets knows his stuff, he will fit into our gang perfectly," added Because.

"That was sure fun to do," smiled Pockets. "I like this job you gave me. Is there anything else you want me to do?"

"There is nothing more to do at this time. Let's wait and see what happened to these guys after you removed their memories of you and your lamp," Hannibal went on to say.

"I'm not sure what the rest of you think, but I think we should celebrate by having a party," exclaimed I'm Not Sure.

"I like parties. At this moment, I don't know if there is anything to celebrate," reasoned I Don't Know.

"Hannibal, can't we have a party with liquor and women? Without liquor and women, it's not a party," reasoned I'm Not Sure. "What's wrong with having a party to celebrate? What's wrong with a little celebration?

Ask Pockets that you want to make a wish to get us some liquor and girls so we can have a party. Please decide to let us have a party."

"If you like parties, you should be in congress instead of working at The Detective Agency," laughed Scooter.

"Smiley, why don't you and Whatever go in the kitchen and make some coffee and get the ice cream out of the frig, so we can celebrate?" requested Hannibal. "Right now, we have other problems and don't have time to celebrate with liquor and women. Pockets, is there anything special you would like to have?"

"You mean you're going into the kitchen to get the food, instead of wishing for it?" asked Pockets.

"That was the plan," replied Hannibal. "You did your work for the day. Now it's our turn to treat you."

"Can I at least supply a cake that goes with the ice cream," cried Pockets.

"If that is what you wish to do," laughed Hannibal.

"What kind of cake does everybody like?" asked Pockets.

"I want white cake with lots of chocolate frosting," demanded Scooter.

"Forget the chocolate frosting on Scooter's piece of cake. I really think he would prefer brown paint instead," insisted Hannibal.

"Hannibal, I make a few silly mistakes and you never let me forget it," cried Scooter. "You have never ever let me forget about making a bomb in Rex Tarillo's Chemistry Class and throwing it out the window into the parking lot, blowing up Rex's brand new car. Something like that can happen to anybody."

"Oh you think so," answered Hannibal. "How about after that, when Rex took us to The Dean's Office, you broke his expensive statue twice. The second time you broke it after The Dean glued it back together. Those things don't just happen to anybody. They just happen to you."

"That's just your opinion and you may be right. I still wish you would stop telling me that over and over," exclaimed Scooter. "Oh why don't you go to Africa and get your head shaved on the way? Then when you get to Africa, you can lock lips with a gorilla."

"Scooter, you used the word wish," asked Pockets. "Do you wish me to send Hannibal to Africa with his head shaved and when he gets there, he can lock lips with a gorilla?"

"No, Pockets. I don't want you to do that to my best friend," answered Scooter. "We always talk to each other that way."

"As you wish, Scooter," replied Pockets.

Chapter Twenty One

Give Me Back My Tuesday

As Dr. Fine and Charlie, The Chill were taking in some groceries, they bought into their apartment, in downtown Davenport on East 3rd Street, they continued to talk about the lamp with the magic genie. After they set the groceries down on the kitchen counter, they stopped talking.

Dr. Fine then blurted out while looking at Charlie's head, "When did you have your head shaved?"

"What do you mean?" I never got my head shaved," answered Charlie as he reached up to feel his head. "What do you think? I had my head shaved the same time your head was shaved."

"What are you talking about. There is no way that I would get my head shaved," replied Dr. Fine as he reached up to feel his head. "We both have our heads shaved. What's going on here? How? Why? When? How do you explain it?"

"I can't explain it," answered Charlie. "This is very scary. To get our mind off of this, I think we better keep an eye on the rumor about Michael, alias Dr. Zodiac coming to Davenport, to get something valuable that he left in the house that he sold to The West Side Kids Detective Agency."

"Before I forget to ask you, did you pay the apartment rent?" inquired Dr. Fine. "Today is Tuesday, May 6th and tomorrow it will be late."

"No I didn't," replied Charlie. "I'll go pay it now." A couple minutes later, Charlie was standing in front of the desk clerk.

"May I help you?" asked the desk clerk.

"Yes," answered Charlie. "I would like to pay my May rent for apartment 6015." "You're a day late," explained the desk clerk. "I'm going to have to charge you a $25.00 late fee."

"You must be mistaken," answered Charlie. "Late charges won't start until Wednesday. This is Tuesday."

"No sir. Today is Wednesday, May 7th and you're a day late," insisted the desk clerk.

"What have you been smoking?" asked Charlie. "Do you have today's paper? If that is what it takes to convince you. Get it and show me the date."

"Yes sir," replied the desk clerk. "It says right here at the top of the front page, Wednesday, May 7th. Now along with your rent, I need $25.00 more. You are responsible for that."

"Do you mind? I could have bet dollars it was Tuesday, May 6," answered Charlie.

"Well you might say you lost $25.00 just now. So pay up," demanded the desk clerk.

"If it's Wednesday, I'm pretty sure I paid you. What happened to Tuesday?"asked Charlie, shaking his head. "What happened to Tuesday. If the flies are out of my house, I will have a happy life."

"That's very good. Are you feeling OK or do I need to call a doctor?" asked the desk clerk.

"Give me back my Tuesday," pleaded Charlie. "Give me back my Tuesday. I know what happened to it?"

"What happened to it?" answered the desk clerk.

"You're not going to believe what happened," answered Charlie. "I don't like to blow the whistle on anybody, but they're asking for it, because they started it. They don't get along with anybody. They fight all of the time, because they have a faulty digestive system. That's what makes them so mean and ornery."

"I never thought of that. That's a good theory," replied the desk clerk. "I still need $25.00 more."

"Either Dr. Zodiac took it or Scooter Hickenbottom stole it. They make me so mad. I think they're at the bottom of all this. At least they had a small part in it. They did a very bad thing, very bad," replied Charlie as his face turned bright red. "If they only knew what they did to my Tuesday and how important it is to me. You see they will never learn. Why don't they leave me alone?

That was a very dumb thing that they did. Now that I lost my Tuesday, I want it twice as much. Well, they are not going to get away with it. No, we don't do that kind of thing. Anybody who thinks they can get away with it, better think twice. I know what they have done and I'm going to handle it. They did a very bad thing."

"I didn't know that. Don't take it so hard. It's OK. You sit right here in the chair sir. I'm going to call an ambulance," insisted the desk clerk.

After the desk clerk called an ambulance, he then called Charlie's room mate, Dr. Fine.

"Hello, is this Dr. Fine," asked the desk clerk.

"Yes, this is Dr. Fine speaking. Who is it? May I ask who is calling?"

"We have a big problem here. This is important. I want to get right to the point. Please come down to the lobby immediately," demanded the desk clerk.

"Just what did happen?" asked Dr. Fine.

"I think you should get down here as soon as possible to straighten things out," explained the desk clerk. "Your room mate, Charlie is sitting on a chair here. He seems very sick and I had to call an ambulance. He keeps repeating things over and over."

"I didn't know that. Tell Charlie, I'll be there right away," replied a nervous Dr. Fine.

A couple minutes later, Dr. Fine walked off the elevator into the lobby.

"Hold it! Hold it! What's the problem here? Somebody getting mugged?" asked a

desperate Dr. Fine. "What's going on here? Charlie, do you remember me? What's wrong?"

"Look at today's newspaper. The date," gasped Charlie. "They did a very bad thing."

"Sit down and we'll talk about it. Here's the whole thing in a nut shell. I don't know

what's wrong with Charlie. That's why I called an ambulance. I figured it was an emergency, but I think he will be alright." explained the desk clerk. "All I know is, I told Charlie that he was a day late on his rent and I had to charge him a late fee. He insisted that he was paying on time because it was only Tuesday, May 6th. I told him it was May 7th and showed him the newspaper.

After he looked at the date in today's paper, he just blew up and started talking crazy about a Dr. Zodiac and a Scooter Hickenbottom and then his face turned bright red."

"Let me see that paper," demanded Dr. Fine.

After looking at the date in the newspaper, Dr. Fine reasoned, "That date can't be right. The newspaper printed the wrong date in the paper. I'm going to make an exception. What I don't see, I don't know."

"May 7th is the right date. Today is May 7th and I have to charge you and Charlie a late fee," explained the desk clerk as the paramedics arrived. "Ask these paramedics what the date is?"

"Sir, what is today's date?" asked Dr. Fine to the paramedic. "I heard it from the desk clerk. Now I want to hear it from you."

"May 7," replied the paramedic.

"I suppose I should, but I didn't know that. Just take it back," reasoned Dr. Fine.

"Thank you for your honesty."

"I knew that, replied the paramedic.

Dr. Fine's face then began to turn bright red as he mumbled, "What happened to Tuesday? What happened to Tuesday? Scooter Hickenbottom has got it. I don't understand these kids today and they don't understand me. They can't treat me like that. The smell is getting into my underwear.

Make Scooter give me back my Tuesday. He's a real problem case. He makes me so mad. He has done a very bad thing. If Scooter doesn't have my Tuesday, Dr. Zodiac has got it. Then make Dr. Zodiac give me back my Tuesday. They're going to do it again and make a fool out of me."

"Do you want me to help you? That's what I do best. Why don't I speak to you? Do

you think I can?" asked the paramedic. "I have a theory. Do you want to hear it?"

"Not necessarily. I don't need anybody's help, because nothing is going to get by me. First I said I have to get out of here. Then you go away. You must get out of here," scolded Dr. Fine. "I have everything under control. Didn't I tell you I could handle things like this? Don't ever tell me I don't know how to handle these problems. I will be right on top of the situation. Then Scooter will have to give back my Tuesday. Dr. Zodiac will have to give back my Tuesday.

That would be a very nice gesture. Well, they are really not going to do it. They have done a very bad thing. They have done a very bad thing."

"What? Did I say something wrong?" asked the paramedic.

"No, I don't think it has anything to do with what you said," answered the desk clerk. "When Dr. Fine and Charlie looked at the date in the newspaper. We, you saw what I saw."

"I don't know why the date in the newspaper would make these two react like that?" answered the paramedic. "Who is this Dr. Zodiac and Scooter Hickenbottom they are talking about? Why would they think these two people could take a day of the week away from them? Are these two loony or on drugs?"

"No, I'm sure they're not loony or on drugs," answered the desk clerk. "After they started to talk like this, they became the clumsiest people I ever saw. I just never seen them this way before."

"Only a doctor should be able to find out for sure what their problem is. I think we better get them both to the ER right away," reasoned the paramedic.

Burlington By The Book

Chapter Twenty Two
GO BACK JACK. DO IT AGAIN

"It is now Tuesday, May13, 11 a. m. and Chris is back in his store, Burlington By The Book starting his day at work. As he walked behind the counter of his store, Michael, his twin brother walks in.

"Hello Chris," greeted Michael. "When did they release you from the hospital?"

"Yesterday, at four o' clock." answered Chris as the telephone rang. "Kelly came to the hospital to bring me home, little brother. Hello, Burlington By The Book. We're located at 301 Jefferson and open until five."

After Chris hung up, Michael began scolding Chris saying "I wish you would quit calling me little brother. Just because you're a few minutes older than me, it doesn't make me your little brother."

"Well, that makes me your older brother," laughed Chris.

"That's not funny," insisted Michael. "You have been calling me little brother since you could talk. You have also been calling yourself my older brother since you could talk. I don't like it and I never have. Why don't you just quit your talking and read a book."

"There are just no way around it. I am your older brother and always will be your older brother," replied Chris as Kelly entered the store.

"What are you two doing that you're fighting about this time?" asked Kelly.

"It's the same thing we have been fighting about for years," answered Michael. "Chris keeps saying that he is my older brother and I'm his little brother. He just won't stop and I think he is overdoing it."

"Wait a minute. Chris must be feeling better and bouncing back since he is able to remember calling you his little brother. He is mighty active for someone who has lost their memory." observed Kelly. "Michael, the doctors couldn't find out why Chris had a loss of memory about Tuesday and Wednesday of last week. They said to let him return back to the things he normally does. He has an appointment to go back and see his doctor in a week.

The doctor is going to try and relieve Chris of those foolish fears of losing his memory that scares him and that time has finally caught up with him. It's a mistake that Chris has to live with. So far, the doctor has given Chris the seven rules of life that are:

1) Smile
2) Be kind
3) Don't give up
4) Don't compare
5) Avoid negativity
6) Make peace with your past
7) Take care of your body and mind

Let the glow in your heart reflect in your soul. It seems to me that Chris has to let the past die or it won't let him live. Quit being so sensitive. Time goes on. Chris, whatever you're going to do, do it now. Don't wait. You're as young as you feel. If you do these things, you can still live until you're ninety and still have kids."

"That's just what I want to hear, that I can still have kids when I'm ninety," reasoned Chris. "And they will all have wrinkled noses. You know up to now, I have never had anything wrong with me."

"You mean to say that you think you had this coming?" asked Kelly.

"No, I'm asking why me? I was mad. I thought about it and now I'm over it," reasoned Chris. "The doctor gave me the answers to my loss of memory and I'm going to take the doctor's advice now that I know there is more than one way to swing.

I just want to start doing things on my own again. You are going to see a lot of changes in me. You know me one way and now you're going to know me another way."

"Who cares, because I'm not putting you down. I don't think I can blame you. I like you the way you are," answered Kelly. "Just for old times sake, do it for me, your sister and don't change who you are. I just want everything to be perfect for you."

"Oh! I never said such a thing. The important thing is, I haven't changed," replied Chris. My life is the same as it always was. I have done pretty much what I wanted to do."

"There is one change that you made since you lost your memory of losing Tuesday and going to Davenport that I don't like," exclaimed Kelly. "Obviously it's a mistake. I'm sorry things didn't turn out the way you planned.

You never want to go anywhere anymore in the first place and do you know why? It's because you don't like people anymore except for your customers."

"Yes I do," answered Chris.

"No you don't," insisted Kelly. "You would rather sit around in a torn dirty old tee

shirt and swirl beer while you watch TV."

"I'm sorry, I don't do that. I never do that. Besides, I'm happy the way I am," reasoned Chris. "Now, do you believe me?"

"I don't want you to be like your brother Michael when he was different and became known as a strange guy, as Dr. Zodiac," cried Kelly. "Michael wouldn't listen to me and it seemed like it didn't matter anymore. If he hadn't been caught by The West Side Kids and the police, he would have continued to stay evil. Now Chris, I'm expecting you to listen to me."

"I guess it leaves it up to me to go to Davenport to get my winning lottery ticket from the house I sold to The West Side Kids Detective Agency, since my older brother can't go" reasoned Michael. "Although I may be your little brother, I will get the job done and I will remember what I was doing. Now that I think of it, maybe Chris may lose his memory about being my older brother and me his little brother. The problem with doing nothing is that Chris never knew when he was finished."

"Oh brother! Stop it," demanded Kelly. "Is that all you guys have to do, is sit around and talk about things like that? Maybe you should go to Davenport. Michael, If you're not around, you will quit your fighting."

"OK, I will go," answered Michael. "I have to ask you something Kelly.

"If it has anything to do with getting the winning lottery ticket, I don't want to get involved," replied Kelly.

"I want you to help me get the winning lottery ticket by loaning me your car," asked Michael.

"I'm looking at the facts and I don't like it. That's being involved. No Michael, take the bus to Davenport. I need my car," insisted Kelly.

"That has nothing to do with it. Why are you being so stubborn?' asked Michael. "If you loved me, it would mean so much to me if you would lend me your car."

"I'm not being stubborn. I'm just saying no, because I need my car," reasoned Kelly.

"Why can't any of my family members ever want to help me out and do a favor for me?" boomed Michael.

"Now what are you two fighting about?" asked Chris.

"I want to borrow Kelly's car, so I can go to Davenport," replied Michael.

"Now wait a minute. Another reason I'm not lending you my car is that you're a terrible driver," insisted Kelly.

"How do you know I'm a terrible driver? You have never ridden in my car with me?" answered Michael.

"Who is the jerk that parked in front of the store?" asked Chris.

"That's my car," answered Michael. "I'm going to buy a new car, because I need one."

"That's a nice car. What's the matter with your old car? Why do you need Kelly's car when you have one of your own?" questioned Chris.

"Because I wrecked my car," answered Michael."

"When are you going to take care of those parking tickets?" asked Chris.

"No time now. I'm in a rush. The check is in the mail for the parking tickets," answered Michael. "Now I have to call the bus station to see when the next bus leaves for Davenport."

"Don't call on this phone. This is for business only," teased Chris. "Use the phone in the telephone booth at the entrance to the store."

"You know that phone isn't hooked up. I have to use this phone," scolded Michael.

"I forgot. It must be due to my loss of memory," insisted Chris.

"Very funny, big brother or should I say older brother?" answered Michael. "Now move out of my way, so I can use the phone."

Five minutes later, Michael hung up the phone after calling the bus station.

"When is the next bus leaving for Davenport?" asked Kelly.

"At one o'clock," replied Michael. "Would you take me to the bus station. Because like it says in the Beatles song, "I've Got A Ticket To Ride."

"I never did like those songs the Beatles sang," laughed Chris. "Every time I heard one, I wanted to call an exterminator."

"You are so funny, Dummy," insisted Michael. "You always liked the Beatles. They have always been your favorite artists."

"You're right, little brother. You're never far from my thoughts," answered Chris. "Sure. Do what you want. Now, go catch that bus to Davenport if you can and go as far away from my thoughts as you can. On your mark. Get set. Get out of here and remember to come back with that winning lottery ticket.

Would you mind repeating after me? Today is Tuesday, May 13. Today is Tuesday May 13. In fact, you better write yourself a note saying today is Tuesday, May 13. and put it in your pocket. Remember, time flies like an arrow. Fruit flies like a banana."

"Don't you two ever stop?" asked Kelly. "Come on Michael. "You better go home and pack a few things. We need to get you to the bus station where your coach is waiting."

"You two sure make a great comedy team," laughed Michael. "You two should go on stage and do your act instead of selling books."

"Maybe we will if you will be our agent," laughed Chris. "You know that after selling books all these years, I can read your mind."

"Come on Kelly. Here we go again. Let's get out of here before I write a book called, The Over Bearing Big Brother," laughed Michael.

Michael, Alias Dr. Zodiac

Chapter Twenty Three

GOING FOR THE LOTTERY TICKET

It is now one o' clock and Michael found his seat on the bus. He is sitting next to the window looking out, as the bus begins to leave for Davenport. After a while, Michael decides that it is time to call the West Side Kids Detective Agency to see if they will let him in their house, so he can look for the winning lottery ticket. As the phone rings, the gang is sitting in the kitchen eating.

"Would you hand me the pot of coffee?" asked Hannibal. "Not you Scooter, I don't want a cup of paint. Go answer the phone."

Scooter then went into the office and answered the phone, "The West Side Detective Agency. How do you wish me to help you?" laughed Scooter. "Chief, I think it's Michael, alias Dr. Zodiac calling again."

Hearing what Scooter said, Hannibal ran into the office and grabbed the phone out of Scooter's hand.

"Let me talk to the patient," demanded Hannibal. "This is the President of The West Side Detective Agency. How can I help you? Hmm?"

"This is Michael Murphy. You know, alias Dr. Zodiac," said the caller. "I'm coming to Davenport and would like to stop by your house that was once my house and is now your house."

"And why do you want to stop by my house that was once your house and is now my house? Hmm?" asked Hannibal.

"There was just too much confusion at the time," explained Michael. "When you bought my house, I was in jail. My big, older brother, Christopher Murphy was involved in selling you my house and moving all of my things out of the house. I have this personal thing hidden in the house that he didn't know anything about. This really bothers me that you may not let me back in the house to get this."

"I don't know if I want to let you back in the house," laughed Hannibal as he remembered having this same conversation before. "You know how it is. I don't trust you, because of the trouble you gave us and now they set you free at your trial."

"When I find this personal thing, I was going to ask you if I can hire you to escort me safely back to Burlington?" asked Michael.

"What is so important about hiring us to take you back to Burlington safely?" asked Hannibal. "Does this have something to do with that personal thing you have hidden in the house?"

"I can't tell you," insisted Michael. "I'm willing to pay you $3,000 to get me there safely. I would need the services of two of you, but not that crazy Scooter."

"I don't know. Who would you suggest?" asked Hannibal.

"I don't know. I'm not sure," replied Michael.

"I'm afraid that I Don't Know and I'm Not Sure can't go," answered Hannibal. "The only ones that are available to take you is me and my friend as we all know him, Crazy Scooter."

"What? Because I don't want Scooter to go, I'll give you $4,000 if you can get somebody else to go in Scooter's place," pleaded Michael. "Who else can you get?"

"Who, What and Because can't go neither," replied Hannibal. "It has to be Scooter and yours truly for $4,500 and you must tell me what this hidden treasure is."

"You don't say. Whatever?" insisted Michael.

"They can't go neither," answered Hannibal.

"Who can't go? I don't even know what we're talking about. Are you trying to be funny or are you just playing with my mind?"questioned Michael. "You are just as nuts as Scooter."

"Come on now. That was an insult comparing me to Scooter," scolded Hannibal. "Who, What, Because, I Don't Know, I'm Not

Sure and Whatever are just nick names of our gang. Now, as I said it's $4,500 to hire Scooter and myself and you have to tell me what this hidden treasure is, if you want to make a deal."

"If I tell you, can you take me back to Burlington tonight?" asked Michael.

"I'll have you back to Burlington so fast, you won't even remember going there. It will be like magic," reassured Hannibal. "Now what is this hidden treasure that is so mysterious?"

"I guess I have to tell you. I don't have any choice," reasoned Michael. "If I tell you, you will have to stick to our deal of $4,500. It's a winning lottery ticket worth millions.

Now that you know much. I better tell you the rest. I don't want Jerry Dickerson and his crooks to find out about the winning lottery ticket or Dr. Fine and Charlie, The Chill. If they find out, they will try and take it away from me. That's why I need a safe escort back to Burlington."

"What time will you be here?" asked Hannibal.

"About four o'clock," answered Michael. "After I find the winning lottery ticket, will you be ready to leave for Burlington?"

"Absolutely. For $4,500 we can leave right away," insisted Hannibal.

"OK. I'll be there at four," promised Michael. "You and Scooter be ready to go right away. I don't want to take any chances of Dr. Fine and Charlie, The Chill to find out about me coming to Davenport. Jerry Dickerson is another rat I want to avoid finding me in Davenport."

It is now four o' clock and Michael is knocking on the door to The West Side Kid Agency Office. As he steps inside, Ace and Lefty is looking through the office window where they can see Michael.

"Are you ready to go like you promised?" asked Michael.

"We are ready, believe it or not," replied Hannibal. "You will be on your way before you know it after you do me one quick favor."

"I thought we already made a deal. I didn't expect another condition," reasoned Michael. "Why should I do a thing like that? Just what do I have to do?"

"Because that's how it happens," answered Hannibal. "This is a new member to The West Side Kids Detective Agency. I want you to meet Pockets. Look Pockets in the eye and say these same exact words that you wish to go back to your brother's book store, Burlington By The Book in Burlington, Iowa."

That's a strange request, but I'll do it if I must," promised Michael. "I wish to go back to my brother's book store, Burlington By The Book, in Burlington Iowa."

In a flash, Michael was standing in front of the counter in his brother's book store.

"Lefty, did you see that?" asked Ace. "You know something about this?"

"I do and I don't," answered Lefty. "I didn't see anything. I didn't hear anything. I don't know anything and I don't want to know anything."

"First Michael was standing there talking to Hannibal and this Pockets guy and poof, he's gone," explained Ace.

"I'm glad you told me what you saw first. I sure wasn't going to say anything," reasoned Lefty. "I didn't want you to think I was crazy."

"We better get back and tell Jerry what we saw. He isn't going to believe it," muttered Ace. "After we tell him, he will think we're both crazy."

Chapter Twenty Four

A FLIMSY EXCUSE

Back in Burlington, Chris was looking at Michael and said to his brother, "I didn't hear you come in. That didn't take you very long. Did you find the winning lottery ticket?"

"No I didn't," replied a confused Michael. "The last thing I remember, I was talking to Hannibal at my old house. Hannibal introduced me to some dummy called Pockets. Hannibal asked me to look this Pockets in the eyes and say, I wish to go back to my brother's book store, Burlington By The Book in Burlington, Iowa and here I am."

"That's a flimsy excuse," replied Chris. "How long did it take for you to dream that one up? Were you afraid to go back to the house to face Scooter again? If you really didn't want to go, you should have said something."

"Search me how that happened. I tell you, I was there. If you don't believe me, call Hannibal. Let him tell you," pleaded Michael. "Hannibal should still be at the house."

"OK, I will, just as soon as I wait on this customer here at the counter," insisted Chris as the phone rang. "Burlington By The Book. Can I put you on hold?" questioned Chris.

"Are those two books all you want?" asked Chris.

"That's all I want for now," replied the customer. "Can I put these books on my credit card?"

"You sure can. Set your credit card on the counter and put the books on them," laughed Chris. "Never mind. Hand me your credit card. Those books will be $34.95."

"I was going to paint my bathroom. I decided to buy these books instead," reasoned the customer. ""So when I get home I'm going to forget painting the bathroom, because these books aren't going to read themselves," laughed the customer."

"That is a wise decision," replied Chris. "Thank you. Come in again whenever you

have the urge to paint your bathroom."

Picking up the phone, Chris said to the caller, "I'm sorry you had to wait. How can I help you? 301 Jefferson. Yes I can order that for you. We're open till five. Thanks for calling Burlington By The Book. Good Bye."

"Now that there are no more customers in the store and you're done talking on the phone, hurry up and call Hannibal," pleaded Michael.

"OK, little brother. Don't get yourself into a snit," replied Chris. "I'm calling him now. The phone has rang six times. I don't think anybody is there. Oh, hello. May I talk to Hannibal?"

"This is Hannibal. Who's calling?" asked Hannibal.

"This is Chris Murphy, Michael Murphy's brother," replied Chris. "Did my brother Michael come to Davenport to see you today?"

"Just a minute," answered Hannibal as he put his hand over the phone. "Scooter it's Chris Murphy on the phone. Hurry, go get the gang while I put the phone on the speaker. Sorry Chris, what did you want to know?"

"Did my brother Michael come to Davenport today?" repeated Chris. "He was suppose to come to your house today to find a personal belonging that was left behind."

"That's the first I heard of it," replied Hannibal. "The last time I saw your brother, I was at his trial in Burlington. What time is Michael suppose to be here?"

"Four o' clock," answered Chris.

"It's four thirty right now. I'll be watching for him," reassured Hannibal.

"It's not necessary. Michael is standing right next to me," explained Chris.

"Why did you call and ask me if Michael was coming to Davenport, if he is standing next to you?" protested Hannibal. "Are you having fun with me?"

"No, no, it's nothing like that," answered Chris. "It's a long story. Nothing you would be interested in hearing about. That's all I want to know. Thank you for your help. I have to go. There is a customer coming into my store. Good bye."

"Well. Well. Well. What did Hannibal tell you?" asked Michael. "This is the hour of truth. He told you I was in Davenport, didn't he?"

"Why would he tell me that you was in Davenport when you didn't go. What was that suppose to be, Davenport humor? I guess you really don't want that winning lottery ticket or never had one," scolded Chris. "Hannibal told me that the last time he saw you, was at your trial and you weren't there in Davenport. Now tell me, how far did you go before you got off the bus?"

"Here we go again. That's a lie what Hannibal told you. I didn't get off the bus until I got to Davenport," insisted Michael. "I tell you, I have a winning lottery ticket and I was in The West Side Kids Detective Agency Office. That's all I remember.

Hymn, now that I think about it, you had the same problem when you went to Davenport. When you came back you not only lost your memory about going, you lost a day. Something funny is going on. You don't and never did need a doctor and I'm not crazy."

"I think Kelly should go to Davenport next," suggested Chris. "She may be able to bring back the lottery ticket and solve the mystery of us coming back to Davenport and remembering how we did it."

Chapter Twenty Five

SCOOTER AND THE VOICE

Back in Davenport, The West Side Kids are celebrating with Pockets about returning Michael to Burlington.

"So that is what Michael has been up to all this time," exclaimed Hannibal. "So there is a hidden winning lottery ticket hidden somewhere in this house. Pockets, if I made a wish, can you produce the hidden lottery ticket?"

"No Hannibal. I can only try to make a duplicate for you," answered Pockets.

"OK gang, we know that the hidden ticket is here behind the dark room of the office," Everybody get a flashlight and spread out in this room to look for it," ordered Hannibal.

"Hannibal, do you want me to help you?" asked Scooter.

"Scooter, I don't need your help. You stay in the office lock, the door and man the phone," demanded Hannibal. "I don't want anybody in our house while we look for this mysterious lottery ticket. You got that?"

"I not only got that. I'm going to run with it," laughed Scooter.

"Just do what you're told or I'm going to stuff your head down your collar," ordered Hannibal.

"How are you going to do that? I'm just wearing a tee shirt?" laughed Scooter.

"How about we play Chicken Farm and I smear an egg all over your face," scolded Hannibal.

"Alright, already Chief. I will be sure and take care of everything you told me while you go on your treasure hunt," reassured Scooter.

Ten minutes later, Dr. Fine and Charlie, The Chill was standing behind Scooter.

Dr. Fine put his hands around Scooter's head and covered his eyes and said, "Greetings again. Anybody home?"

"Hey! What are you doing here?" asked Scooter.

Guess who? I hope you don't mind me coming here?" answered the voice.

"You don't sound like Who. I know who it is. You sound more like Willy, The Wino," reasoned Scooter. "I want you to get out of here."

"Oh, that's good. That's really good," replied the voice. "Did you know that a morning cup of coffee has an exhilaration of the afternoon cup of tea?"

"Are you trying to play a joke on me?" asked Scooter.

"What if I am," said the voice behind Scooter. "This time I got you and I got you covered."

"I don't know who you are, but what are you doing here?" asked Scooter. "You scared the wits out of me. What do you mean, sneaking in here like a thief? There is no point of you being here. You know that you're not suppose to be in the house."

"You never told me that," answered the voice.

"I must have told you a couple of times," insisted Scooter.

"Well, I never listened," laughed the voice. "I don't know if you noticed, but I haven't been around the last few days."

"It's been nice. That's what I thought," insisted Scooter. "You're not saying that to make me feel better?"

"Actually, I've been around. I just haven't been around you," replied the voice.

"How did you get in? What are you doing here?" asked Scooter. "Didn't I tell you to get out of here? The door was locked. Why didn't you knock on the door?"

"We didn't have to. The back door wasn't locked," laughed the voice.

"Oops, I didn't know that," yelled Scooter.

"I knew that," laughed the voice.

"Oh boy, Hannibal is going to be mad at me again!" yelled Scooter. "I thought I told you to get out of here! I don't have any time to discuss anything with you! I 'm in a hurry to get you out of here!"

"Come on. Come on. Would you hold it down? Remember, you've been warned," instructed the voice. "I'm really serious about this. If you don't talk more quieter, I'm going to make you a little more sluggish where you are absolutely harmless and then you're going to pass away. Then I'm going to take a picture of you and try to find out how hard it is for a stiff to say cheese. You need to be more casual about how you talk."

"I don't know why I was so loud, maybe because I'm really shy?" reasoned Scooter.

"Why? Because you're short, you wear glasses and you look like you're going to trick or treat?" asked the voice. "OK, I just have a few questions to ask you. The second question is going to be a little bit harder," insisted the voice.

"After we saw the lamp with the genie, we got all pepped up. The saying is, you can lead a horse to water, but you can't make him drink. Now, we're thirsty little horses. Now tell me, where is the lamp? I don't intend to leave until you give me the lamp and? you will never see me again.

See how easy that can be. If you don't tell me where the lamp is we're going to take you with us back to our apartment, because it's going to be a mercy mission. This is the last time you're going to bull doze me again, so don't turn me down."

"So that's your little game is it? Aren't you finished yet? OK, now you're in a lot of trouble. You're not telling it right. I'm not turning you down. Stop that noise and get out of here. I said I'm telling you that you have to get out of here," insisted Scooter.

"Are you calling me a liar?" asked the voice.

"I ain't calling you nothing. You just have to get out of here," Scooter continued to say. "Would you kindly leave so I can lock the back door and then come back later through the front door after I unlock it? I'll meet you later and then we can talk."

"Sure I will, as long as you give me the lamp with the genie," replied the voice. "You are a very stubborn man. I took an advantage of a situation and you have every right to be angry. It's going to cost you a bundle. Now pony up or I'm going to unscrew your toes. Knock knock."

"Who's there?" asked Scooter.

"Dr. Fine and Charlie, The Chill," answered the voice.

"Now, I recognize the voice," laughed Scooter. "It's you, Mister Dr. Fine. Hello Dr. Fine. Good bye Dr. Fine.

Next time, call before you come," muttered Scooter as he turned around to see Dr. Fine and Charlie, The Chill. "So you're the knock knock joke."

"Who did you think we were?" asked Charlie, The Chill.

"Thirsty little horses," answered Scooter. "Now, I know what thirsty little horses look like. It seems the thirsty little horses didn't only go to the water to drink, they fell in and you two just look like you flew over the coo-coo's nest."

"Do you believe what Scooter just said? You take that back!" yelled Charlie, The Chill. "If you ever repeat this, I will take a very dim view on this. A very dim view."

"I don't know anything about a lamp with a magic genie. All I have are two books about genies. They are called, "The Forbidden Wish" and "Three Wishes".

If I had three wishes, my first wish would be that you two would go away, far, far away and quit bothering me. My second wish would be that I remembered to have locked the back door. Then let's see. My third wish would be that I had a lamp with a magical genie to make my first two wishes."

"Don't you have that backwards?" laughed Charlie, The Chill. "Your third wish has to be your first wish in order to get your other two wishes."

"I didn't know that," replied Scooter.

"I knew that," insisted Charlie, The Chill as Hannibal and The West Side Kids walked into the office.

"Scooter, what are these two dummies doing here in our office?" yelled Hannibal.

"Hannibal, I'm certainly glad to see you. You got here just in time," insisted Scooter. "I was just stalling for time."

"I thought I told you to lock the front door." boomed Hannibal.

"I did Chief. I did lock the front door like you told me," answered Scooter. "They did it. I was just giving them a piece of my mind, because they came in the house on their own."

"You told us to come in," replied Dr. Fine.

"I did not," insisted Scooter. "Hannibal, you don't think I would do that, do you?"

"Did to!" boomed Charlie, The Chill.

"Yes I do. What are you looking for, sympathy?" asked Hannibal.

"I'm sorry. I didn't mean to upset you. I told them to get out of here," answered Scooter.

"Did not," replied Charlie.

"Did too," insisted Scooter.

"Then, may I ask, how did these two gentlemen as I use that term lightly, get into our office?" Hannibal screamed.

"It's your fault they are here, not mine," reasoned Scooter.

"OK, numskull. Explain that one to me," insisted Hannibal.

"It's very simple. You forgot to tell me to lock the back door," answered Scooter.

"OK gentlemen, may I escort you on your way out the door?" replied a disgusted Hannibal. "Your presence is no longer needed or wanted."

Charlie, The Chill then pulled a gun out of his pocket and pointed it at Hannibal and said, "Me and Dr. Fine came here for the lamp with the magic genie. We're not leaving, until you hand it over."

"Oh, we're playing that game again. Well, this is a fine how do you do," replied Hannibal. "So what? OK, you asked for it. Next Christmas, I'm going to see that a tree drops on your heads. I guess this leaves The Genie free to come after you. Pockets give these gentlemen what they deserve."

"Right on it Chief," answered Pockets. "OK dummies, do you mind stepping over here for a minute?"

"I don't get your play," replied Dr. Fine.

"You have nothing to worry about, he is just bluffing," reasoned

Charlie, The Chill. "This guy isn't a genie. The real genie comes out of the lamp."

"I didn't know that. I would like to believe that," answered a nervous Dr. Fine.

"I knew you would see it that way," laughed Hannibal.

"Where do you wish to go after you leave here?" asked Pockets.

"Back home to our apartment," replied Dr. Fine.

"Charlie, The Chill, Dr. Fine, beat it if your scared. Return to your home immediately and don't waste time," wished Pockets.

In a flash, Charlie, The Chill and Dr. Fine vanished from The West Side Kids Detective Agency and were now standing in the living room of their apartment.

"Oops, they did it to us again. Wait until I get my hands on Hannibal," roared Dr. Fine. "One way or another, we have to come up with another plan to get that lamp, with the magic genie."

Back at The West Side Kids Detective Agency, everybody was cheering for Pockets.

"Did you find the winning lottery ticket?" asked Scooter.

"I'm Not Sure found it and he gave it to me," replied Hannibal. "I decided to hide it someplace else until we can cash it in. I don't want to take a chance of Michael finding it if he should come back to Davenport again. After that, we are all going to be rich."

"Where did you hide it?" asked Scooter.

"I'm not going to tell you," answered Hannibal. "I said we are all going to be rich, not stupid."

"Don't worry," added Pockets. "If Michael comes back, he won't have even a small chance of finding the winning lottery ticket. I will return him back to Burlington faster than I can say, I'm a slave of the lamp."

Chapter Twenty Six

THERE IS A BASEBALL GAME TONIGHT

"I've been thinking about it Pockets," beamed Hannibal. "There is a baseball game tonight at the stadium by the river. How would you like it, if all of us took you to see the game tonight?"

"I would like that," replied Pockets. "Who is playing?" "Who is not playing. He is going with us to watch the game," answered Scooter.

"What I mean to say is, what teams will be there tonight?" asked Pockets.

"I don't know," answered I Don't Know. "Do you know who is playing, Because?" "Like Scooter said, Who is not playing, because he is going to watch the game with us," replied Because.

"You don't say," added You Don't Say. "All I know is there is going to be two teams on the field tonight."

"Then tell me the names of the teams that are playing there tonight?" asked Pockets.

"Whatever teams that are playing tonight, it should be a good game," insisted Whatever.

"I wish somebody would tell me the teams that are playing there tonight," laughed Pockets.

"I don't know who is playing tonight," insisted I Don't Know.

"Pockets, even though I'm not sure about the teams playing tonight, I know you will have a great time," reasoned I'm Not Sure."

"Whatever you think," added Whatever. "I just want to go so I can get some peanuts, popcorn and Cracker Jacks, then I don't care if I ever get back."

"Well, I'm ready to go," announced Pockets. "Come on. Take me out to the ballgame."

Chapter Twenty Seven

It's True. We Couldn't Believe Our Eyes

Ace and Lefty just returned to Jerry's apartment to tell him what they saw.

"Jerry, Lefty and myself went to The West Side Kids Detective Agency like you told us," exclaimed Ace. "When we looked in the window to the office, there was Michael, alias Dr. Zodiac standing there as big as life. He was looking and talking to some strange looking dude."

"That's right," broke in an excited Lefty. "Like Ace said, Michael was standing there and poof he was gone like he never was there. I kid you not. I couldn't believe my eyes and I still can't believe my eyes."

"Your glasses must have cataracts. I don't understand this whole matter. I think it's strange, very strange! In fact that's the craziest thing I ever heard of!" screamed Jerry.

"Do you expect me to believe a story like that? Isn't it possible that you both could be mistaken? How many times do I have to tell you to stay out of the tavern! You must have had a very good time. If this gets out, you're both going to look like a couple of yo-yews.

Maybe you and Ace need to hook up with that dumb Scooter or join those dummies, Dr. Fine and Charlie, The Chill. You two jerks might just fit in with their dumb schemes."

"We can explain," replied Lefty.

"Then make it a good one so we can discuss this whole sorted affair," pleaded Jerry.

"On my honor as an Ex Boy Scout, we never did go into any tavern," insisted Lefty. "Boss, what I'm telling you what we saw is on the level."

"Boys, stop it! Listen to me!" yelled Dixie. "Either that house that The West Side Kids own is haunted or they do have a lamp with a magic genie!"

"That's right boss. That does make sense," replied Ace. "I say that if we all had our heads shaved and lost our memory of a couple of days, that should explain our vision of the vanishing Michael."

"Jerry, now what are we going to do?" asked Danny. "It seems like every time we make plans, something weird happens and throws a wrench into what we were planning to do."

"Ace when you and Lefty looked in the window, did you see a lamp?" asked Jerry.

"No boss. All we saw was all we saw and we didn't see any teapot or lamp or anything out of the ordinary except for Michael disappearing before our very eyes. Isn't that right Lefty?" asked Ace.

"Right on Ace," replied Lefty. "All we saw was Michael doing his disappearing act right before our eyes and that was all we saw. I tell you, after that, we didn't see anything."

"OK. Time out. Since it looks like our plans aren't going to work out, we need to change our plans to a different game plan, but never the goal" insisted Jerry. "Ace, you and Lefty continue to keep an eye on The West Side Detective Agency. Danny, you and Mugs keep an eye on these two window peepers, Ace and Lefty. Shorty, you keep an eye on all four of these dummies. I want you to keep a sharp eye out for anything that looks suspicious. I'm going to keep my eye on all of you. You have your work cut out for you and I expect results.

Dixie, you go to Burlington with me. Is that clear to everybody?" asked Jerry. "Any questions? None. Good. Dixie, pack your bags. We're on our way to Burlington."

Burlington By The Book

Dixie Doneright

Chapter Twenty Eight

DO YOU FEEL LUCKY?
WELL, DO YOU?

It was now 1 p m and Jerry and Dixie were just entering Burlington.

"Look Dixie, there is the casino and our motel," exclaimed Jerry. "I thought we might as well have some fun as long as we had to come to Burlington. Let's go to Burlington By The Book and see what we can find out about Michael. The store closes at 5 p m. Later on we can check into this motel, get something to eat and do a little gambling. Do you feel lucky Punk, I mean Dixie? What do you say?"

"Why are you calling me punk, Jerry?" answered Dixie. "I didn't do anything wrong." "I didn't mean anything by it, Dixie," explained Jerry. "I was thinking of the movie,

Dirty Harry, that Clint Eastwood was in where he said as he was pointing his gun at a bank robber, "You've got to ask yourself one question, punk. Do you feel lucky? Well do you punk? Did I fire five shots or six?"

"Jerry, that was a very good imitation of Clint Eastwood. You know what they say.

Imitations are a sincere form of flattery. I always liked Clint Eastwood in the movie, Dirty Harry and I have seen it at least five or six times,"replied Dixie.

"Well you should see it some more," answered Jerry. "That should make you lucky, because that will be the sixth or seventh time you've seen it. When we get back to Davenport, would you watch that movie again if I rented it?"

"I would love to see it again. Now that I think of it, I don't remember if I've seen Dirty Harry, five times or six times. Oh boy. Lucky me," laughed Dixie. "How close are we getting to Burlington By The Book?"

"We should be there in a few minutes," answered Jerry. "When we get there, I don't want to park in front of the store in case Michael, alias Dr. Zodiac is there. He would recognize us in a minute. We need to look though the window first. If Chris is there by himself, then I think it would be safe to go in."

Five minutes later, Jerry was parking his car at the end of the block where Burlington By The Book was located.

"Dixie, you go look in the window of the book store," instructed Jerry. "I will follow you a short distance behind you. If the coast is clear, motion me on ahead and then we will go in the store."

After Dixie approached the window of the store, she looked inside. There was nobody in the store but Chris, with a silly looking fly costume on, holding two books in his hands.

"Come on Jerry. Look in the window," laughed Dixie. "You'll never believe this." Jerry then walked over and looked in the window. "What in blazes is that?" asked Jerry.

"It's either Chris playing Halloween in May or a very large fly that escaped from the exterminator," laughed Dixie. "I know that Chris has a twin brother, but he's not crazy enough to put on a costume like that. He is more into doing impressions of a zombie."

"Well, if you're sure that it's Chris, let's go inside and talk to him," laughed Jerry. "I know you're good at reading minds, but do you like to read books? Maybe there is a book about Dirty Harry that Chris has in stock. If that is the case, does he have five books or six books?"

Once inside the store, Chris walked up to Jerry and Dixie and asked, "May I be of some help to you?"

"You sure can, Mr. Fly. Do you have any books on lamps with genies?" asked Dixie.

"Oh, this fly costume. Looking at me, you must think I'm nuts. I was just trying to use this costume to promote these two books about flies. I like the saying, "Time flies like an arrow. Fruit flies like a banana. I'm Chris Murphy. I own this book store."

"Before I forget to ask," insisted Jerry. I am feeling lucky about this. Do you have any books about the movie, Dirty Harry, with Clint Eastwood? Well do you?"

"I should have some books about the movie, Dirty Harry. They should be over two aisles to the left from where we're standing. I don't remember if I have five or six books," laughed Chris.

"You don't say?" reasoned Jerry. "You don't happen to be related to a Michael Murphy? I read in the paper that he was accused of murdering a couple of people."

"Yes, I'm afraid so. Michael is my twin brother. The jury couldn't prove he murdered anybody and he was set free," explained Chris. "Right now, Michael is living with me, until he can get back on his feet. I also have a younger brother, called Tim and a sister, named Kelly."

"That's very interesting about your family," replied Dixie. "What's it like to have a twin brother? I always thought I would like to have a twin sister."

"There are good, bad and ugly things about having a twin brother," answered Chris. "The good thing is to have a twin brother, who is truly my friend. The bad thing is to have some people mistake me for my twin brother, Michael. And the ugly thing is for five or six people to ask me if I'm the well known evil, Dr. Zodiac? That's the good, bad and ugly things of having a twin brother. Most people don't know us. My brother is really a nice guy and my customers know and like Michael and me."

"Talking about your brother Michael, is he interested in lamps with magic genies? I'm sure he would be, if he believes in the super natural like he says he does," asked Dixie.

"No, I don't think so," replied Chris "If he did, he would be reading the books I have about lamps with magic genies."

"Does he ever plan on coming back to Davenport for any reason or even moving back to Davenport?" asked Dixie.

"Why are you asking me all these questions about my twin brother?" boomed Chris "You don't even know my twin brother. I don't know. Maybe you should ask Michael all these questions. Now, do you want me to help you find those books?"

"I'm sorry about Dixie asking you all those personal questions about your twin brother," insisted Jerry. "You know how it is. Women are just plain busy bodies."

"Now, do you want me to help you find those books?" asked Chris.

"No, we're just going to take our time looking," answered Jerry.

"I should have a couple books on the subject of lamps and genies. Check down that aisle halfway down on the left," instructed Chris.

"Jerry, don't forget to ask about lottery tickets," added Dixie.

"Oh yes. Do you sell or know where we can buy some Iowa Lottery Tickets?" beamed Jerry.

"I don't sell them, but there is a gas station on the river road towards the bridge that sells them," answered Chris.

"Jerry, can we come back another time and look for these books?" asked Dixie. "I didn't eat lunch and I'm getting hungry. I'm really wishing very hard that you will take me to get something to eat. Well do you plan on taking me? Well do you?"

"I guess we will be going to get something to eat and have to come back later," answered Jerry. "How late are you open, five or six?"

"Five o'clock is when I close up shop and then I make a bee line home," laughed Chris. "I open again tomorrow at eleven."

"I know we have plenty of time to come back, but there are other things we want to do while we're here in Burlington. I guess we may have to come back tomorrow," replied Jerry. "We have a room at a motel here in Burlington. I guess after we eat, because I feel lucky, we're going to the casino. We also wanted to go see Snake Alley."

After Jerry and Dixie got into their car and drove away, Dixie asked, "Did you feel lucky enough that we pulled it off that to fool Chris into what we wanted to know?"

"I don't think he suspected a thing. I didn't find out as much as I wanted to find out," replied a puzzled Jerry. "I think tomorrow, we should be gad a bouts and drop in from a distance and park close to the store. We might be able to detect a few things that we overlooked and see if Michael shows up. If he does, I want to keep an eye on him.

Nothing gets by me. When it comes to finding out things I need to know, I practically have radar in my nose."

"By the way, what did you mean that women are busy bodies?" asked Dixie.

"That was the only thing I could think of to say to cover up the reason for all of your questions," answered Jerry.

"Well in that case, if this is really any of my business, I'm going to make you pay for what you said," boomed Dixie. "I want you to take me to a restaurant where I can order a very expensive steak dinner."

"Then how about Mexican food?" asked Jerry.

"Mexican food is too hot and I'm all the fire you can handle," replied Dixie.

"How about eating at the casino. Their meals are expensive," laughed Jerry. "You can have anything you want to eat at the buffet. Then you know what's going to happen? An hour after you eat, you're going to be hungry for me again. Then here I come, ready or not."

After we're done eating, remind me to call Ace to see what's going on in Davenport. I want to see if he is keeping an eye on The West Side Kids Detective Agency."

Betty Snyder and Kelly Murphy

Chapter Twenty Nine
Kelly Goes To Davenport

It is now Tuesday, May 20. Chris, Michael, Kelly and Tim are standing in the book store, to try to decide who is going to Davenport next.

"It's been a week now since Michael went to Davenport to get the winning lottery ticket," Kelly went on to say. "I think we should try a different angle on getting that lottery ticket. I was up all night and was so excited, I couldn't sleep. Now, I have an idea and I think I've got it."

"Kelly, I'm laughing already. What's your idea? Go ahead. Do me a favor and lay it one me. What did you have in mind?" asked Chris.

"All my ideas are good ideas. A good place to start is from the beginning," reasoned Kelly. "I'm going to start all over with a new plan. This time, I have a plan that's got to work and this will have a happy ending. Now, I feel like celebrating.

"I think I should go to Davenport next and pretend to hire The West Side Kids. I will pretend I don't want anything else," answered Kelly."I don't think it's too late in the day to go. Michael, if you tell me where the lottery ticket is, I will try and find a way to get it. I'll bet a buck there is nothing to it, but you won't let me do it."

"Oh man, you can't do that. I don't want to seem insensitive. How can you possibly do
   that? What do you know? Let's talk about this sensibly," insisted Michael. "If you go, I'm afraid they are going to take you away to the Funny Farm."

"What do you know? I was right. You are deliberately wrong," answered Kelly. 'You had a chance to bring back the winning lottery ticket. Why didn't you do it yourself?

I keep hearing about how stupid this Scooter is. It's a beautiful, beautiful plan. With my plan, I will show you how easy it is, because I'm going to be the captain of the ship," replied Kelly.

"Yes, The Titanic," reasoned Michael. "With Scooter, you can have almost an impossible talk and not get a thing accomplished, because you're playing with fire."

"Why are you being so negative?" asked Kelly. "I can be a fun person to be with. People are crazy about me. When I'm around, the fun begins.

Maybe if I begin with the romantic approach on him and show him we are a matched couple, he will gladly give up the winning lottery ticket. Maybe that's the way I should handle it."

"I know that. One sense of humor with one brain," laughed Michael. "It may seem like a good idea and then it might just backfire. I am dead set against this sort of thing happening."

"Michael, you just refuse to give me credit for anything I do. I have a better plan than you and the word for that is jealousy" cried Kelly.

"I just feel that I shouldn't be dumping my problems on you," replied Michael.

"That's silly," insisted Kelly.

"It's not silly," replied Michael. "Maybe I should go along dreaming of something else, because my whole life just fell apart. Maybe it's good this happened. Maybe I'm glad this happened."

Underneath that hostility, you really have a heart of gold," reasoned Kelly. "I told you I was going to do this. In the meantime, why don't you just leave me alone so I can plan this the right way?"

"Are you crazy? Just out of curiosity, why?" asked Michael. "You're the most unthinkable woman I have ever known."

"Michael, you don't need to be upset. I get it. It sounds like a good idea to me. It takes a lot off my mind. In fact, this is a good idea," reasoned Chris. "I'm sure things will eventually work out. If it's any consolation, Kelly, I'm proud of you."

"Chris, I knew you would believe in me," reassured Kelly. "If it's worth it to you, then it's worth it to me to try. I may just luck out on this one."

"What I love about Scooter is, you never know what he is going to say or do next. You may pull one over on Scooter, by asking him for the winning lottery ticket. I still wouldn't count on getting it," added Chris. "Just watch out for Hannibal, because Hannibal is a different story. I know you're excited about your plan, but let them set the tone."

"If that is a problem, that could be a thought. How are they going to turn me down if I take my girlfriend Betty Snyder with me?" explained Kelly. "This calls for a rendezvous with destiny. It will be a trip to remember. Between the two of us, I'm sure they will be defenseless."

"I don't know. This, I gotta see," exclaimed Tim. "It sounds kind of risky to me. I don't

think it will work. It just can't be done. I don't really think you want to go to Davenport."

"Tim, how dare you! How dare you! Is this a conspiracy? This is a terrible shock.

What are you doing here? Trying to minimize my idea of getting the job done by claiming I can't do it," insisted Kelly. "If this works out, it will be no thanks to you. Tim, I think you are still living in the stone age."

"Just a minute. You don't have to get so snippy about it," replied Tim.

"I'm not trying to be unreasonable, but it is demeaning to me to say that I can't do it. That's the story of my life. Tim, I think we have grown apart. This is a closed matter," insisted Kelly.

"I'm on your side, but I'm still hearing snippy!" boomed Tim. "I'm willing to let bygones to be bygones!"

"I know I may seem frustrating to you, but you don't have to scream!" shouted Kelly.

"In that case, I would say you were very well restrained," answered Tim. "But since I tried to talk to you, I can see your mind is made up. I have a feeling you're right. But when something has gone on this long, it's hard to change it. Why don't we go for a walk and talk about it? Are you coming?"

"Although this isn't a good time. I might as well as long as you are wising up. I'm sure Betty and I can get the job done," reassured Kelly. "If I thought everybody was happy, I would drop it. But don't you realize, I have a choice. I need to challenge Hannibal and Scooter about getting that winning lottery ticket.

I don't think I need to spell it out. I know what happened when Chris and Michael tried to get the lottery ticket and it didn't work. Betty and I are going to make up the mess where our other two brothers have failed."

"I appreciate what you and Betty are trying to do for me. This is as good of a time as any," insisted Michael. "You're the greatest sister a guy ever had. OK. I know you don't want to do this, but be strong. I'm glad you are doing this for me, because we all need this lottery ticket. For what it's worth, good luck."

"I'll see what I can do," reassured Kelly.

"Chris and I don't want you to see what you can do. We want you to do it," insisted Michael.

"It's no bother. When Betty and I get back, I hope to have some good news for you," reasoned Kelly. "Well, this is it. I'm going to call Betty right now."

"Here we go again," boomed Michael.

Two hours later, Betty and Kelly were on the bus heading for Davenport.

"Let's get this show on the road? This should be a fun trip," exclaimed Kelly. "When we get to Davenport, I want to present us as a fun couple who are a good time, fun loving folks, in trouble. This can be the most hilarious moments of our lives. That's why they will enjoy us so much."

"That's a different kind of an idea," replied Betty. "I know people like that."

"I'm going to put on the charm for Scooter. While I'm doing that, you go after Hannibal the same way," explained Kelly. "Get him to take you out to eat and to a movie, while I work on Scooter."

"What's this Hannibal like?" asked Betty.

"He's not exactly tall, dark and handsome. He's not bad looking and on the short side," explained Kelly. "He's the leader and the smarter one of The West Side Kids. We just need to keep Hannibal separated from Scooter in order to get what we're after."

"You're talking about the winning lottery ticket. Right," replied Betty. "As you explained it, if we can get the winning lottery ticket, you were going to give me a share?"

"Yes, if you do your part in getting the ticket," insisted Kelly. "Chris and Michael each came to Davenport to get it and failed. Now, it's up to us to get the ticket. I'm out to win. Are you with me, girlfriend?"

"I sure am," answered Betty. "After we cash in the winning lottery ticket, I'm going to have a pocketful of riches."

"I think its time that I called The West Side Detective Agency and make an appointment to see them," laughed Kelly. "After I call them, I am going to pretend to hire them. I am going to tell them that you and me are sisters and we live in Muscatine."

"Hello. Is this the West Side Kids Detective Agency?" asked Kelly.

"Yes, how can I help you?" asked Scooter.

"My name is Kelly Snyder. My sister, Betty and me would like to make an appointment to come and see you for a job this afternoon," replied Kelly. "We were coming to Davenport on some other business and also want to come and see you in a couple of hours, say four o'clock. A friend of ours recommended your agency for the job and gave me your phone number and address. We are fun people and you sound like a big strong man and should be right for the job."

"Hannibal isn't here right now. I will call him on his cell phone and tell him you're coming," promised Scooter. "I'm glad to do any job you have to give us."

"OK, I will see you at four," insisted Kelly.

"Who was that you talked to?" asked Betty.

"That was Scooter," answered Kelly. "After we get to Davenport, I'll tell you what we are going to do."

It was now five o' clock and Kelly was knocking on the door of The West Side Kids Detective Agency. Knowing who was coming at four, Scooter rushed to answer the door.

"Knock, knock," said Kelly.

"Who's there?" answered Scooter.

"We're the fun people, Kelly and Betty," answered Kelly.

"Hello ladies, come on in," insisted Scooter. "My name is Scooter Hickenbottom and that is Hannibal sitting here at the desk."

"Hello ladies. You're an hour late. How may I assist you?" asked Hannibal. "Hymn."

"We met this other couple on the way here and started to talk to them," answered Kelly. "One thing led to another and we didn't pay any attention to the time. It completely slipped our minds. You understand, don't you?"

"It's no big deal. Well, what do you know? Would I be presumptuous that you are the fun people we were expecting?" asked Hannibal.

"We're the fun people you were expecting," answered Kelly. "My name is Kelly Snyder and this is my sister, Betty."

"Anybody want coffee?" asked Hannibal. "Make yourselves comfortable. How about that I give you one of our best drinks or would you like something else to drink?"

"We didn't expect you to go to any trouble," replied Kelly. "We would both like to have a bottle of water. Isn't this a charming, nice place you have here? Doesn't this all look wonderful? I'm so glad you invited us in."

"We're very proud of this place," replied Hannibal.

"It's wonderful to finally meet you. I feel I know you already," insisted Kelly. "You can't have a detective agency without people talking about you. Hannibal, what do you do for a living? What's it feel like to be a celebrity?"

"Just fine," answered Hannibal. "I haven't heard any complaints."

"I want you to know how uncomfortable Betty and I feel about asking you this. We need your protection. I was wondering if we can talk to you for a few minutes. It's kind of personal," explained Kelly.

"We all have problems," replied Hannibal. "Me and my detective agency are people helping people. That is what this country is all about. Tell me anything you want to. I would like to hear what your problems are."

"Both of our boyfriends are in a motorcycle gang, in Muscatine," explained Kelly. "We don't want any more to do with them. We lucked out and escaped. They think we was trying to avoid them because they are dull, when Betty and me are fun people. They think we're the life of the party and they're not."

"You know that feeling? Don't you Scooter?" asked Hannibal. "Kelly, why did you leave them?"

"We thought they would come after us," replied Kelly. "Three hours ago we jilted our boyfriends and broke their hearts. We left them and are no longer part of their life. They said they did have the right to know why we did that and wanted the truth. They deserved an explanation and wanted us to say we were sorry. They could always tell when we were lying to them and would not be handling this with so much dignity."

"So go back to them," suggested Hannibal.

"Not on your life. It doesn't matter because we don't want to see them. If we went back to them with an explanation, it would turn into an ugly scene," replied Kelly. "You don't understand. It was just a little dumb thing that came between us, so they threatened to hurt us real bad if we didn't continue to go out with them. It may be a very serious problem. They really scare us. I wish they would leave us alone."

"I don't know if they can. At least not completely. It depends on what you do," answered Hannibal. "I think maybe you're right. You made your point. If you do go back to them, you may regret this the rest of your life."

"My boyfriend told me that it will be the day that I would choose a clown over him," Kelly went on to say. "He make me so mad. There isn't a man alive who does not have someone in his past that he doesn't think about."

"My boyfriend told me that it would be a great day if I choose a ding-a-ling over him," added Betty. "I don't know if we will ever see them again. I know the nice thing about people like that is you don't care."

"Then don't go back to them. Am I crazy or is this a stand off? It must be tough to

make decisions like that. You would be surprised how simple it is. But you're right. Either you will or you won't, you do or you don't or you can't or you're crazy," insisted Hannibal. "At least try to make a decision."

"OK! I will. Forget it, I can't," answered Kelly. "Hannibal, you don't think I'm terrible for thinking that way, do you?"

"Not at all," replied Hannibal.

"Hannibal, you really mean that?" insisted Kelly.

"I never know. What's the big deal. If that's the way you feel, are you asking me to help you?" asked Hannibal. "It just sounds like a stupid, meaningless relationship that both of you got into. It will take time, patience and friends and you will get through it."

"That is what I am afraid of. I never would have thought of it that way," replied Kelly. "You are a generous guy. I'm glad that this is a wonderful moment. The point is if this happened before we had a chance to meet you, I don't know what we would have done."

"Have you gone to the police about this?" asked Hannibal.

"Yes and they told us that there was nothing they could do, until something happens to one of us," answered Kelly. "Both Betty and me have been crying for the last week now, because we are both scared for our lives."

"I'm not going to suggest anything else. Right now, everything is alright. Everything is fine," replied Hannibal. "How many are in this motorcycle gang?"

"I would say about fifteen or sixteen," reasoned Kelly.

"If that is all there is? Well, cry no more. Thanks for getting us involved. I just wish it had been under better circumstances. Since you two are terrific people, me and my detective agency will do everything we can to protect you," promised Hannibal. "We expect your fullest cooperation. Between Scooter and myself, we can take care of them for you."

"I know you two are big strong men. We just need someone to be in charge. We thought since you don't have a regular job, you would have the time to take care of us," reasoned Kelly. "You were somebody we never thought of until we heard about you. Betty and I are counting on you, because we know you won't take your job lightly. Just what are you going to do about it? How can the two of you go up against fifteen or sixteen people in the motor cycle gang?"

"Wait, everything will be OK in a couple of days. We can do it.

We have our ways. I'm going to think about this, because I want to coordinate a plan," replied Hannibal.

"My boyfriend said that anybody who would protect Betty and me from his motor cycle gang must be a saint," boomed Kelly.

"He didn't use the word saint," corrected Betty. "He said insane."

"Say no more. This is a proud day for our detective agency to be working for girls like you," insisted Hannibal. "In my business, I go a lot of places and meet a lot of different people."

"Betty and I are looking forward to having you protect us from our boyfriends," replied Kelly. "Betty and I was told that we couldn't do any better than to use Hannibal to protect us. I admire a man who does what he says."

"I'll do my best," replied Hannibal.

"Hannibal, what do you have planned for us the rest of the day? We don't have any plans. We thought we would wait to see if you had some."

"I've given this some thought and this is what I've come up with," reasoned Hannibal. "For starters, why don't you let Scooter and myself take you out to eat and then to a movie?"

"That sells me on it. I would like that very much," reasoned Betty. "Hannibal would you take me? I haven't had a bit to eat all day and a movie would take my mind off of my troubles."

"Betty and I have to admire you for the things you do," insisted Kelly.

"What a nice thing to say," answered Hannibal. "Kelly, are you sure you won't change your mind about going with us?"

"If it matters to anyone. I am not hungry. Right now, I am having second thoughts and want to think things out. I'm really confused right now and have a lot of mixed feelings. I am not feeling good and I want to ralph," insisted Kelly.

"You want to what?" asked Hannibal.

"I am very depressed right now and feel like I want to ralph, vomit," answered Kelly.

"I sure don't like being around depressed people," replied Scooter.

"What are you confused about?" asked Hannibal.

"Many times when I watch a detective show, they inspire me. It must be written all over my face. Scooter makes me crazy. I am very attracted to Scooter and I would like to stay here and get to know him better," exclaimed Kelly as Pockets entered the office.

"I've been meaning to spend more time with depressed people. Kelly, are you here by some stroke of luck?" asked Scooter. "Any friend of Betty's is a goddess of mine. We have been so critical in this day of age, we can't profess our feelings for each other. If there is anything you need. If you need a hand to hold, a shoulder to cry on, a warm body to cling to, I will be here for you."

"Betty, I'll be ready to go in a minute. Scooter, why do you look like that?" asked Hannibal. "Why are you standing there with that dumb smile all over your face? What is so funny?"

"I'm not smiling," insisted Scooter.

"If you're not smiling, you need to get rid of that Halloween Mask," ordered Hannibal. "Betty and I have a date. We have our whole evening planned. I know the reason you are smiling. After Betty and I leave, you know what is to come. You mind your manners with Kelly.

Ladies, this is one of our members of our agency. His name is Pockets. Pockets, this is Kelly and Betty Snyder. They are hiring us to do a job for them. Their ex boyfriends threatened to hurt them.

I am taking Betty out to eat and to a movie. Kelly is staying here with Scooter. So I'm leaving you in charge. I want you to keep an eye on Scooter. If there is any trouble of any sort, you know what to do."

"Yes master, I mean Hannibal. I will see that everything goes well while you are gone," answered Pockets.

"Well Betty, what are we waiting for? Your carriage is waiting," laughed Hannibal as he went out the door with Betty.

Scooter and Kelly Murphy

Chapter Thirty

Scooter and Kelly

"Isn't it a small world? Scooter, you really made my day. Isn't this exciting? This is a very nice place you have here," insisted Kelly. "Now that we're alone, let me have a look at you. Would you like to show me around?"

"Why sure. I will be glad to show you around," answered Scooter.

"After you show me around, what should we talk about?" asked Kelly.

"I like to talk about lamps with magic genies," answered Scooter. "I have two of these books in my room about lamps and genies. Would you like me to go get them for you?"

"I would love to see those books," insisted Kelly.

"Come to think of it Pockets, I was going to show them to you and I can't remember where I put them," Scooter went on to say. "Would you come with me and try to help me find them?"

After Scooter and Pockets left the office to go into Scooter's bedroom, Kelly began to search for the switch that would open up the door in the wall, behind the office desk. After finding the switch, the door in the wall began to open.

Knowing she didn't have much time, she took a flashlight out of her purse and went in the room behind the office desk. In seconds, she reached the wall where the winning lottery ticket was hidden, only it wasn't there. She immediately left the room and sat down in a chair by the desk with the door still open. A couple minutes later, Scooter returned to the office with Pockets at his side.

Returning to the office, Scooter exclaimed, "Pockets helped me find my two books, "The Forbidden Wish' and 'Three Wishes". Hey, why is that door open behind the office desk?"

"I accidentally opened it. I feel terrible about this," answered Kelly. "I needed something to write with and I didn't think you would mind if I looked through the desk to find a pen. I hope you're not so sensitive that you feel anything bad of me for doing that. I guess I'm just scattered brained and didn't know how to close it. You have to forgive me. I'm just feeling sad and my mind isn't functioning, OK. I guess I'm really out of it."

"Really?" asked Scooter. "Is everything alright? You seem like a very nice person?"

"Not really," replied Kelly.

"That's quite OK, Kelly. I'm so sorry to hear that. Hey, it's not the end of the world," insisted Scooter.

"It's the end of my world," cried Kelly.

"Would you calm down? Just what are you talking about? I know it is none of my business and I don't know what to say," answered Scooter. "Are you asking for my opinion or telling me that it is the end of your world?

Oh, what's the difference. If worse comes to worse, you can always tell me what happened? You can't expect life to stand still because you have big problems."

"I am very much mixed up. Now, I don't know what to do," replied Kelly as she continued to cry. "I'm glad you're talking this over with me. My boyfriend is always criticizing me, getting me upset. I have some stories to tell you."

"That isn't necessary. I'm sure you don't want to be out of it," answered Scooter. "I'm always being accused of doing stupid things around here and always being out of it. Not that I'm calling you stupid. I think you're very attractive and I would like to get to know you better."

"That's very sweet of you to say that," insisted Kelly. "I wish my ex boyfriend was like you. I want you to know that I never went into that room.

As I was sitting here waiting for you to come back, I was wondering what that hidden room was used for. That is a funny looking layout. I never knew there were hidden rooms in houses."

"It was a dark room, a very dark room when we bought the house," Scooter went on to say. "We had a light installed in this room even though we don't use it for nut in."

"You mean nothing don't you?" asked Kelly.

"That's what I said, nut in," answered Scooter.

"What were you planning on doing tonight?" asked Kelly

"I was going to put rockets in my pants and send up flares," laughed Scooter. "Would

you like to go in this room to see what's in there? Won't you come into this room, said the spider to the fly?"

"I not only would like it. If you bring two chairs in there, we can sit and be alone. Do you want to give it a whirl?" exclaimed Kelly. "Are you on a solo trip or do you have a main squeeze? If you really want to get into things, you have to go where it is happening."

A couple minutes later, Scooter took two folding chairs and set them down in the middle of the room.

"You are quite a gentleman. Are you having fun so far? I know I am. I am really happy, because it's our chance to be friends," insisted Kelly.

"I can't tell you what it does to me to know that you are this happy," replied Scooter.

"Are you as happy as I am?" asked Kelly.

"I'm happier than you are, because you told me that you are so happy," reasoned Scooter.

"Then this is truly a happy day for both of us," answered Kelly. "I'm not hungry, but

could I have a cup of coffee?"

"I'm glad you're having a good time. Your wish is my demand, I mean command," replied a nervous Scooter. "If you don't need me for anything else, I'm going to be gone for a few minutes. You wait here, because I have to go into the kitchen and make some coffee."

"Thanks. That is sure swell of you. Take your time Honey, because we have got all evening. I'll just sit here and hang loose," insisted Kelly, as Scooter was leaving to go into the kitchen.

After Scooter left, Kelly took out her cell phone from her purse to call Michael as Pockets stood outside the door, listening.

"Michael, What are you doing right now? I can't find the winning lottery ticket. Are you sure the winning lottery ticket is hidden in the room behind the desk?" asked Kelly.

"You need to go back over our game plan. Have you thought about what you're going to do about that?"insisted Michael.

"Well, it's not for sure yet. Let me think about it. No, I haven't," answered Kelly.

"The winning lottery ticket should be where I told you it was. You are looking in the right spot?" asked Michael. "What's the matter? Are you getting nervous?"

"That's great, really great. You would bring that up. I wouldn't be this nervous if I wasn't snooping around. I only have a few minutes. I'm going to turn my camera on my phone to show you where I'm looking," replied Kelly. "How about right here?"

Looking on his phone, Michael replied, "You,re looking in the right place. It should be there. I don't know who could have done it. Take another look around to see if somebody moved it."

"Oh, you think so. Well, it's not. I don't like this set up. Something is haywire. It looks to me that you left the winning lottery ticket right into somebody's lap. I'll have another idea how to find it. This is a sure fire idea that can't miss," insisted Kelly.

"Are you sure? Sometimes your ideas have a way of kicking back," reasoned Michael. "Here we go again."

"Don't worry. This idea is going to work. First I want to find out what Scooter knows about this. Scooter's coming with my coffee, I have to go," insisted Kelly as Pockets stood in the doorway.

"What are you doing in there?" asked Pockets. "What's the big idea? Come out of there right now. Scooter, I don't think it's a very good idea to leave this young lady alone in this room."

"Here is your coffee. I forgot to ask if you wanted your coffee black," beamed Scooter.

"Of course I want it black. Who ever heard of white coffee?" laughed Kelly.

"I don't know why, but I'm very attracted to you," blurted Scooter.

"That's the same way I feel about you," replied Kelly. "Scooter, you are deep. I can't believe how deep you really are. I think we are a well matched couple. You came back early. I'm anxious. I'm ready. I wanted you to kiss me from the moment we met. I think we have a lot to talk about and we're going to be a great couple."

"You're the first girl that has ever said that to me," blurted Scooter. "It's going to take a while for me to get used to you saying things like that. I always thought I was too stupid for any girl to like me."

"You stupid? Come on! You sound like a very smart man to me," answered Kelly. "You know? I feel very safe with you. This gives me a nice safe feeling with you. As long as I'm with you, I don't have to worry about my ex boyfriend."

"Oh, you're just saying that," insisted Scooter. "All my life, I have always been afraid to fight anyone, because I might get hurt. If your ex boyfriend was to come here, I would really try to protect you from him. I would make him sit in a chair and keep slapping him until he told me where the lamp was. Then I would break both of his arms and legs and then go and hide.

Several months ago, Hannibal, Detective Rex and Uncle Columbo talked me into wrestling three tough professional wrestlers. I was very afraid of getting hurt."

"Did you get hurt?" asked Kelly.

"No, I didn't get hurt," answered Scooter. "I won all three matches without laying a hand on these wrestlers."

"That's impossible. Are you making this up, because nobody could do that?" reasoned Kelly. "If this is true, how did it happen?"

"Well, I did. I really did," insisted Scooter. "You couldn't know. Before I went into the ring, I drank some chemicals that I made up. These chemicals made me very strong. I did that so I didn't have to worry about getting hurt."

"You're putting me on. Now, I know you're making this up," laughed Kelly. "As the saying goes, it's a nice try, but no cigar."

"I wouldn't tell a nice girl like you a story like that if it wasn't true," insisted Scooter. "Since I was a kid, I always liked working with chemicals and I had a chemistry set. When I got older, I went to The University of Davenport and was in Rex Tarillo's Class.

I made up some chemicals that Rex Tarillo drank and he became a forty inch Small Fry. On the same day, I made a bomb and threw it out the classroom window. It landed on Rex Tarillo's new car and blew it up."

"That can't be true. You're putting me on," answered Kelly.

"Well, it is true. Ask Rex. Ask Hannibal. They will tell you," insisted Scooter.

"If all you're telling me is true, then it makes you a bad boy," replied Kelly. "I like bad boys. I'm attracted to bad boys."

"I hate to tell you this. But if it makes any difference to you, I'm a stupid bad boy," added Scooter. "It's because I am always doing stupid things that make me a bad boy."

"Don't be silly. How can a smart man like you do stupid things?" asked Kelly. "As an example, what would you do with a winning lottery ticket. Would you hide it in a hidden room like this or do something else with it?"

"I would give it to Hannibal to hide," answered Scooter. "If I had it to hide, something awful would happen to it. Then Hannibal would be mad at me for what happened to it."

"OK, so you gave the winning lottery ticket to Hannibal. What would he do with it?" laughed Kelly.

"He would find a place in this very room to hide it and he wouldn't tell me where he hid it," replied Scooter.

"I didn't know that," answered Kelly.

"I knew that," replied Scooter.

"As long as we're here, we can tighten up and do something funky," explained Kelly.

"Funky? What is funky?" asked Scooter.

"Funky means feeling loose. Feeling cool. Getting back and staying loose," answered Kelly. "Come on. Try it. Go ahead and try it. Can you dig it?"

"No, I can't dig it, but you sure can shovel it," laughed Scooter.

"OK, let's start by playing a game," suggested Kelly. "If you really want to keep up with the times, you have to go with where the action is.

So far, you have been telling me that you do stupid things. Since I met you, I think you're big, strong and very smart.

Let's pretend that Hannibal really did have a winning lottery ticket and he hid it in this very room somewhere. I want you to show me how smart you are and try to find the kind of hiding place Hannibal would put the winning lottery ticket. If you pretend to find it, I want you to show it to me to prove you found it.

I'm going to give you a time limit of ten minutes. If you can't find it, we can shut the door to this hidden room and then begin to know each other better."

"That sounds like fun," laughed Scooter. "This is better than what I wanted to do, like take you bowling."

"Oh, that sounds a lot better. That's the point of this whole evening. You don't dig nothing, do you? Because in this game of mine, winner was to take all and I was going to Ooh, Ooh, Ooh with you if you know what I mean?" promised Kelly. "Then I was going to ask you to take me out to eat after that. What do you think of this game?"

"It's a lot better than bowling. When do you want to start?" asked Scooter.

"Well stay cool Super Fox. You will have exactly ten minutes. I need your watch for this game," Kelly went on to say. "Now that I have your watch, on my go, I will tell you when to start. Are you ready?"

"I'm more than ready," answered Scooter.

"Then go!" yelled Kelly.

Scooter then ran to the wall, looking for a pretend winning lottery ticket.

"I can't find it," laughed Scooter.

"Did you look everywhere on that wall? What are you doing over there?" asked Kelly. "I don't think you really get it. I think you should look over here."

"Thank you. I'll see what I can do. I'll get it. I'll get it," replied Scooter. Within a couple of minutes, Scooter pulled a piece of paper out of the wall and Scooter replied, "I found it."

"You did? What's that you found?" asked a surprised Kelly.

"I have the pretend missing lottery ticket," laughed Scooter.

"You have? Let me see it." As Kelly looked at the piece of paper, She saw it was the missing, winning, lottery ticket.

"What do you have in your hand?" asked Scooter.

"It's just an old piece of paper. It looks alright. They're good. You did find the pretend winning lottery ticket. That shows me how smart you are," answered Kelly.

"I get it. It's like a decoy," replied Scooter.

"I guess now you have to take me bowling," beamed Kelly. "Tell me where the bathroom is so I can freshen up and then we can go."

"The bathroom is in the kitchen, first door to the left," explained Scooter.

Chapter Thirty One
YOU'RE COMING WITH US

After Kelly left to go into the kitchen, Pockets walked up to Scooter and said, "I was listening here in the office about what you and Kelly were talking about. When you went in the kitchen to make some coffee, Kelly called somebody on her cell phone by the name of Michael and she talked about a hidden winning lottery ticket. She has been snooping and she looked in the walls of the hidden room and couldn't find it. That piece of paper you gave her was the winning lottery ticket."

"I didn't know that," replied Scooter.

"I knew that," replied Pockets. "I think you should take the winning lottery ticket away from her. Then, I will send her back from wherever she came from."

"Well, I never, I never. I thought she was a nice girl who truly liked me," replied Scooter. "When she comes back, I will get it from her. Whatever you do, don't tell Hannibal. He will really be mad at me."

While Scooter and Pockets were waiting for Kelly to come back to the office, Kelly ran out the back door. There waiting for Kelly was Dr. Fine and Charlie, The Chill.

Charlie grabbed Kelly from behind and put his hand over her mouth and said, "I don't know who you are young lady. That's as far as you go. Don't scream if you want to live. You're coming with us."

Just as the three of them walked around the house and past the garage, there stood Jerry Dickerson and his gang.

Seeing Jerry Dickerson and his gang, Kelly asked, "Make him take his hands off of me."

Pulling his gun out and pointing it at Dr. Fine and Charlie, The Chill, Jerry replied, "You heard what she said. Take your hands off of her and hand the woman over to me. Now, I want both of you to get in your car and leave."

After Dr. Fine and Charlie, The Chill left, Dixie said to Jerry, "I know who this woman is. She is Michael's sister, Kelly."

"I didn't know that," replied Jerry. "Well, Kelly. It seems that we have a situation here where you're going to have to come with us. Ace, put a blindfold on Kelly."

"What do you want with me?" asked Kelly. "Michael may be my brother. I don't even like him anymore for murdering people."

"You're still coming with us," answered Jerry. "You know things that we want to know. Do you know what I mean?"

"What makes you think that? I can't tell you anything," promised Kelly. "I didn't go to see Michael at his trial. I never heard Michael tell me anything. I know nothing."

"I didn't know that," insisted Shorty.

"Me neither," insisted Mugs.

"Well, I knew that," replied Ace.

Fifteen minutes later, Kelly, Jerry and his gang were in Jerry's apartment.

"Ace, take the blindfold off of Kelly. Welcome to the wild kingdom," laughed Jerry. "Dixie, see what Kelly has in her purse."

Grabbing Kelly's purse from her, Dixie dumped all the contents of the purse on the coffee table. Immediately, Dixie spotted the winning lottery ticket.

"Look what we have here. Just look what she brought us," laughed Dixie. "A lottery ticket. According to the date on it, it's seven months old. It's got to be worth some kind of big money. She sure surprised us all."

"No, you must be mistaken. Maybe you need to get some specs. It wasn't a winner," lied Kelly.

"In that case, you won't mind if I tear it up," laughed Dixie.

"No, don't do that. How dare you! That is very expensive and a winner. It's worth millions. Give it to me," insisted Kelly.

"That's interesting, very interesting," replied Jerry. "I'm dying to hear the rest of it." "Wait, that's not the best part. I'll share the winnings with you," exclaimed Kelly.

"Not you lady. Oh, that's a good one. That's the craziest thing I ever heard. Why should we do that, when we can have it all," asked Jerry. "You act like you know what you're talking about. What's the matter? Can't you handle it? Who do you think I am, The Welcome Wagon? Maybe we should have a barbecue and invite the whole neighborhood. To do it justice, maybe we need an hour to talk about it.

Now if you can answer a few more questions and help us get a certain object from The West Side Kids Detective Agency, I'm not saying, but it's possible. I'm just saying that it's possible if I decide that I will give you back the winning lottery ticket. I mean, if there is another way, I'm going a whole different direction."

"What do you want me to do to get back the winning lottery ticket?" asked Kelly.

"Just sit here and let me tell you what I want you to do," instructed Jerry. "Now this may sound crazy to you, but The West Side Kids have a lamp with a magic genie that comes out of it and I want it. I had possession of the lamp and the genie a couple of days ago and we all saw and talked to the genie when he came out of the lamp. We all want the wishes that the genie can give us. That is way worth more than your lottery ticket. If I wasn't interested in the lamp and the magic genie, you wouldn't be here."

"Anything, anything! If you think you're going to lose something, you want it twice as much. If you need it, you will have it. It will not be a problem, because I think I can do the job. I give you my word," insisted Kelly.

"I'll get what you want if you promise you won't tell anybody about my winning lottery ticket. Just give me back the lottery ticket. That's what I am hoping for. I don't want anybody else to know about this," replied Kelly as she reached for the ticket.

Pulling the lottery ticket away from Kelly, Jerry offered a deal to Kelly.

"Guess what? I don't work that way. Now, I'm going to have to include you in my plans. I don't know what business you have, but it can't be more important than the business I have with you. I'm going to tell you one time. I'm going to give you twenty four hours to get me the lamp or you're going to be in serious trouble. That doesn't leave you with much time."

"I will never forgive you for making me go through this," boomed Kelly.

"This is your idea, not mine. You may think that you don't have to go through with this. From running away from this confrontation, you will only make things worst," answered Jerry. "The confrontation for the anticipation exceeds the actual event."

"I can fix that," reasoned Kelly. "This time I'm going to run away again. Just this last minute, I decided to leave for Alaska."

"You hope not. Do you realize the opportunity you're missing out on? Save it for later," insisted Jerry. "I'm not going to forget about it. For one thing, I'm going to tear up the ticket.

OK, let's put our cards on the table. I can make it easy on you. Here is you're chance to get the winning lottery ticket. When you get the lamp, I will trade you this lottery ticket for it. Then I want you to promise me that you won't tell anybody about the lamp and the genie. Now, you're on your own," promised Jerry as Kelly and the lottery ticket disappeared.

"Did somebody just see what happened? Hey, this is getting to be a habit," exclaimed Ace. "I 'm getting a little riled up. The genie did it to us again. He must have gotten wise and double crossed us at the last minute. Now what are we going to do?"

"Keep your shirt on. Never mind. No harm has been done. Somehow we need to get that lamp with the genie," insisted Jerry. "There are a dozen ways that Hannibal and Scooter can cross us up with the genie. In the meantime, we just have to sit tight."

Chapter Thirty Two

The Missing Lottery Ticket

Just minutes after Kelly went into the kitchen to find the bathroom, Scooter said to Pockets, "That didn't go well. Kelly really made a fool out of me. We need to get that lottery ticket back from Kelly before Hannibal gets home. If he finds out what happened, he is really going to be mad at me. What do we do next?"

"I should have done something sooner," replied Pockets. "We have a lot of time to make up. As a new member of the gang, Kelly also made a fool out of me. She made me look like Pop Smith in the nursing home."

"How can we prove Kelly took the winning lottery ticket?" asked Scooter.

"We can't," replied Pockets. "I wonder what happened? She is taking a mighty long time in there. Why don't you go into the kitchen and just ask Kelly?"

"All right, I'm going, I'm going," insisted Scooter. "I'll see what's keeping her."

Scooter immediately went into the kitchen looking for Kelly. A couple minutes later, Scooter returned to where Pockets was standing with a funny look on his face.

"You sure are acting kind of strange," insisted Pockets. "Why are you so quiet? What's the matter with you? You seem far away? Is there anything wrong? I mean, do you have a problem?"

"I do. It's my problem, yet it's not my problem," reasoned Scooter. "You know me. I better tell you before I bust. For old times sake, I will tell you, then let me know what happens.

I can't find Kelly. She is not around. I looked everywhere, she just is not around. We hit it off great, because of the fantastic communications we have. It was like we had ESP."

"Where do you think she is?" asked Pockets.

"I have no idea," insisted Scooter. "I can't believe she is gone and we don't know where she is. Although she says she is a fun person, she seems so shy, simple and innocent and then there is her ex boyfriend, quite the opposite. She must be a brave little thing, because her ex boyfriend must have found her in the kitchen and took her away. I hope she's OK.

When you see a poor helpless creature, you say, I'm going to help. I don't know why we didn't try to stop her from going into the kitchen by herself. I think it's our fault we didn't keep a better eye on her. We have got to find her. I just don't feel good about this. I'm sorry, but I can't help worrying about her."

"You just have to believe we will find her and she will be fine. Did you look in the kitchen?" asked Pockets.

"Of course I looked in the kitchen," answered Scooter. "I know I have a problem and I know I have a kitchen. I can't tell you where she is, because it is so hard to talk about it. I am never going to tell nobody nothing again."

"Most people ignore me. I am really grateful for what you and Hannibal have done for me. I've grown attached to this place and do you know why?" exclaimed Pockets. "You and Hannibal made this my home away from my home by taking me out of the lamp. When I hear Hannibal scream at you, it makes me feel alive.

This is an emergency. Don't panic. I'm going to do something that I should have done from the start that I never thought about. I'm going to put a stop to it by bringing Kelly back with the winning lottery ticket."

In an instant, Kelly was standing in front of Pockets and Scooter with the lottery ticket in her hand.

"How did I get here?" asked a confused, embarrassed Kelly.

"Oh, there you are. I have been looking all over for you," sighed Scooter. "Now that I found you, everything is fine."

"I was sitting in a chair talking to Jerry Dickerson and the next thing I know, I'm here," replied a surprised Kelly.

"You must be dreaming," replied Scooter. "You have always been here. Don't you remember? You just went to the bathroom off the kitchen to freshen up and just came back. Who is this Jerry Dickerson?"

"I must have been dreaming. I can't tell you who he is," reasoned Kelly.

"What is that piece of paper in your hand?" asked Pockets. "I know you took it out of the room you was sitting in and I want you to give it back to me."

Looking down at her hand, a surprised Kelly saw the lottery ticket and gave it to Pockets.

"Now that I won the game, are you ready to go bowling?" asked Scooter. "Would you like to go in my 1980 Dodge Aspen that is parked in the garage or on my motorcycle?"

"I really don't want to go bowling at all," cried Kelly. "There is something I have to tell you. I have a confession to make. It's a long story. I am going to tell you the short version, the quickest way I know how.

I am really Michael, alias Dr. Zodiac's sister. Betty and I really don't have any ex boyfriends in Muscatine. I really came to Davenport to get that piece of paper I just gave to Pockets.

That is a winning lottery ticket that belongs to my brother Michael. You don't know what I have gone through to get this winning lottery ticket. I'm sorry and I hope you understand. I would like for you to give it back to me."

"What? What? What? That is very funny. I thought you were serious," laughed Scooter. "You got me again."

"I am serious," cried Kelly. "I feel rotten, because I did a terrible thing."

"Aha. Aha. Of course you do," answered Scooter. "I'm not upset with you. I'm not going to make a big deal out of it, because it wasn't your fault."

"I'm going to make it up to you," exclaimed Kelly. "It is very difficult for me to open up to a stranger and I don't want anybody to see me like this."

"Oh yeah. You don't have to worry. There is nobody here except Pockets and myself," insisted Scooter.

"I see this is making you uncomfortable. Maybe I must be getting soft. I do have a confession to make," added Kelly as she continued to cry. "Do you realize what an attractive man you are?"

"You confessed enough. You got me again for a second time," laughed Scooter. "I don't know what you are talking about. We can talk about it later."

"I think we should talk about it now. I just want to say that I'm really sorry how I tricked you into giving me that lottery ticket," cried Kelly. "I was playing a game with you to get the winning lottery ticket. Well, that's the story. I don't like to spill my gut out to you. Scooter, are you disappointed in me? I know you're feeling as awkward as I am. You understand, don't you?"

"I'm relieved that you're telling us about what you did," answered Scooter. "I have been thinking what you said. It's the right thing to do."

"Does that mean we can still be friends?" asked Kelly.

"The past is past. There is no reason we still can't be friends," insisted Scooter. "We have to put what you did out of our minds and live for today."

"I'm glad you appreciate it. I'm sorry I had to put you through all of this to try and get the lottery ticket," explained Kelly. "I have been making a lot of soul searching and evaluation of myself and I made a decision what I'm going to do next. I hate to tell you this, but I have to leave. I'm sorry things didn't work out.

If it's all the same to you, my mind is made up. My decision is final. I'm going to leave now. I hope there won't be any hard feelings."

"Your leaving? Your walking out on me? That's awful!" boomed Scooter. "I don't believe it. Aren't you ashamed of what you're doing? I wish you would stop it. If your mother could see you now."

"I'm going to tell you one more time and get it out of the way. I'm leaving. Somehow it seems like a bigger jester at this time," reasoned Kelly. "I don't think I'm who you are looking for."

"Well, I do. I'm not going to tell anybody about what you did," reassured Scooter. "I wish you would stop it. Kelly, what are you doing?"

"Looking at you," laughed Kelly.

"Don't you think you can see me better from over there? " insisted Scooter. "This is just another trap. Are you sure you,re not doing this to put up a brave front?"

"I wish I were. I just had a minor setback, but nothing has changed," reasoned Kelly.

"You have been terrific with me and now I am relieved. You care about me and I appreciate that. I never had so much fun in a long time.

Both of my twin brothers each came to Davenport to get the winning lottery ticket and failed. Now I'm going to leave a failure. It was only a tip of the ice berg. Both of my brothers returned to Burlington without the ticket and didn't even know how they got there. They even lost a day of the week and couldn't remember what happened.

I thought it was my turn to come to Davenport to try and trick you into giving me the lottery ticket. I should have told you who I was and why I came from the start. I can't talk to you anymore. I have to go now, because you're not going to give me back my brother's winning lottery ticket."

"Well, I don't know. I didn't say that. Well, Pockets. How do you like that?" beamed Scooter.

"Scooter, I think you handled that really well," replied Pockets. "Kelly, it's obvious for whatever reasons, you have lost your values. In that case, I can't make any promises if you will get the winning lottery ticket back. When Hannibal gets back, you will have to ask him about giving you the lottery ticket. We'll just have to wait and see."

"I think that's enough for one day. While we are waiting for Hannibal, I still would like to spend the time talking to you," beamed Scooter. "Can I take you out to eat?"

"That's too much trouble, but I would like that very much. I really do like you," replied Kelly. "Now that I told you why I really came to Davenport, it is a big relief and I can be myself."

It is now nine p m and Kelly, Betty, Pockets, Scooter and Hannibal are sitting in the office talking.

"I know. I wasn't honest with you why I came to Davenport. I won't be a problem to you anymore," Kelly began to say. "My twin brother's Chris and Michael both came to Davenport to get the winning lottery ticket and failed. I knew I had to try and get it because it belongs to my brother Michael. I didn't know what else to do. My brothers are expecting me to come home with the winning lottery ticket.

What I don't understand is how my brothers returned to Burlington and did not remember coming to Davenport."

"You don't say. I didn't know that," insisted Scooter.

"I knew that," reasoned Pockets. "Scooter, you knew that as well."

"I didn't know that," exclaimed Scooter. "Pockets, do you want Hannibal to get mad at you? You know that you're not suppose to tell anybody about you being a real genie and that you sent Kelly's brothers back to Burlington with the loss of their memory of coming to Davenport."

"Kelly don't pay any attention to what Scooter is saying," pleaded Hannibal. "You should know Scooter well enough by now that he is always joking around. He likes lamps and genies so well, that he is always pretending that one of the gang members is a real genie."

"Now, I remember. I was kidnapped and taken over to Jerry Dickerson's apartment a couple hours ago," exclaimed Kelly. "Jerry Dickerson took my winning lottery ticket away from me. When I asked for it back, he wanted me to get the lamp with the magic genie from you. Then he offered to trade my lottery ticket for the lamp and the magic genie.

Now, I know it's true. Because you have a magic genie, you don't need the winning lottery ticket. One of you is a real genie and I know how I was brought back to your house with the winning lottery ticket. I think Mr. Pockets is the genie."

"Are you crazy? It's simply impossible. I don't have a magic genie. Are you trying to make us look guilty of having a magic genie? There is no such thing as magic genies," laughed Hannibal. "That's a good one. If Mr. Pockets was the genie, he would be in the lamp, not standing in front of you. The way you tell it, you can convince anyone that there are magic genies. If you think Mr. Pockets is a real, genuine, genie, make a wish, any wish. It won't hurt a thing, because it won't come true."

"I can't do that. I would feel real funny believing Mr. Pockets is a real genie and asking him to grant me a wish," said an embarrassed Kelly.

"You wouldn't have had those problems if you had gone to the movies with Betty and myself," replied Hannibal.

"I thought it would be more fun if I had stayed here with Scooter," answered Kelly. "I was wrong."

"I'll tell you what I will do for you," exclaimed Hannibal. "We made a deal with your brother Michael that Scooter and myself would escort him safely back to Burlington for $4,500. I will give you the same deal to escort you back to Burlington safely. I will do that and give you back your winning lottery ticket for say $1,000,000.00 tax free and you forget all about lamps and magic genies.

Jerry Dickerson and his cut throats really believe we have a lamp with a magic genie. So does Dr. Fine and Charlie, The Chill. We have enough problems with these people without adding somebody else's, to our troubles. Because of the problems these people are giving us, Pockets is going with myself and Scooter to take you to Burlington tomorrow morning.

If we had a genie, I wouldn't be asking for the $1,000,000.00 tax free that I'm asking from you to do this job. My gang, The West Side Kids and me wouldn't even have to run a detective agency, because we would have all the money we needed to live. We wouldn't even have these other problems with these above mentioned morons that want a lamp and a magic genie that we don't have. We would just wish for more money and wish these morons out of our lives."

"OK. OK. I believe you. I'm just so excited that you're giving me back the winning lottery ticket!" yelled an excited Kelly. "It's not just because you are a good guy that I will give you $1,000,000.00 tax free. I think you're talented enough to get Betty and me with the winning lottery ticket back to Burlington safely.

I just can't explain how my brothers returned to Burlington the way they did, with a loss of memory about coming to Davenport."

"I don't know what to tell you. I have enough troubles trying to run our agency without worrying about anybody else's problems," insisted Hannibal. "It's getting late. Tomorrow is the big day. If it's all the same to you, we need to be up and out of here by nine tomorrow. I guess one way or another, we will know if tomorrow is going to work out.

There is no reason for you and Betty to stay at a motel. We have an extra bedroom here for you and Betty to stay in."

"I would really like that very much. This is going to be great," replied Kelly. "Now I can get to know Scooter better and this time I will mean it. I know it's crazy, because this will give me time to try and figure out how to tell Scooter how I fell for him after I met him. If he would ask me to marry him, I think he should meet my father."

"Why should Scooter meet your father? asked Hannibal. "Does he need your father,s permission to marry you?"

"Not at all," replied Kelly. "I just want Scooter to see what my mother did to my father. Hannibal, what if Scooter is the right person for me? Since you're his best friend, what do you think I should tell him?"

"No way. I'll bet everything I own that Scooter isn't the right person for you," laughed Hannibal. "It sounds to me that he shouldn't let a judge marry you without a jury. The first thing you should tell Scooter is that I'm not his best friend."

"I feel the same way about Hannibal," added Betty. "Don't you just love it. I am as excited as you are. I had a great time with Hannibal and I would like to know him better."

"Scooter, look alive," demanded Hannibal.

"I thought I was alive," answered Scooter.

"I know this is short notice. I just gave the girls your bedroom to stay in for tonight," laughed Hannibal.

"Jeppers! Your kidding!" boomed Scooter.

"Of course I'm kidding," laughed Hannibal. "I'm going to give the girls the extra bedroom down the hall from your room."

Chapter Thirty Three
On To Burlington, We Must Go

It is now Wednesday, May 21, 9 a m. and the gang is climbing in a Dodge SUV. Hannibal is driving with Betty sitting in the front passenger seat. Scooter is sitting behind Hannibal and Kelly is sitting behind Betty with Pockets sitting in the third row of seats with his lamp in a paper bag.

Ten minutes later, they are going west on River Drive, past Credit Island in Davenport. Following them are Jerry Dickerson and his gang in a 2010 white Cadillac SUV and following Jerry are Dr. Fine and Charlie, The Chill in a 2015 red Honda Civic.

"Well, today is the day. Pockets, watch to see if anyone is following us," asked Hannibal.

"OK Chief. Just what am I looking for?" answered Pockets.

"Watch for any strange car that is following us from a distance," replied Hannibal. "Scooter, you help Pockets. I want to get these girls back to Burlington safe and sound with their winning lottery ticket. If we do, that will be worth a $1,000,000.00 tax free to us. That will more than replace the money you lost at the casino. Kelly, how are you doing?"

"I'm very nervous," replied Kelly.

"This time, I'm going to take the money to the bank my own self. Kelly, how soon are you going to cash in the winning lottery ticket?" asked Hannibal. "We really need the money to pay some bills."

"Kelly, when are you going to cash in the winning lottery ticket?" asked Betty. "Don't forget, you promised me a share of that money if I helped you to get the winning lottery ticket."

"So that's what it was all about," reasoned Hannibal. "With the both of you coming to Davenport, you were as good as had the lottery ticket in your hands."

"Yes we did," replied Betty. "And you, Hannibal was my bonus. After you take us back to Burlington, will I ever get to see you again?"

"Me? You mean me? You mean you really want to see me again?" insisted Hannibal as his face turned bright red.

"Yes you, Mr. Leader Of The Pack," replied Betty.

"Pockets, take a look. Do you see anything yet," asked Hannibal.

"Hannibal, there is a white car that has been following us since we left Davenport," reported Pockets. "I thought you would want to know right away."

"Thanks Pockets. I knew it. I knew something like this would happen. We are a mile away from The Blue Grass ramp. I'm going to take that exit. Watch to see if that white car follows us into Blue Grass," ordered Hannibal. "Scooter, you help Pockets."

"They know we're following them," reasoned Jerry. "We'll just have to stay a safe distance away from them for now."

"In that case, What are we waiting for? Let's go nab the lottery ticket and now," reasoned Lefty.

"Not so fast. Since we know Kelly has the lottery ticket, she will have no reason to help us get the lamp," insisted Ace. "Jerry, do you have a plan as to how we're going to get the lamp?"

"Not exactly. We just have to wait for our chance to get the lamp, before they use the genie to side track us," replied Jerry.

Five minutes later, the gang is two blocks away from the Blue Grass Business District.

"What are we stopping for?" asked Kelly.

"There is a used car lot straight ahead," observed Hannibal."I'm going to pull into that used car lot and park to see if we can lose them. When we get there, everybody put your heads down."

A few minutes later, everybody sat up and looked around. As they all sat up, out walked the salesman of the used car lot.

"Hello, my name is Friendly Freddy. I'm here to help you. I'm glad I caught you on my used car lot."

"What are you doing here?" asked Scooter. "I thought you owned a used car lot on Kimberly Road in Davenport."

"Oh, it's you, the deal breaker. Oh, I'm sorry. I don't want to do business with you," scolded Friendly Freddy. "Get off of my lot. I was just on my way out to deliver a car to a customer."

"We want to buy a car that will at least make it to Burlington," replied Hannibal. "We need to get these girls back to Burlington safely and we need a car that will get us there."

"Please Mr. Freddy. Please help me and my friend Betty," pleaded Kelly. "Won't you help us?"

"For you and your friend, my dear lady, I will sell you a car," answered Freddy. "I just don't want to deal with these two rascals. I sell the finest used cars money can buy. I have a Ford Taurus I can let you have for a $1,000. This is a limited time offer. Isn't it a beauty? A cream puff. That car is a real honey. This car is special to me. I was going to give it to my daughter for her birthday. My wife drives one just like it and she loves it."

"I've heard that line from Mr. Freddy before," laughed Scooter. "Every car he has on his lot is a beauty and a cream puff. His daughter must have a very big garage, because Mr. Cream Puff is going to give all of his cars to his daughter for her birthday."

"We don't have time to haggle over the price of your cream puffs. We'll give you $500.00 and you know you will take it," exclaimed Hannibal. "You go in your office and fill out the paperwork and I will be there shortly to sign the paperwork and pay you."

"I guess I can discount $500.00 off the price. I just want you to know I'm losing money on this deal," replied Freddy.

"If I recall, you told my friend Scooter that if he didn't like the car you sold him after a week, you would give him back his money," insisted Hannibal. "After I take these girls to Burlington, I'm going to come back and return your car so you don't lose any money on this cream puff as you call it."

I, I, I, don't know if I can take it back," reasoned Freddy.

"Don't bet on it. You'll take it back, because you will try to sell your cream puff to some other sucker for $1,000.00," laughed Hannibal. "Now go get the paperwork ready. I will be there in a minute or two to sign the paperwork."

As Freddy went into his office, Hannibal began to talk about his plan to get the girls to Burlington safely.

"I think that was Jerry Dickerson following us. That means we didn't fool him," Hannibal began to say. "Scooter, you have work to do and this is what I want you to do. I want you to get out of here while I do something different. I want you and Pockets to take highway 61 into Muscatine and then go to Wilton Junction on highway 6. Call the gang to meet you in Wilton Junction and then go back to Davenport.

I am going to take the girls to Burlington in this cream puff. I am not going to tell you what highway I'm going on. What you don't know, you can't tell Jerry Dickerson if he happens to stop you. I don't have $500.00 dollars on me. I need everybody to anti up so we can pay for this car.

Pockets, I want to talk to you privately. Now that we're away from the girls I want to tell you, I have a special job for you. I want to make a wish that that car we just bought will run like a cream puff, in fact like a new car, so I can get the girls safely back to Burlington. Scooter, call the gang while I go pay for this beautiful pile of junk."

Ten minutes later, Hannibal was back out in the used car lot, with the keys to the Ford Taurus.

"OK. Is everybody ready?" asked Hannibal. "I'm coming out. Scooter, you and Pockets leave now in our Dodge SUV. Watch for Jerry Dickerson and make sure he follows you. OK. Move out."

Two minutes later, Scooter pulled out of the lot, while Hannibal and the girls watched.

"There goes Jerry," boomed Hannibal. "There is a surprise. It's Dr. Fine and Charlie, The Chill following in their 2015 Honda Civic. By golly, I think it is. I better call Scooter on his cell phone and let him know about our other friends pulling up on the rear.

Hello Scooter. Watch your step. Apparently you have someone else following you. You have extra company following you in a red Honda Civic," announced Hannibal. "It's Dr. Fine and Charlie, The Chill."

"Thanks Hannibal. I will have Pockets keep an eye on them,"

replied Scooter. "This proves what I always say. Some people are garbage. This is people saying I can get away with something. I wonder how long this is going to last where Jerry continues to follow us? Is this going to keep up or do I have to have Pockets wish them back to Davenport?"

"No, leave them be. It is a challenge. At least we know where they're at. I don't want anybody getting lost. Just don't do anything stupid where it gets you into trouble," answered Hannibal. "I would rather have you send them on a wild goose chase."

"I'll be careful," insisted Scooter. "My pal, Pockets will protect me if I do something dumb."

"Call me if you have any problems. I have to go," boomed Hannibal. "Girls, are you ready? Get in the car. We have to go and now."

After Betty, Kelly and Hannibal were in the car, Kelly asked, "Are we going to take highway 61 to Burlington?"

"No, Kelly. I'm going to drive down to the river road and go into Muscatine," explained Hannibal. "When we get to Muscatine, I'm going to take the bridge into Illinois. Then, we will take the Illinois roads to Burlington."

"Hey, this is a lot better," insisted Kelly.

"Kelly, I want you to call your brothers and tell them what is going on," instructed Hannibal. "When we get to your brother's book store, Burlington By The Book, I want your brothers to take you and Betty some place where Jerry Dickerson and Dr. Fine can't find you.

I don't believe they will come to Burlington anyway. With Scooter taking them on a wild goose chase, they will forget all about Burlington."

"You are so cleaver," reassured Betty. "I never would have thought about wild goose chases and all that."

"Well, at least I'm returning home with the winning lottery ticket," exclaimed Kelly. "My brothers made fun of me about going to Davenport to get the winning lottery ticket. The saying goes, "Whatever you can do, I can do better. I can hardly wait to tell my brothers that I succeeded, where they failed."

"Only we had a secret weapon to get the job done," exclaimed Betty. "It was Hannibal."

"Don't forget Scooter. He helped," laughed Kelly.

An hour and a half later, Hannibal and the girls were sitting in the Ford Taurus in front of Chris Seven Murphy's book store, Burlington By The Book.

"OK, girls, you're here safe and sound," boomed Hannibal. "After you get out of this cream puff, I'm going back to Davenport."

Tim Murphy, Kelly Murphy and Christopher Seven Murphy

"Here is the $50 million winning lottery ticket.
Wouldn't it be nice to have one of those?"

Burlington By The Book

Michael, Alias Dr. Zodiac

Chapter Thirty Four
WAIT! DON'T GO YET!

"Wait! Don't go yet!" insisted Kelly. "Isn't that both Chris and Michael I see in the store? Hannibal, I want you to come in the store to talk to Chris and Michael about our $1,000,000.00 tax free deal. I want my brothers to know you gave me the winning lottery ticket when you didn't have to.

I also want you to tell my brothers about the evil people chasing us to Burlington. It's amazing how they can't be unforgiving. That was wonderful how you risked your life for us."

"Kelly, it wasn't like that. They weren't chasing us and Hannibal didn't risk his life for us," replied Betty. "They were not evil people and they were following us at a safe distance, because they just wanted the winning lottery ticket."

"Come on girls, lets go into the store so I can feel that I finished the job," instructed Hannibal.

A couple of minutes later, everybody was in the store talking to Chris and Michael.

"Hey brothers, I brought some company. What I want to tell you is that Hannibal is alright because he brought Betty and me here with the winning lottery ticket," exclaimed Kelly.

"You did it Kelly. You did a great job. Isn't this a wonderful day? You know how long I waited for this?" insisted Michael.

"I didn't expect you back until tomorrow. Michael and I weren't sure we would be seeing you so soon," answered a surprised Chris. "Hey, you seem pretty happy here. I'm sure you were happy to get back home safely with the lottery ticket."

"I'm glad to be back. I told you, Betty and I could get the job done if we tried something different. We not only brought back the ticket, we also didn't lose a day of the week or our memory," exclaimed Kelly.

"It sounds like you were having your usual good times. Oh crying out loud. You did it," reasoned Chris. "You are quite a rebel rouser. Michael and I thought you were crazy. I know we can't control your thinking. You pretty much have a mind of your own. When you have a problem, you confront it. You knew what you had to do and you did it."

"I know we have a relationship that we don't tell each other what to do," replied Kelly.

"Is that what you're telling us?" asked Michael. "Chris and myself thought that you should have given up before you left for Davenport. We thought this had all the ear markings of a radical. There is one thing about progress. You can never tell when it's going to happen."

"I thought you were right, but I had an idea and decided to do it anyway," answered Kelly. "There is one thing about doing nothing. You can never tell when anything is going to happen."

"Kelly, you can't take all of the credit," reasoned Betty. "Hannibal and Scooter are both alright. It goes to show you. You can never tell what will happen. If it weren't for Hannibal and Scooter, you wouldn't have that winning lottery ticket in your hands to give to your brothers. You were totally helpless.

Both Hannibal and Scooter have been very thoughtful. They have been wonderful. In fact, they have been great. I think you need to thank these guys for helping you."

"Hannibal, it's nice to have you here. I don't know how to show you my appreciation for helping Kelly. Is there no end to your thoughtfulness? Would a handshake be good enough?" asked Michael.

"Oh, it was nothing," answered Hannibal.

"I'll never forget you for this," added Betty.

"You're probably just saying that, but thank you anyway," replied Hannibal.

"Kelly, I hope this whole thing has taught you a lesson," exclaimed Chris.

"If I didn't stick to the things I believed in, I couldn't have done this," insisted Kelly.

"That's what the lesson is. If you didn't stick to the things you believed in, you couldn't have done this," laughed Chris.

"Kelly, you better tell your brothers everything, because we may be having more trouble coming our way," reasoned Betty.

"What other problems could there be? You got the ticket and now we're all going to be rich," stated Michael.

"I'll tell you what kind of problems in one short sentence," answered Hannibal. "Jerry Dickerson, his mob, Dr. Fine and Charlie, The Chill."

"Oh, them," replied Michael. "How did they find out about the winning lottery ticket?"

"I'll tell you what Betty and I went through, so you can say, aha, aha," explained Kelly. "First, Dr. Fine and Charlie, The Chill tried to kidnap me when I tried to run out the back door of The West Side Detective Agency. After we walked past the garage, there stood Jerry Dickerson. He took me from this Dr. Fine and Charlie, The Chill. Jerry blindfolded me and took me to his apartment. His girlfriend, Delores went through my purse and found the winning lottery ticket."

"Her name is Dixie, not Delores," corrected Hannibal.

"OK, Dixie went through my purse," Kelly continued to say as Tim walked into the store. "After Jerry realized the ticket was a winner, he started to question me about some sort of silly lamp with a magic genie. He wanted me to go back to The West Side Kids Detective Agency to find that lamp and bring it to him. He said that if I did, he would trade me my ticket for the lamp. If I didn't do as he asked, he would tear up the winning lottery ticket.

Then for some odd reason, I was standing in front of Scooter and this guy by the name of Pockets in the kitchen of The West Side Detective Agency and I didn't know how I got there. Then, I began to believe that Jerry Dickerson was right about a lamp with a magic genie."

"Jerry Dickerson really did a job on Kelly. He was playing a game with Kelly to make her think that there are lamps with real magic genies," added Hannibal. "When I talked to Kelly about lamps with magic genies, Kelly insisted that I had one.

I think Jerry was just trying to find a reason to keep the winning lottery ticket. That is why Jerry tried to follow us back to Burlington. I had Scooter lead Jerry on a wild goose chase in our SUV. I bought the Ford Taurus in Blue Grass and brought the girls safely back to Burlington. I was really proud of Scooter taking Jerry Dickerson on a wild goose chase.

Since I don't have a lamp with a magic genie, I have a new deal with Kelly. For $1,000,000.00 tax free, my share of the winning lottery ticket, I gave the ticket to Kelly. I was suppose to bring them back to Burlington safely for that $1,000,000.00. What are you going to do now that you have the ticket? When are you going to cash it in?"

"If you will wait right here, I will call the lottery officials right now," answered Michael as he picked up the phone of the book store. "I don't want to take any chances of losing it to Jerry Dickerson or Dr. Fine."

"Michael, how many times have I told you not to use the store's phone," laughed Chris. "Let me give you a quarter and you can use the phone in the phone booth in the hallway."

"Chris, your are always a comedian. You know that phone isn't hooked up," insisted Michael. "How would you like me to disconnect you from the lottery ticket winnings?"

"Hannibal, they're at it again!" yelled Kelly. "They just never stop."

"I understand that," answered Hannibal. "Scooter and myself are always doing the same thing. Don't pay any attention to them. That's what friends and brothers do."

"If that's the case, Michael and Chris have been doing that all their life," added Tim. "I would never treat my brothers and sister like that."

"Don't believe a word Tim says," laughed Kelly. "He's the worst of my three brothers."

"Am not," replied Tim.

"Am so," insisted Kelly.

"Stop it Kelly and Tim," demanded Chris. There are customers coming in the store."

"I just talked to the lottery officials," boasted Michael.

"How did it go?" asked Kelly.

"Our ticket is a winner," answered Michael. "I'm going to Des Moines tomorrow by bus to cash it in."

"Hannibal, can we hire you for one more job?" asked Kelly. "This is ridiculous because Michael has lost his memory of a day of the week, would you accompany Michael to Des Moines to cash in the ticket? If you do, I think we can give you another $1,000,000,00, tax free."

"This is my lucky day. It sounds like a good idea to me. I'll do it," yelled an excited Hannibal. "Right now, I think I'm going to stay at the hotel at the casino to celebrate. My problem is I'm broke from buying that Ford Taurus. Is there anyway I could get an advance on what you owe me? Say $500.00."

"Let me see what I have in the register," answered Chris. "This winning lottery ticket is getting expensive. It looks like I have $500.00 to give to you. Thanks again."

"Thank you sir. Michael, I will be picking you up tomorrow in front of the book store at eight o'clock. I will be leaving now," replied Hannibal. "When I get to the car, I'm going to call Scooter to see how he is doing."

A couple minutes later, Hannibal was sitting in his car calling Scooter on his cell phone.

"Scooter, where are you at?" asked Hannibal.

"I'm in Wilton Junction right now," replied Scooter. "Because and the gang just pulled up right behind me."

"Where is Jerry Dickerson," asked Hannibal.

"He left as soon as the gang was here. Dr. Fine never stopped. He just kept going, following Jerry back to Davenport," explained Scooter. "We sure outwitted them this time. The gang scared them both away. Where are you at?"

"I'm in Burlington, sitting in my car in front of Burlington By The Book," answered Hannibal. "The girls are safe and sound inside the store with the lottery ticket. For another $1,000,000.00 I was hired to take Michael to Des Moines tomorrow to cash it in. Now, I am going to get a room at the casino hotel and stay the night. I am even planning on doing a little gambling to celebrate. Are you going back to Davenport?"

"I'm on my way right now. Tell Kelly I would like to see her again," replied Scooter.

"I will tell her," answered Hannibal. After you get back to Davenport, you and the gang keep an eye out for Jerry and Dr. Fine. I will see you in a couple of days."

Chapter Thirty Five
THAT CAN BE THE ONLY EXPLANATION

After Hannibal left the store, Kelly said to Tim, "What's eating you?"

"I was thinking about what you said about Hannibal having a lamp with a magic genie," replied Tim. "From what you told us, I think Hannibal has convinced you that there is no such thing as a lamp with a magic genie. I think his story is phony. We'll soon find out."

"Come to think of it, I think you are on to something, Tim," reasoned Michael. "There is just something wrong with the story Kelly told us. You don't go from one place to another in a couple of seconds without realizing just what happened to you. I sure would like to know how it happened. I know. It happened to Chris and myself."

"The West Side Kids have to have a lamp with a magic genie," insisted Chris. "Michael, that can be the only explanation as to how we came back to Burlington and not knowing how it happened. It also explains losing our memory and losing Tuesday. It happened that way, because The West Side Kids have a genie. It was pretty smart of them, wasn't it? Now that I remember that, I know that I'm right."

"On top of that, I know this Jerry Dickerson and Dr. Fine," reasoned Michael. "They wouldn't be after the lamp with a magic genie if it wasn't true."

"I think I've got the answer," reassured Chris. "When I went to

Davenport to get the winning lottery ticket, I found a pot. No, it was a lamp and I threw it in the wastebasket.

Scooter would know it was a lamp when he saw it. I'm sure he didn't know there was a genie in the lamp anymore than I did. He pulled the lamp out of the waste basket and I sold it to him for $5.00. Neither Scooter or myself knew he was getting a bargain."

"I bought that lamp at a yard sale. I always had it in the back of my mind that there could be a genie in the lamp," exclaimed Michael. "Let me just say one word. If you're not interested, I'll never mention it again. The word is lamp."

"No. Michael, you might as well forget about the lamp. I'm not interested. OK?" insisted Chris.

"Maybe I need to say more words. The West Side Kids have my lamp with a magic genie and I want it back," demanded Michael.

"No. I strongly advise you to forget the lamp with the magic genie," reasoned Chris. "Besides, with our winning lottery ticket, it's just as good as having a genie."

"What in the world are you talking about?" asked Michael. "Why do you keep saying no, every time I want to do something? I think you're being mean and insensitive."

"There is something else I want to explain to you. You're not going to understand this," explained Chris. "You shouldn't be the one to complain. Since you bought the winning lottery ticket, now, we will be living the life of Riley. Nobody is going to try and take our winnings away from us except maybe our family, friends and greedy people. Then, we might run into some people that might be off the beaten path.

That's the problems of the rich. There is nothing we can do about it and it can't be helped, even if we had a pocket full of wishes. I'm beginning to think we're better off not having a winning lottery ticket or wishing we had a magic genie."

"Is there a way out?" asked Tim.

"I have no idea," answered Chris. "Don't you think you should give this a little more time? What do you expect?"

"Well, nonsense. Well, what are we waiting for? Haven't we uncovered enough evidence about the lamp with the magic genie? I want the lamp with the magic genie," boomed Tim. "And I'm going to

Davenport to get them both. Kelly, since you were in The West Side Kids Detective Agency, would you draw me a diagram of the house so it would give me an idea where to look for the lamp?"

"When you come up with an idea, why do you always dump it on me?" asked Chris.

"Because you're my brother and my best friend," replied Tim.

"I don't want to be your best friend," answered Chris.

"Why are you so reluctant to help me," asked Tim.

"This is not a good time," objected Chris. "I think you should just have to wait awhile."

"When is a good time?" growled Tim. "This is really a very important thing for me to do."

"Tim, that's the only thing you care about. You're looking for more trouble than you can handle. I don't know if I can talk to you anymore about this," reasoned Chris. "Kelly happened to luck out to bring back the winning lottery ticket. With Michael and I, it was another story. Michael believed in the supernatural and it turned on him and me. I think you better leave well enough alone."

"Why are you so mad at me?" asked Tim. "What's the matter with you? Don't you ever stop being angry at everything? You are very rude."

"I have to be honest, because it will turn out exactly the way I know it will," answered Chris. "You are a little pushy and also very arrogant. What I'm trying to say is, you live by the sword. You die by the sword."

"But if I get the lamp and the magic genie, the possibilities are endless," replied Tim. "Not only can we have what we want, look what we can do for Burlington. OK. You are right. Like it or not, this was my idea and I have responsibilities. The only thing left for me to do, is what I have to do."

"I agree with Tim," insisted Kelly. "It's really not a bad thought. I know the house and I know how Hannibal and Scooter thinks."

"I guess if you feel that strongly about it, you can try it," reasoned Chris.

"See, it's not so hard to give," added Tim.

"I know the house even better," boomed Michael. "I think if Tim wants to go to Davenport to get the lamp and magic genie, I will accompany my brother to Davenport."

"Oh, that's dumb. Michael, haven't you forgotten something?" asked Chris. "You're getting a little too careless with your thinking. You can't go to Davenport with Tim, because you're going to Des Moines with Hannibal tomorrow."

"I get you. You're way ahead of me. You're right, it is dumb. I just wasn't thinking," answered Michael. "Tim, before you go, can you wait for me to come back from Des Moines? I wish you would wait until I can go with you.

Now that I think about it, Tim won't need me to go to Davenport with him, because Hannibal will be with me. He just doesn't want to run into Hannibal. All Tim has to do is deal with Scooter. Well, I admit, I like the idea."

"Then it's settled. I heard enough to make my decision. I'm handling things myself and am leaving for Davenport right away while I have a better chance to get the lamp with the magic genie. The sooner, the better," announced Tim. "I think you have heard everything I have to say."

"Then you better have a plan, a good plan," explained Michael. "Remember, you're going to have to compete with Jerry Dickerson and Dr. Fine to get the lamp with the magic genie. What are you going to do now?"

"Don't worry. I have a good idea how to get the lamp and the magic genie. None of these people in Davenport knows who I am. That will be in my favor," reasoned Tim.

"Just watch yourself and don't be too overconfident," noted Chris. "We don't want you to return to Burlington like my little brother Michael and I did with the loss of your memory."

"I'm willing to take that chance, because I think I can pull it off," reasoned Tim. "I just want all of you to know that anything Kelly can do, I can do better."

"Tim, you are so full of it," replied Kelly. "You don't realize it, but you have a big job ahead of you. A big, big job."

"Kelly, from what all of us talked about, I think it is going to give me a chance to do the big, big job," answered Tim.

"OK, go for it. I know you will get the job done because you are a Murphy," exclaimed Chris. "There is something we didn't talk about and that is the rest of The West Side Kids you will be dealing with. Remember, there are eight of them to deal with."

"I never thought about that," answered Tim. "I guess I'll have to deal with them one way or another when I get there. One thing is for sure. I know about them, but they don't know me. I've got work to do. They are in for a big surprise. I'll be there when they least expect it. They will be surprised alright.

Tomorrow, I'm going to the house to get the lamp. I don't have time to explain. Now I have to run if I want to get the lamp with the magic genie."

"Here we go again," boomed Michael. "Tim, I hope everything turns out the way you hope that it will be."

"Now, what's Tim up to?" asked Kelly.

Search me," answered Michael. "It sounds like trouble. But, if there is trouble, Tim is going to be right in the middle of it."

Chapter Thirty Six
HEY! PUT MY LAMP DOWN!

The next day, Tim pulled up to the property of The West Side Kids Detective Agency. Tim decided to sit in his car to see if anybody was in the house. After sitting in his car for a half hour, Tim climbed out of his car and walked over to the house and began to look through the windows. There sat the lamp on the kitchen table.

"It looks peaceful to me. Now I ought to have a clear field to get the lamp," said Tim to himself.

Not seeing anybody around, Tim walked into the back door and approached the kitchen table. As he picked up the lamp, Pockets walked into the kitchen.

"Hey, put my lamp down!" yelled Pockets. "That's my lamp."

Tim then began to walk out the back door with the lamp as a puff of smoke filled the lamp.

Hearing Pockets yell, Scooter ran to the kitchen just in time to watch Tim leave with the lamp. A race began as Tim raced to his car with the lamp, with Scooter following.

Sitting in his car down the street, Jerry Dickerson and his gang watch as Tim with the lamp, climbs into his car, started the engine and drives away. Jerry Dickerson starts his car and follows Tim.

Scooter gets in his car and follows Jerry Dickerson and Tim.

Parked down the other side of the street is Dr. Fine and Charlie,

The Chill. After they watch what happens, they follow Tim, Jerry and Scooter. And the race is on to Burlington.

Tim calls Chris at his book store, Burlington By The Book and tells Chris about getting the lamp and being followed to Burlington by Jerry Dickerson and Scooter.

Scooter, calls Hannibal who is with Michael Murphy in Des Moines and tells him about Tim taking the lamp and Jerry Dickerson following him.

"I don't know who that was that took the lamp," said Scooter to Hannibal. "It looks like he is leading us to Burlington. How soon can you get to Burlington?"

"Michael and myself are an hour and a half away," replied Hannibal. "I will step on it and try to get there sooner. In the meantime, call The West Side Kids and have them follow you. We may all end up in Burlington."

"I know who has the lamp," insisted Michael. "It was my brother Tim, who went to Davenport to get the lamp from you and Scooter. None of us ever figured that Jerry Dickerson and his mob would be following Tim back to Burlington. I better call Tim and warn him that he is being followed by Jerry Dickerson and then, I better call my brother Chris."

As Scooter is talking to Hannibal, Jerry sees Dr. Fine in his rear view mirror and calls him.

"Dr. Fine, This is Jerry Dickerson. I don't know who this Mug is that has the lamp in front of us. I know you want the lamp as much as we do," exclaimed Jerry. "We are both having trouble grabbing the lamp from Scooter.

I'm particular who I put in with. Let's make a deal and go on this together as partners, instead of fighting over who gets the lamp. Maybe, we would be working for the same end at that. What do you say?"

"That's a good idea. I'm willing to help anyway I can. Why are you telling me all of this?" asked Dr. Fine.

"That all depends on you. This game is not over yet," answered Jerry.

"What makes you think so?" asked Dr. Fine.

"All I want is a chance to work together," answered Jerry.

"I'm for it," reassured Dr. Fine. "If we can get the lamp, the genie should grant all of us the wishes we want. How do you propose we get the lamp? You had your chance to get the lamp before. What stopped you?"

"I have no idea," replied Jerry. "All I know that, since this Mug doesn't know who we are, that may be our chance to get the lamp. Just stay a safe distance behind us, so you won't be spotted. It's not going to be a picnic.

Now remember, if anything happens and we fail to get the lamp, because this Mug turns the genie on us, it will be up to you to grab it from this Mug. They made a pack of fools out of all of us by using the genie. They used the genie and got us all messed up by having our heads shaved."

"He can't turn the genie on us," reasoned Ace. "Remember, only Scooter and Hannibal, together has control of the genie. That is something we shouldn't overlook."

"That's right. I'll find out for myself," insisted Jerry. "Scooter is following me and Hannibal is no where to be seen. Now is our chance to get the lamp."

Forty five minutes later, Tim is on highway 61 going up the curve in the road leading to the top of the hill, west of Muscatine, followed by Jerry Dickerson and his gang, Scooter, Dr. Fine and Charlie, The Chill. Again, Jerry calls Dr. Fine on his cell phone.

"Dr. Fine, this is Jerry calling again," Jerry went on to say. "It looks like this Mug is going to Burlington with the lamp. I just wonder if he knows Michael and Chris Murphy."

"It's possible," answered Dr. Fine. "We will just have to see where he leads us. How far do you think Burlington is from here?"

"I just saw a sign that says thirty nine miles," replied Jerry. "If he goes to Burlington By The Book in Burlington, that will be our opportunity to grab the lamp. If that's the case, me and my boys will try to park our car in front of the store and go in first to try and grab the lamp.

Are Charlie and myself going after this Mug into the bookstore with you?" asked Dr. Fine.

After we go in, wait a few minutes to see what happens next. If we get the lamp, then you and Charlie, The Chill grab Scooter when he gets out of his car," instructed Jerry. "After that, we will all go to Davenport as fast as we can and go to my apartment. Then we need to get Hannibal to come to my apartment so that Scooter and Hannibal, together will turn the lamp and the genie over to us."

"What if Hannibal and Scooter turns the genie against us?" asked Dr. Fine.

"They won't, because when we get back to Davenport, we will kidnap one of their gang members and not tell Scooter and Hannibal what we did with him," replied Jerry. "Those boys care very much about each other. Hannibal and Scooter will sacrifice the lamp for the safety of one of the members of their gang."

"I like your plan. It looks like we are finally going to get the lamp," reasoned Dr. Fine. "What if this Mug goes someplace different than the bookstore?"

"We'll deal with it if that happens," answered Jerry. "I really think this Mug is going to the book store. In case, if you get lost, do you have the address to Burlington By The Book?"

"No, I never been there before," replied Dr. Fine.

"The address is 301 Jefferson in downtown Burlington," answered Jerry.

"OK. I'll see you when and if we get to the book store," replied Dr. Fine.

Thirty minutes later, Hannibal and Michael pulled in front of Burlington By The Book and went into the store.

"Hi Chris," said Michael. "What's the word? Did Tim tell you he had the lamp? He did a great job. I didn't think he would make it here with the lamp."

"Yes he did and he should be here in a couple of minutes. I sure would like to know when he is going to show up," replied Chris.

"What's your hurry?" asked Michael.

""I just can't stand this waiting, waiting, waiting," answered Chris. "I hope no customers come in the store after he gets here."

"Jerry and his gang is right behind Tim. He is looking for the lamp. I think I'll have some fun and let him find it," exclaimed Michael. "Chris is that baseball bat still in the store room?"

"It's somewhere in that room," replied Chris.

"Then, I have a plan. The going is going to be mighty tough for Jerry and his pirates. Jerry is a tin horn crook and he is really asking for it," insisted Michael.

"This, I have to see," boomed Chris.

"OK. Let's get ready for them. I'm going to wait in the store room at the end of the store with that ball bat," explained Michael. "Hannibal, there is a hallway at the end of the store that leads to the art center and bathrooms. You wait there. Chris, when Tim comes, send him our way with the lamp. Jerry and his gang will follow Tim and when they do, I will hit each of them on the head with the bat. When they reach the hall, Hannibal, sock em a good one. Chris, after they all walk past you, call the police. Hannibal, there's Tim. Let's go."

As Michael and Hannibal ran to the end of the store, in walks Tim and Scooter.

"Tim, run out to the hallway in the back of the store! Hurry!" yelled Chris.

"Hey mister, you've got my lamp and I want it back," screamed Scooter as he followed Tim to the back of the store.

Next Jerry, Ace, Lefty, Danny, Shorty and Mugs came rushing through the front door of the store as Dr. Fine and Charlie, The Chill watched from their car.

"There he goes with the lamp! Look at him run!" yelled Jerry. "Get that lamp!"

As Jerry walked past the supply room, Michael hit him in the head with the bat and Jerry staggered out in the hall as Scooter raised his arms and yelled, "Get him Hannibal!"

Hannibal then socked Jerry, knocking him down.

As Ace, Lefty, Danny, Shorty and Mugs passed the supply room, Michael hit each one in the head with the bat as Scooter repeated, "Get him Hannibal! Get him!"

Each one then walked blindly in the hallway, where Hannibal socked each of them in the jaw where they all fell down on each other.

The Blue Gin then appeared in the hallway and grabbed the lamp out of Tim's hands. He then rubbed the lamp and a puff of smoke came out of the lamp.

"I don't know who you are," said Scooter to The Blue Gin. That's my friend Pockets and that's my lamp." Give it back to me," ordered Scooter.

"Who is this stupid crazy human being ordering me around like that?" asked The Blue Gin.

"That's my friend Scooter. Don't do anything to him," asked Pockets. "He has been very kind to me. That is Hannibal standing behind me. They have both been very good to me."

"You and your lamp are coming with me," replied The Blue Gin.

"Before you take me away, can I grant Scooter and Hannibal one wish?" asked Pockets.

"Just one quick wish and then we're leaving," replied The Blue Gin.

"Because I always wanted a lamp of my own, with a magic genie, I wish Hannibal to be put in a lamp and replace you as my genie," wished Scooter.

In a flash, a second lamp appeared with Hannibal inside it.

"Let me out of here! Let me out of here!" screamed Hannibal.

"Hannibal, you wanted a lamp and now you have one," laughed Scooter.

"Rub the lamp and let me out!" yelled Hannibal.

"Hannibal, I will rub the lamp if you want to come out of that broken down tea pot and promise me that you will follow my rules. One of my rules is not to do anything stupid," insisted Scooter. "You have to grant me all my wishes and quit calling me stupid. Now, I finally have a pocket full of wishes of my own."

Printed in the United States
by Baker & Taylor Publisher Services